more than than one way to be A Girl

DYAN SHELDON

INTERNATIONALLY BESTSELLING AUTHOR

D0063651

"Glittering with wit and charm." *Publishers Weekly* on *Confessions of a Teenage Drama Queen* (New York Times Bestseller)

"Outrage and delight in a curious rich mix distinguishes Dyan Sheldon's fiction. Her ear is tuned, her eye is clear, she is smart and generous, tough and funny." *New York Times Book Review*

"A great read that'll have you hooked from the start." *The Sunday Times* on *Confessions of a Teenage Hollywood Star*

"Constantly funny, splendidly witty: a bull's eye." *Kirkus Reviews* on *The Truth About My Success*

LOVE

Other books by Dyan Sheldon

more than than one way to be A Girl

Dyan Sheldon

WALKER
BOOKS

First published 2017 by Walker Books Ltd
87 Vauxhall Walk, London SE11 5HJ

2 4 6 8 10 9 7 5 3

Text © 2017 Dyan Sheldon
Cover photographs © Iryna Hramavataya/Alamy Stock Photo,
YAY Media AS/Alamy Stock Photo and Mikalai Bachkou/Alamy Stock Photo

This book has been typeset in Berkeley

Printed and bound by CPI Group (UK) Ltd, Croydon, CR0 4YY

British Library Cataloguing in Publication Data:
a catalogue record for this book
is available from the British Library

ISBN 978-1-4063-6303-6

www.walker.co.uk

MIX
Paper from
responsible sources
FSC® C020471

For Terence

ZiZi

Books aren't the only thing that begin with a "B"

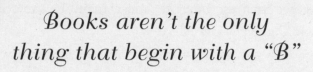

Towards the end of my freshman year in high school, Jude Fielder touched my breast.

So you don't get the wrong idea, there was nothing sexy or romantic about it. It wasn't like we were in some passionate clinch in a dark corner of somebody's basement. We were in the town library. I was looking for a book for my history assignment. I guess I left it a little late, because by the time I got around to finding something, everything under three thousand pages had been taken out of the school library. I begged the librarian to see if maybe there was one little, reasonably sized book that hadn't been shelved yet or was in the back waiting to have its spine fixed or something, which he did (he was always very helpful). But there wasn't. He was really, really sorry, but what could he do? The problem wasn't what he could do, but what I had to do. This was one of those times when you couldn't just slap something together from the Internet. You actually had to read a book. *Quel pain in the butt.*

So anyway, there I was on a Saturday morning, when I could've still been in bed or on my way to the mall, standing in the world history section of the public library, hoping to find something no thicker than a crispbread for my assignment, when Jude Fielder came up beside me. I knew he was looking at me, but I was used to guys looking at me, so I acted like the only thing next to me was air. He sighed, he looked, he took a book off the shelf, he put the book back on the shelf. And then, instead of reaching for another book he wasn't interested in, he suddenly put his hand on my breast. Just like that! It was really quick. I was so surprised I could hardly believe it. I'm not really sure, but I think he may have pressed. Lightly. He laughed, like it was a joke, and then he apologized. "Sorry," said Jude Fielder. "I just wanted to see if it was real." I didn't think there was much I could say to that. (*What made you think it wasn't real? Do I look like a robot?*) Or much I could do. I know I'm not supposed to say this (at least I know it now!), but I was kind of flattered. I mean, what's the point of push-up bras and cleavage and low-cut tops if no one notices? If you don't want to be noticed, you wear baggy turtlenecks and dungarees.

And anyway, I guess I was a little embarrassed (even if I wasn't sure why). I figured he was probably embarrassed, too, for doing such a dumb thing, but I wasn't too worried about how he was feeling right then. I just wanted to get out of there. So I took the book I'd been flipping through (which turned out to be more boring than white socks) and left without opening my mouth. As I said, I was used to guys looking, but nobody'd ever groped me before. And anyway, the library isn't where you'd ever expect something like that to happen. Seriously? You don't exactly go into the library thinking, *Wow, I wonder if someone's going to grab my boobs while I'm looking for a book on the Romans.* So even though I wasn't really mad or anything, I was kind of shocked. But it wasn't a gigantic big deal because Jude Fielder was pretty okay. When our science class had to get garbage out of the river for Earth Day, in middle school, Jude Fielder let me carry the bag while he did all the work and got dirty. Plus he was one of the better-looking boys in my year. Not gorgeous, but not gross like some of them, either. (Just the thought of one of the creeps from the deep touching me would've made me throw up.) So anyway, I got out my book and left. I didn't run (in case my breasts bounced too much – that always gets looks) but I walked pretty fast. I was halfway to the sidewalk when I heard this kind of wounded-animal cry and then someone shouted, "What the hell, you crazy bitch!"

That made me stop and turn. There were other people around (like the background crowd in a movie), but right behind me were Loretta Reynolds and Jude Fielder. They were staring at each other like they were checking out flaws in a mirror. Jude Fielder was red in the face. Loretta Reynolds was her usual colour (wet, unbaked pastry). Loretta said, "Sorry. I just wanted to see if it was real." She said it really loud.

Quel day for surprises! You could've knocked me over with an eyelash.

Jude Fielder looked pretty surprised, too. (You wouldn't have needed a whole lash to knock him over.) He didn't laugh that time. What he did was stomp off, shouting at me as he passed, "Your freakin' dyke friend's crazy, you know that, Abruzzio? Like two hundred per cent certifiable!"

Here's the thing: Loretta Reynolds was not my friend. I knew her from being in school with her since for ever, just like Jude Fielder did. I didn't dislike her (most people like her okay even if they think she's pretty weird), but I didn't really know her. I could've picked her out of a police line-up, and if I'd run into her at the airport on my way to Paris, I would've said hello, but that's it. Loretta is the girl who always sits at the front of the room and is either first with her hand in the air to give an answer or the only person with a question. (That's from primary school on.) She's really smart and never cared who knows it. And she's always been confrontational. My first vivid memory of Loretta disagreeing with a teacher was in Year Two when she argued with Mrs Dansk about whether or not cats and dogs can think. (Loretta won. Yes, they can.) But until that fateful Saturday, if I ever spoke to Loretta directly it was only to say sorry for bumping into her. (Although, like just about everyone else who'd ever had a class with Loretta, I'd more than once muttered under my breath "Please shut up" when she was yammering away about something, or "Please don't start" when she was about to.)

So, as Jude Fielder stormed away, I screamed at him, "I'm really sorry. And she's not my friend."

The next thing I knew, Loretta Reynolds was shouting at me. (*Quel ironic!*)

"Are you out of your tiny little mind?" she roared. "What the hell is wrong with you?"

Me? What was wrong with *me*? How did I get to be the one who was nuts? The one who had something wrong with her? I didn't do anything.

"Excuse me," I said, "but I'm the innocent victim here."

"If you're such an innocent victim, maybe you could

explain to the incredulous TV audience why *you* apologized to *him*!"

"Excuse me, but I wasn't apologizing for me. I was apologizing for *you*."

"Oh, thank you so much." (In books, people's voices drip with sarcasm. But not Loretta's. It poured.) "You apologized for the one person in this little drama who has nothing to apologize for." She said that really scornfully. "And just to clarify things, Giselle Abruzzio, you are not an innocent victim." Only teachers or parents who are mad at me call me Giselle – everybody else calls me ZiZi. "What you are is an unconscious enabler. How come you just stood there like a doll and let that jerk maul you?"

I said I didn't let him – he did it without asking me. Plus, he didn't maul me. Maul was an exaggeration. (Exaggeration is a Loretta Reynolds trademark. She should patent it.) And anyway it wasn't exactly the crime of the century. "Chrissake, it's not like he hit me or ripped off my blouse." I was poised and calm, not enraged and waving my arms around like some people. "All he did was touch me." Really lightly. "And, anyway, what about you? What did you do to *him*?"

"Tat for tit," said Loretta. "If he'd grabbed my breasts, I'd've decked him."

Yeah, right. Only no boy was going to go grabbing

Loretta Reynolds' breasts. He'd have to find them first.

I thought she was seriously overreacting (something else she's known for). He didn't really grab my breast. (Already I knew better than to mention the possibility of a squeeze to Loretta.) I said it was more like someone brushing against you at the mall when it's really crowded. Like when there's some big sale on or it's Christmas.

Loretta flapped her hands in the air some more. It was amazing she didn't take off. "Except that someone shoving past you in the mall isn't deliberately going for your private person! He had no right to do that. That counts as assault."

I didn't think so. It was more an imposition than an assault. I mean, it wasn't like Jude Fielder went into the library planning to go for my private person. I figured he acted on impulse. Like when you buy a pair of shoes you know you can't walk in because they look so cool you just can't help yourself.

That argument scored in the high nineties on the Loretta Reynolds' contempt meter.

"So if I have the impulse to push somebody in front of a car, that's okay because I didn't plan it?"

I still don't know anyone else who can scream and sneer at the same time. I said that was like comparing lipstick to leggings. He wasn't trying to kill me. I think

I shrugged. Philosophically. (Loretta's not the only one who can be philosophical.) "If you ask me," I said, "getting all warped out about what happened's dumb. It's like being mad at the cat for scratching you when you're dangling a piece of string in front of it. He was just being a boy. They can't help it."

Talk about dangling a piece of string in front of a cat. If Loretta had been a cat, I'd've been covered in blood.

"Don't tell me," shouted Loretta. "Let me guess. You think it's cool when guys gawp and make comments when you walk down the street. You think it's part of being a girl."

Not all girls. It for sure wasn't part of being Loretta Reynolds. But she was annoying me with her attitude, like she was the only one who could ever be right, so I gave her what I knew was the wrong answer. "It is kind of a compliment. You know, unless they're saying your butt's too big or you have a nose like a pelican or something like that. They're letting you know you're attractive. What's bad about that? I mean, unless it's some ugly old loser with a beer gut or someone really creepy. That would be pretty gross."

The contempt meter went through the stratosphere.

"You hear that sound?" bellowed Loretta. "You know what it is?"

I didn't hear anything besides traffic and normal people talking in normal voices about normal things as they walked past us. And Loretta. They could probably hear her in Florida. I pictured all these old people sitting by their pools, looking around trying to figure out who was making the big racket.

"I'll tell you what it is." If you don't know something Loretta feels it's her duty to fill in the gaps. "It's the sound of Emma Goldman rolling in her grave!"

I had no idea who Emma Goldman was, but I figured the smart move would be not to ask. Not that Loretta gave me a chance. She answered anyway.

"In case you're interested, she was an outspoken champion of women's rights."

I wasn't interested, but I knew better than to say that, too. So I tried to lighten the mood. "Does that mean we can thank her for miniskirts and sexual liberation?"

"You can thank her for more than that," snapped Loretta. And away she went again. We stood there while half the town passed by and Loretta lectured me on male violence and aggression and female passivity – and at least a dozen things that started with the word "gender". Which wasn't a word I was used to hearing in everyday conversation. I didn't know what she was talking about. It was like when you have a couple of years of school

French and then you go to Quebec and the only things you understand when someone talks to you are hello, no and goodbye. I figured God probably didn't know what Loretta was droning on about either. If He was smart, He'd tuned out after the second sentence the same as I did.

"Maybe it's this sweater," I said when she finally stopped. That's what I'd been thinking about while she gabbled away. My sweater was orange.

"Sweater?" Loretta blinked. "Maybe what's this sweater?"

"The reason Jude did that. Bright colours make you look bigger."

Which could be considered the first fashion tip I ever gave her. And the first she totally ignored.

"So the whole thing was really your fault, is that what you're saying? That you were right to apologize?"

See how she twists things?

"I told you, I was apologizing for *you*, not for me."

You know how sometimes your parents look at you like they're wondering if the babies were switched in the hospital? That was the way Loretta was looking at me. Then she closed her eyes and counted to ten. When she was done counting, she opened her eyes again and said, "Okay. Let's start over. I guess at least you're right about it not being planned. If he'd planned it one of his friends would've been at the end of the aisle, taking a picture. And then it'd be all over the Internet."

So there was some good news.

I said I was the one who should've taken a picture. The next time she did something like that she should give me some warning so I'd have my phone ready.

Loretta laughed. "His face was great, wasn't it? You'd think I'd just hit him with a dead fish."

I laughed, too. "More like the entrails."

When we stopped laughing Loretta asked if I wanted to go somewhere for a coffee.

I guess because we were laughing like normal people my guard was down. I said, "Sure."

Quel day for firsts.

Loretta

You never know what's going to happen next

Although there is a lot of randomness in the universe, I am the sort of person who likes to know what's going to happen next. I'm not happy bobbing along on the ocean of life, waiting to see where the current takes me. I make lists, schedules and plans – and I keep to them. If I say I'm going to do something, I do it. If I say I'm going to be somewhere at a certain time, I'm there no matter what – because I'm also the person who always takes the variables like weather, traffic and unexpected events into consideration. Which means I knew all the things I was doing that Saturday – and becoming friends with Giselle Abruzzio was not on my agenda.

We'd known each other since we started school, but ZiZi and I had never been what you'd call friends. Not the kind who walk together if they happen to be going the same way, and for definite not the kind who eat lunch together and go to each other's house to play. I don't remember ever having an actual conversation with her, but in primary school we were always in the same groups for reading, etcetera, so we must have said something to each other sometime. I do remember that once – in Year Three or Four – some boys in our class threw her backpack up on the roof, expecting her to burst into tears or go running to a teacher, but she just climbed up and got it. In Year Five, she and I tied for first place in the school-wide Math Marathon. And in Year Six we were in the group that did a project on the effects of oil spills on ocean life for the Science Fair (we won second prize). What I'm trying to say is that, in my memory, ZiZi Abruzzio used to be smart and feisty (and really good at things like Science and Math). But when we got to middle school I guess she discovered there was more to life than reading, independence, algebra and environmental degradation. There were clothes, make-up and boys. Which means that she went from being a person who could shimmy up a pole to the roof of the school to being a Girl with a capital "G". Girls with a capital "G" are so bouncy and energetic that even if they aren't cheerleaders, they seem like they are – cheerleaders when it's always half-time in an important game. I've always thought of them as the Misses Bubble. They talk a lot, shop a lot, talk about shopping a lot, talk about boys even more, and laugh as if they're in a laughter competition – especially if it's at some unfunny joke by a guy. For reasons I don't understand, they don't like to be seen to be smarter than boys – especially ones they like. The only climbing they do is into or out of a car. After we moved up to middle school I know for definite that ZiZi and I didn't talk to each other. Not until The Assault in the library.

The night before The Assault, I'd watched a documentary about Emma Goldman, the twentieth-century American political activist, philosopher and orator who led the struggle for workers' and women's rights. File under the heading: *Positive role model*. I fell asleep thinking of her. I dreamed that she was giving a speech on a street corner. There was an enormous crowd gathered to listen – mesmerized by her eloquence and passion, and surrounded by policemen. Suddenly, it began to rain and people started to run for shelter, until I was the only one left – I had my emergency rain hat with me – and Emma continued as if I was a multitude. It was better than the dream where I win a Nobel Prize. When I woke up, Emma Goldman was still in my mind.

On my list of things to do that day were a couple of odd jobs in town – I did everything from mowing lawns and putting up screens to rewiring lamps and putting up shelves. I started fixing things around our house when I was eight or nine. My dad and mom are both great at their jobs but they're fairly useless when it comes to basic household upkeep. They can change a fuse and clean out the filter on the washing machine, but that's their limit – and as far as the car goes, their expertise stops at putting in petrol. Somebody had to be able to do necessary maintenance and repair, and the cats weren't interested. I taught myself basic plumbing and carpentry, the man next door had a vintage motorcycle and he taught me basic mechanics. Our middle school offered an elective in woodwork and I took it – I was the only girl. I started fixing things in other people's houses and putting the money I earned away for college when I was twelve – which may sound a little extreme but, as I said, I make plans and one of them is to take several college degrees.

On my way home that Saturday, since she was still on my mind, I decided to go to the library to see if it had a book on Emma. It didn't, which wasn't exactly the surprise of the year. Howards Walk isn't what anyone would call a bastion of radical thinking. I was on my way out when I glanced down one of the non-fiction aisles and there were Giselle Abruzzio and Jude Fielder. I don't know whether I stopped because the sight of either of them in the library was so unusual that I wanted to be certain my eyes weren't deceiving me, or because Jude Fielder wasn't actually looking at the shelves of books as Zizi was, but at ZiZi's breasts. And then he grabbed one – a breast not a book. To be fair to ZiZi, she looked as shocked as I felt. My first thought was: *What would Emma Goldman do?* Zizi didn't do anything. She just stood there as if she'd been turned to plastic. Jude Fielder laughed. Then he said, "I just wanted to see if it was real." Which made me think that he's probably even more stupid than I'd always thought. ZiZi had a half-smile on her face, like she wasn't sure what had just happened, but she must have been sure because she left so quickly she might have been on wheels. Jude Fielder waited a few minutes – presumably because he was at least smart enough to give her time to get away in case she recovered the power of speech and not because he'd suddenly discovered a love of books.

I followed him out, still thinking, *What would Emma Goldman do?* As soon as I stepped outside, I knew exactly what Emma Goldman would do if she were alive now. She was an activist, after all – and she wasn't afraid of making a scene. I'm not exactly known for my spontaneity, but I hurried to catch up with Jude, and when I was right behind him I called his name. Jude Fielder stopped and turned. I made a grab for the crotch of his jeans.

He jumped back so fast and screamed so loudly that I didn't actually touch him, but the effect was the same. He was horrified, but, unlike ZiZi, he still had the power of speech; he yelled that I was crazy. I said I was sorry, that I just wanted to know if it was real. I was pretty pleased with coming up with that line; usually I don't think of the really good, zinger response until it's too late. He didn't find that a fraction as funny as he'd found molesting ZiZi. Well, he wouldn't, would he? Then he marched off, yelling at ZiZi about her dyke friend – which would be me, despite the fact that at that time I was neither of those things. And what do you think Giselle Abruzzio, having been assaulted in broad daylight in a public place by a boy whose only documented talent is the ability to run a piece of dental floss through his nostrils (Year Six, cafeteria, absolutely disgusting) did next? Here's a hint: it for definite wasn't what Emma Goldman would have done. ZiZi apologized! Of all the things that had happened in the last ten minutes that I couldn't believe, that was the one I couldn't believe the most. She said, "I'm sorry," and sounded as if she meant it. *I'm sorry?* Was she insane? What the hell was she sorry for? Having breasts? Not letting him grab the other one, too? Not taking off her top? Talk about blaming the victim. Here I was listening to the victim blame herself.

That's when I decided I had to talk to her. She didn't seem to realize that this is the twenty-first century, and women are no longer considered the property or inferiors of men. Not in our society, at least. But, as soon as I opened my mouth, I kind of lost it. I may have shouted. I do tend to shout when I feel strongly about something, and I felt very strongly about what had just happened in the non-fiction section, world history aisle, of the public library. ZiZi didn't want to know. Talk about defensive! Why was I getting on her case? She was completely innocent. If you ask me, she was more comatose than innocent. Why didn't she do something when he grabbed her? Yell, scream, hit him over the head with the book she was holding. Instead, all she did was apologize. *She* apologized to *him*! Had we all fallen down a wormhole? That's when she shifted everything around so that I was the one in the wrong – which I now know is a typical Giselle Abruzzio manoeuvre. She said she was apologizing for my behaviour, not hers. She said that I was overreacting. Apparently, it's flattering to be sexually harassed. According to ZiZi, Jude Fielder hadn't done anything wrong; he was just being a boy. At least she got that part right. I tried to make her see all the other things that were examples of boys being boys and men being men – war, murder, genocide, rape, pornography, colonialism, slavery, torture, domestic violence, paedophilia, recreational hunting, etcetera – but she wasn't listening. She was thinking deeply. I know that because when I finished she said she thought the reason Jude Fielder assaulted her was because of the sweater she was wearing. I felt as if I'd been walking down an ordinary street in an ordinary way and suddenly ploughed into a mastodon eating an ice-cream cone. *Where the hell did that come from?*

I said I guessed that meant she was five hundred per cent right to apologize since the whole thing was her fault – her and her orange sweater. What had she been thinking when she got dressed that morning? Why didn't she wear black? Why didn't she put on something baggy over it like a bathrobe? Maybe she should start wearing a suit of armour. That would make her breasts virtually non-existent. ZiZi smiles the way everyone else breathes. "I wasn't blaming myself," she said. "I was just saying." How can you reason with someone like that? We might as well have been speaking different languages. It was like trying to convince a climate change denier of global warming. I was still thinking of ZiZi as the Koch brothers when she said that next time I did something like that I should give her some warning so she could take a picture. I immediately saw Jude Fielder's face in front of me, looking as if I'd just hit him with a dead fish. And

ZiZi said it was more like I'd hit him with the entrails. We both started laughing.

I think that was when I realized there was hope for ZiZi. She'd been smart and spirited before; she could be smart and spirited again. She was drowning in the frothy, pink sea of girliness, and I was in the solid boat of persondom. It was my duty to pull her aboard.

I asked her if she wanted to get a coffee or something.

File under the heading: *Fate*.

ZiZi

Loretta and I have never been the kind of best friends who act like they're identical twins who were raised by different parents

So after the boob grab, Loretta and I went for coffee. Well, I went for coffee. Loretta went for green tea, a brownie and a cookie the size of a wagon wheel. (The only math Loretta isn't interested in is counting calories!) And that was it really. To look at us, you wouldn't think we have much in common. (Which we don't!) My dad's a store manager and my mom's a receptionist at a vet's. I have two brothers (both of them pretty annoying). I'm feminine. I'm sociable. I try to get along with everyone and don't like to rock any boats. And then there's Loretta. Her dad's some kind of shrink and her mother teaches yoga. She's a pampered only child. Loretta's look is all no make-up and sexless, androgynous clothes. She's super academic and can be kind of stand-offish. She's a girl who would sink the Owl and the Pussycat if she thought they were wrong about something. But even though we're pretty different, we were friends after that. We started walking to school together, and then we started hanging out after school and on the weekends. If we weren't just mooching around or talking about life or whatever, we'd watch movies at her house (she's a major movie freak, so she had about a thousand films I'd never heard of). Because I live in a house dominated by boys, most of our movies illustrate Loretta's views on male violence, but my brothers do have some cool games, so if she wasn't fixing the toaster or helping Nate get his bike going (he'd been working on it since he was fifteen, but until Loretta came along, the only time it moved was when it fell over), we'd play something that didn't involve killing. Here's the thing. The more I got to know her, the more I liked Loretta. Even though we disagreed about a lot of stuff (clothes, make-up, what it means to be a girl and stuff like that), she's easy to be with. Plus, she does have a good sense of humour (when she isn't in lecturing mode). We'd be arguing one minute and laughing the next.

I was between best friends right then and by the Summer Loretta had filled the vacancy. My last best friend was Catie Coulson. Catie and I were like the human equivalent of a pair of earrings. Same colouring and body type. Same taste and style. We spent hours together shopping and looking through magazines and watching fashion vlogs. I learned a lot from Catie about clothes, dieting, make-up, boys, sex – and things like that. I also learned a lot about betrayal. She was always getting me in trouble by telling people what I'd said about them in private. She couldn't keep a secret if your life depended on it. And then, our first year in high school and not even a week after I said I had my eye on a certain boy working in the Starbucks at the mall, she went out with him. *Quel Judas!* I never spoke to her again.

So even though Loretta was nothing like me, we kind of fit together. Like the clasp on a bra. (Not Loretta's bras, though. They don't have clasps.)

Quel example of truth being stranger than fiction!

That doesn't mean there aren't a lot of things about Loretta that drive me crazy. There are dozens.

She's stubborn.

She's opinionated.

She thinks she's always right.

She doesn't like spectator sports.

She's not really great when it comes to compromise.

Just because you're her best friend doesn't mean she'll do you a tiny little favour.

* * *

"Absolutely no way," said Loretta. "Get somebody else. You know a lot of cheerleader types. Get one of them to go with you."

"It's Thanksgiving. The cheerleader types are either going to be at the game, cheerleading, or they're visiting their grandmothers." I gave her one of my really winning smiles. It was our sophomore year, so I knew her pretty well by then, but I was desperate. Plus, I can be pretty persuasive. "And anyway, I want you to come. It'll be fun."

"It's a football game." Loretta sneers a lot for a teenage girl. "Saying it'll be fun is a contradiction in terms."

"But we'll be together. That's what makes it fun. And afterwards we're going for pizza."

"I thought you said pizza's fattening."

Not if you just eat the topping.

"But you love pizza," I reminded her. "Plus, after that, we're going bowling."

Loretta's really good at looking underwhelmed.

"You're making solitary confinement seem incredibly attractive."

I started to plead. "I know you're judgmental, but you can't really judge Kyle when you haven't even met him, Lo. For all you know, he's the boy you've been waiting your whole life to meet."

"I very much doubt that." She treated me to another

sneer. "He's Duane's cousin, ZiZi. Which means it's more likely he's the boy I've been waiting my whole life to avoid."

Duane Tolvar is another thing Loretta doesn't like. I'd been dating Duane on and off since September. Duane was a junior and the star quarterback on the school's varsity football team. Most people thought he was pretty cool. Loretta thought that if Duane was a pond you'd have to dig six feet to make him shallow. (That's a quote!)

"You're being really unfair, Loretta. You hardly know Duane. Maybe he's not going to find a cure for cancer, but he's a nice guy. And you don't know his cousin at all. Both of them might surprise you."

"Only by being worse than I think."

That's what I mean about stubborn.

"Please, Loretta. It's important." Three isn't really a good number for a date. "If you don't come, Kyle's going to feel like a third wheel."

"I don't care if he feels like a training wheel. I'm not going."

"I'd do it for you."

"No you wouldn't. You refused to come to the observatory with me in the Summer."

There was a beach party on. There was no way I was missing a beach party to spend the night looking at stars that you can see any night of the year.

"I didn't know it was such a big deal, did I? And anyway, I did plenty of other things with you in the Summer. We went to that Japanese movie." (Three hours of subtitles. Even Loretta didn't know what was going on most of the time.) "And that play." (Good but so depressing you kind of lost the will to live for a while.) "And that afternoon of jazz in the park." (Which is not my music but there were some very cute jazz guys dotted around on the grass, so at least there was something to look at.)

"Okay, I know the jazz was a challenge, but you said you liked the movie and the play."

"I did, but that's not the point, Loretta. The point is that you could do this one little thing for me."

"I go shopping with you."

"Most people don't think that's a chore."

"I came to your barbecue."

Ate two ears of corn, two veggie sausages and a baked potato, and gave a short but pretty gripping lecture on the life of a battery chicken (Marilee Sokalov had to run inside to throw up).

"I'm begging you. It's an emergency."

"Duane's cousin being around for the weekend isn't exactly the same as being stranded in a blizzard." Said without sneering, but there was some scorn.

"Please, Loretta. As a big favour to your best friend? If it's just me and them, they'll blather on about football all night and I could end up asleep with my face in the pizza."

"I don't know, Zi. It's not that I don't want to help you out…"

Loretta's stubborn, but she's a loyal friend. I could tell she was weakening. Plus, I could tell that something more than not liking football or Duane Tolvar was holding her back. And then it hit me! Loretta's not shy about giving her opinion or standing up for her principles, but she is shy around boys – unless they're asking her to help them with their calculus or get their car started. She doesn't know how to talk to them. (This is the one advantage to having brothers. At least you know what to expect.) She doesn't do chit-chat. The day all the other girls were learning how to flirt, Loretta was somewhere else, unblocking a sink or trying to discover a new planet.

"You know what I think?" She looked like the answer to that question was "No", but I told her anyway. "I think you're afraid to come with me because you've never gone out with a boy."

"You said this isn't a date. I'd just be making up the numbers."

"It isn't a date. But you know what I mean. You don't

know how to talk to boys. You act like you're the rabbit and they're the headlights. You totally freeze up."

"I know how to talk to them. I talk to them all the time. Usually in English."

"At school you talk to them. About school stuff. Or some theory about particles nobody is sure exist. Or how to fix something. But you don't have casual, not-about-anything-special conversations with them."

"What about your brothers? I talk to them."

"About motorcycles and games. And anyway, my brothers don't count. Nate's too old and Obi's only twelve. Your problem is that you don't know how to hang out with boys our age."

I could tell from the way she was sucking on her bottom lip that I was right.

"Come on, Lo. You have nothing to lose. Think of Duane's cousin as practice. It's like learning to swim in the kids' pool before you go to the ocean."

She opened her mouth and shut it again.

Home team one, visitors nil.

When it comes to disasters, the not-a-date with Duane and his cousin wasn't as bad as a plane crash. Everybody survived in one piece. But it was close.

The guys-in-helmets-and-shoulder-pads-tackling-each-

34

other part wasn't too bad. Loretta and I were a little late getting there (I couldn't find the green leggings I'd planned to wear and had to totally change my outfit at the last minute), so we were spared having to think of things to say to Duane's cousin before the game. And Kyle is sweet. He'd saved us seats and acted like he was really glad to meet Loretta. I sat between them, and Loretta spent most of the game doing stuff on her phone. (Kyle was so into the game that the only thing that would have distracted him would have been if a bunch of giraffes invaded the field.) So Part One was no talking by anyone and everyone pretty happy doing their thing.

Part Two was the drive to the pizzeria. I sat up front with Duane, and Loretta sat in the back with Kyle (but as far away from him as she could get and still be in the car). Duane and Kyle went on and on about the game. Unlike Loretta, I tried to look interested. Duane kept taking his hands off the wheel and his eyes off the road (the way he does) to explain some play to Kyle, and I'd hear these little gasps from Loretta behind me. She'd never ridden with Duane before so she looked kind of terrified. (I guess I should've warned her, and assured her that you get used to it.)

In the restaurant (Part Three), I sat next to Duane and Loretta and Kyle sat across from us. I should mention here that Duane and Loretta had had a couple of disagreements in the past. (The one I remember is when Duane said guns don't kill people, they're just a tool. Loretta said guns aren't a tool to put nails in the wall, they're a tool to kill people. Duane said cars kill people, too – was she going to ban cars and put all those autoworkers out of jobs? Loretta said it was just as well she didn't have a gun or she'd be tempted to shoot him.) But Duane is very forgiving (if he weren't a boy, he'd be a dog), so, even though he thinks Loretta's a little weird, he didn't hold it against her. He started off by asking her how she liked the game. Loretta can make honesty look like a fault. She said she wasn't really paying attention. Still wagging his tail, Duane asked Loretta what she did for Thanksgiving. Loretta said (and I quote!), "We had dinner and then I worked on a talk I'm giving at the Astronomy Club." Duane thought she was joking and laughed. Kyle said he was starving so we should order an extra-large pizza. Maybe half meatball, half pepperoni. I was on a diet that week so I said I wasn't hungry and was just going to have a salad. Loretta said, "I don't eat meat." That time it was Kyle who laughed (he'd never met a vegetarian before). Over our pizzas, I tried to show Loretta how you talk to boys by example (while Loretta just sat there, chewing slowly). I started by asking Kyle all about himself. School. Sports. What he and Duane had been doing. That kind of thing. He and Duane told us all about the thriller they'd watched the night before (Loretta's chewing got slower). Then Kyle said he was going to do some travelling after he graduated in June. I said I wanted to go to France. Kyle said he was thinking of Mexico. "I always wanted to see South America," said Kyle.

And that was when Loretta joined the conversation. "You're going to have a problem, then," said Loretta.

Kyle grinned. "Why's that?"

"Mexico isn't in South America."

"Did they move it?" he laughed.

"Sure it's in South America," said Duane. "They speak Spanish."

"They speak Spanish in Spain, too." Loretta was smiling. This was her doing banter. "But Spain's not in South America, either." She got out her phone. "Let's look at the map."

Anyway, it was a pretty fast ride downhill after that. I gave up trying to show Loretta the fine art of heterosexual conversation, and the boys just talked among themselves. Loretta and I went to the restroom while the guys were polishing off their desserts. That's when she let me know that there wasn't going to be a Part Four. She said she was going to ask her mother to pick her up because there was no way she was getting back in the car with Duane. "He drives like an accident waiting to happen."

I didn't believe her. I mean, I know Duane's driving doesn't make you think the driving test is foolproof (too close, too fast, doesn't pay attention, can't parallel-park), but I didn't think that was why she was bolting. Her cheeks were flushed. She only gets like that when she's really wound up about something. "You're stressing."

"I don't know what to say."

"I told you. You don't have to say anything. Just ask them a question. They'll take it from there. All you have to do is listen."

"I don't want to listen." Stubborn or what? "I want to get out of here."

And what was I supposed to tell Duane and Kyle?

She said to tell them she got her period and had to go home. "You can't bowl when you're doubled over with cramps."

So Loretta called her mom and went outside to wait for her. When I got back to the table, Duane wanted to know where Loretta was.

"She had to leave. She's not feeling well," I said. "You know. A girl thing."

"Oh, right," said Kyle. "I was wondering what was wrong with her."

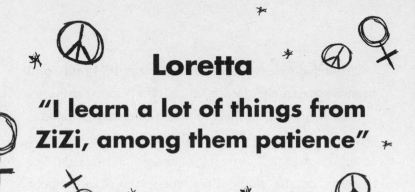

Loretta

"I learn a lot of things from ZiZi, among them patience"

It's not going to knock anyone out of their orbit when I say that I'd never had a friend like ZiZi before. My friends had always been like me – academic, serious, motivated, socially inept. If ZiZi is one of the Misses Bubble, we're the Mses Sticks-in-the-Mud.

Basically, we're like two sides of the same planet: dark and light.

I'm cautious and realistic; I know how easy it is for things to go wrong – and how often they do. That's why I plan my days, my months and my years well in advance. I organize my schoolwork, jobs and extracurricular activities on a weekly schedule. I draw up daily lists of what I need to do. In addition to planning, I worry. I worry about things like my grades and the state of the world and the future. ZiZi, however, has an optimistic attitude to life that borders on the delusional. She sincerely believes that everything always works out all right, and because of that she doesn't go in for too much thinking ahead. The only thing she plans is what she's going to wear tomorrow; her lists are all for shopping; what she schedules are appointments with her hairdresser. Not that she doesn't worry. ZiZi worries constantly about things like how she looks and what she's wearing and what'll happen to her hair if it rains.

I'm the sort of girl who's more concerned with being a person; ZiZi's the sort of person who's more concerned with being a girl. Which works extremely well for her. She's pretty, popular and attractive, and so, naturally, she has this amazing self-confidence. Which, to tell you the truth, is one of the things I like most about her. She's like an emotional heat source; the sun in the form of a teenage girl in short skirts and impractical shoes. ZiZi can walk into a room full of strangers and, within minutes, everybody in there is her friend. I have confidence about my brains and my skills and getting into the college of my choice, but if I walk into a room full of strangers, the odds are that, when I walk out, I'm leaving a room full of strangers behind.

Despite our many documented differences, ZiZi and I balance each other; we work as a team. We're sort of the yin and yang of friendship. Which isn't to say that there aren't things about yang that try yin's patience. There are plenty.

She's obsessed with how she looks.

She has terrible taste in boys.

She has terrible taste in boys *and* she panders to them.

She flirts as naturally as a bird flies.

If there's one thing you can rely on with ZiZi, it's that she's always late.

ZiZi and I were going to the mall together. We set off from her house – ZiZi a step or two behind me because she was looking up something on her phone – talking about the film we'd watched the night before.

"I'm not saying there weren't some clever bits," I said as we turned into town. "I just felt that, though all the leads were women, it was still basically a guy movie." ZiZi didn't say anything. "Don't you think so?" It was when she still didn't respond that I finally realized she was no longer right behind me. I stopped and turned around. ZiZi was four and a half yards back, examining the left shoulder of her jacket in the window of the deli. "Oh for God's sake," I called. "Now what?"

"I thought I felt something hit me."

"Hit you?" I looked up. It was a sunny Spring day. The only things above us were a few wispy clouds but none of them were dropping eggs or frogs or anything like that. "What could've hit you?"

ZiZi sighed to let me know that I was being impossible. "Bird poop, Loretta. I once had a bird poop on my brand-new faux-suede jacket. I not only had to go all the way back home and change, but it never really did come out."

By then I didn't care if an eagle had pooped on her – we were not going back to her house so she could get a different jacket. A different jacket would almost for definite require a different skirt, possibly different shoes as well. On a good day – one when nothing goes wrong and no one else in her family gets into the bathroom before she does – it takes ZiZi at least an hour to be ready to walk out the door. On a bad day – one when she finds a run in her tights or one of her brothers decides to take a shower – it's even longer. I'd already had two cups of tea and two bagels that morning – two teas, two bagels and a long discussion with Nate about the novel *Slaughterhouse Five* – all while I was waiting for ZiZi to get dressed. We'd been friends for a year, which meant that I was used to waiting for her – but I wasn't prepared to wait any more that day.

"There's nothing on your jacket, ZiZi." I didn't look too closely, just in case there actually could be. It wasn't as if civilization would collapse if she arrived at the mall with a spot on her sleeve. "Now come on or we're going to miss the bus."

She didn't budge. "Are you sure there's nothing?"

"Positive. Can we please just get to the mall? Today? The rate we're going, it's going to be shut by the time we get there."

"What'd you get in Advanced Exaggeration, Loretta? A+?" She didn't sigh this time, she huffed – but she started walking again. "You really have to chill a little. The bus isn't even here yet." Which was when the bus passed us, heading for the stop in front of the hardware store. ZiZi waved; the driver waved back. "You see?" smiled ZiZi. "That's Mr Sheski. He's really nice. He always waits."

Maybe time and tide wait for no man, but everyone waits for ZiZi.

She gave Mr Sheski a warm greeting when we climbed on board. Mr Sheski said how good it was to see her – like sunshine after a rainy day. ZiZi beamed; she doesn't always mind when someone exaggerates. Then she asked Mr Sheski how his parrot was. (How did she know he has a parrot? I've lived next door to the Shaunnesseys my whole life and I only found out Mr Shaunnessey has a pet snake the Summer it escaped and wound up in our garage – scaring my cat Alice so much that I'm sure she lost one of her nine lives.) Mr Sheski said the parrot was much better.

Normally, I'd rather square dance in platform clogs than go shopping – especially with ZiZi, who would only spend less than five hours at the mall if it were under attack from gun-toting giant lizards from Mars. She goes to the mall most weekends, but this was the first time I'd gone with her since March, when my boots started leaking. I shop out of necessity, not as a hobby. I'd told ZiZi that my present necessity was a birthday present for my mother. This was largely true. My mother never asks me if something looks good on her or if she's wearing the right colour, but she always asks ZiZi – who, of course, is only too happy to give her expert opinion. Which was why buying a present for my mother with her personal fashion consultant beside me seemed like a good idea.

The other thing I'd told ZiZi was that, while we were there, I thought I might look for something for me to wear to my aunt and uncle's anniversary party. This was mainly untrue. Not that my aunt and uncle were having an anniversary party – they were – but that I needed something special to wear to it. At the end of the year everybody in the Astronomy Club was going out for a meal together. Gabriel Schwartz was in the Astronomy Club. I'd never said anything to ZiZi in case I jinxed myself, but I'd had a crush on Gabriel since Year Nine when he was my lab partner – we always got the results of experiments first. He isn't merely enormously attractive – not movie-star handsome, but his face has a lot of character – he's incredibly intelligent as well. He's also serious and mature, and not one of those guys who's only interested in a girl's looks. Even better, he's as passionate about the universe as I am. Which was why I wanted something a little different from what I usually wore for the Astronomy Club dinner. I was hoping that, if I dressed up, Gabe would notice that I'm not just another high IQ. Who better to help me find something perfect than Giselle Abruzzio – who knows more about looking good than NASA knows about space travel. Only without telling her the real reason, of course. She'd think I was going over to her side if she knew, and then I'd never hear the end of it.

The mall was so crowded you'd think they were giving things away.

"Of course it's packed," said ZiZi. "We live in a consumer society. What you don't seem to get, Loretta, is that it doesn't work if people don't consume. You have to buy, buy, buy. That's the deal."

If capitalism collapses, it'll obviously be my fault.

The way I shop, I know what I need – shoes, a bra, a new drill bit – and I go into a store that sells what I want and, if it has something I like in the right size, I buy it. That's not what you do when you shop with ZiZi. To begin with, you don't only shop when there's something you need, you shop to see if there might be something you'd like to have – or that you would decide you desperately needed if only you knew it existed. You take your time when you shop. You wander through every store as if you're grazing sheep searching for a perfect patch of pasture. When you find something you like, you spend a long time studying it from every angle. You walk away and mull it over. You turn around and examine it again. You try everything on in two sizes.

"You never buy the first thing you see," ZiZi advised, "because you'll only wind up taking it back when you see something you like better."

It took us less than half an hour to find a blouse for my mom that we both thought she was completely going to love.

Getting something for me was more of a challenge – in the way that walking the Inca Trail is more of a challenge than walking to the kitchen.

ZiZi wanted me to get "something really festive". Something colourful and feminine. Something soft and figure-flattering. Something she would wear. "You never dress up," said ZiZi. "Why don't you let yourself go for once?"

I said I was letting myself go – I was going to the party.

ZiZi groaned so loudly that people looked around.

We developed a routine. In every shop, ZiZi pulled dress after dress from the racks, waving them in front of me like pom-poms. *What about this…? Well, what about this…? This one's to die for!* In every shop, I shook my head at every new offering. Too short, too tight, too frilly, too bright. With superluminal speed, it turned into a contest of wills.

I said, "I don't really do pastels." Firmly – and again.

"It's Spring," said ZiZi. "Pastels are the colours for Spring." As if that clinched the argument.

I said, "These dresses all look like the seamstress ran out of material halfway through."

"It's the style, Loretta." Sounding the way bored looks. "Get over it. The Victorian governess's dress is seriously passé."

"I don't actually want a dress," I reminded her. "All I want is a new top—"

"To go with your old, shapeless jeans," she finished for me.

"That's a little dressier than what I usually wear."

"For God's sake, a plain, coloured shirt would be dressier than what you usually wear." She rolled her eyes at an invisible audience. "I swear, Loretta, if designers had to depend on people like you, the only thing they'd have their names on would be their bills."

"It's a family party, Zi, not the prom."

She did her impersonation of a bellows losing air. "It's a celebration, not a funeral."

"But I'm not like you." ZiZi thought that if she wasn't model-perfect, the Four Horsemen of the Fashion Apocalypse would thunder up the street and confiscate her wardrobe. "I don't want to look as if I'm about to have my picture taken for the cover of some fashion magazine."

"No. You want to look as if you came to fix the boiler."

"I just want to look like me."

Which, judging by her expression, wasn't much of a goal.

More eye-rolling; more sighing. "That's the problem. You don't really care how you look."

"That's not true." I'm just as insecure about my appearance as everybody else. "Only I don't agonize over it to the point of Satanic possession the way you do."

"I don't agonize over how I look," declared ZiZi. "I take pride in it. Unlike some people, Lo, I happen to be really glad I'm a girl and not a guy. You don't get it, but girls dress about a million times better than boys. Girls' clothes have personality. They're fun. They're exciting. And they make you feel good. When you put on an awesomely beautiful dress, you feel awesomely beautiful."

"You mean, you do. If I put on one of those dresses I'd feel like a roll that was decorated to look like a fancy cupcake."

"I don't know why you always put yourself down like that." She usually tries not to frown – bad for the image and bad for the future of her face. "What am I always saying? You could look fantastic. You have tons of potential. Only you just refuse to do anything with it."

This was something I could say about all her inner potential, but she didn't give me the chance.

"And anyway, as usual, you're not listening to what I'm saying. Girls get to wear great stuff, but boys' clothes are boring as a power cut. They're so boring they should all just wear the same uniform and save themselves the trouble of having to decide between the blue shirt and the white."

"I a—"

"You know I'm right," ZiZi interrupted. "Men's clothes give them no chance to express themselves. They're just dull and samey. Even guys who think they dress well wear the clothing equivalent of white rice. They spend all this money on some handmade suit and designer shirt, but does that make them feel awesomely beautiful? No, it just makes them feel like they spent a fortune on something that looks a lot like what the guy who bought his suit at Walmart is wearing."

"I think—"

"And what about make-up? Make-up lets women improve what they have and create new looks for themselves. But men can't do that. In nature, it's usually the males who are the knockouts, but not in our world. In our world, men are plain and look exactly the way they looked yesterday. Most men don't change the colour of their hair, or enhance their best features or make their eyes look bigger or more exotic. They don't even really accessorize. A tie is not an accessory, it's just a strip of material that falls in your soup. And – if he's not wearing trainers – nine and a half times out of ten a guy's shoes are either black or brown."

At last, I managed to force a few words into her stream-of-consciousness monologue. "But at least they can run in their shoes."

"So, okay, maybe they can run in them," conceded ZiZi. "But when they stop running, their feet might as well be in the boxes the shoes came in. Seriously? The boxes would probably be more interesting!"

"Zi, could you please shut up for a minute? I don't disagree with you. Not about the limits put on men."

"Seriously?" She looked as if she'd found her closet filled with clothes from the 1980s, a period, she says, when fashion was in a coma. "You don't?"

"Of course not. Men are just as victimized by gender stereotypes as women – and they have far fewer ways of dealing with it. Men are made to think they have to be tough and powerful and make money to be real men. Why should men be the doers and women the carers? What about men's nurturing side? It's not as if they don't have feelings. But they're not supposed to show their feelings, because that's 'being a girl'."

"Like caring how you look is part of being like a girl," put in ZiZi.

"It used to be part of being a man, too. In the past, there have been plenty of societies where men did wear make-up and flamboyant clothes. But our society's idea of how guys should look is more narrow than a shoebox."

ZiZi beamed. "So does this mean you'll get a dress?"

File under the heading: *Immovable as a mountain*.

Eventually – after we'd been in so many shops that everything started to look the same and I'd lost all sense of time – we compromised. I bought a wrap-around, kimono-style top in black and white; which satisfied ZiZi's sense of style and my preferences for simplicity.

ZiZi was studying a window display of women's shoes and I was keeping her company when, out of the corner of my eye, I saw a tall, lanky boy leave the store. He was all in black and his longish dark hair was tied back in a mini ponytail, but I was focused on the out-rageous pair of sandals ZiZi was gushing over and not really paying attention. Until the boy stopped beside me and said, "Hey, Loretta!"

I looked over. "Dillon!" Beside me, I felt ZiZi turn away from the window.

He laughed. "I never thought I'd run into you in the mall. Aren't you the Loretta Reynolds who wrote that article for the school paper about Buy Nothing Day?" He drew his eyebrows together in concentration. "What was the quote? 'Recreational shopping is less fun than watching paint dry, and a lot less productive'?"

"What about you? Aren't you the Dil—" I broke off because I suddenly couldn't remember his last name. "Didn't you say you hate shopping?"

"I can explain." He held up his bag. "Shoes for my feet."

"Me, too." I held up my bag. "Birthday present for my mom."

I felt a poke in my back, and ZiZi moved up beside me. I knew what that poke meant.

"Do you know ZiZi?" I waved towards him. "This is Dillon—"

Dillon nodded at ZiZi. "Yeah, sure I know you. Weren't you in my French class last year? You were the only person Monsieur never ridiculed."

"And the same tutor group once," said ZiZi. "And Biology."

"Right. Biology. You always needed help with your microscope." He smiled at me. "Well I better get going or my brother will leave without me. See you Wednesday, Loretta."

"Yeah, see you Wednesday."

When I looked over at ZiZ, she was staring after him. "See you Wednesday?" She sounded as if she'd just discovered I had a secret life. Possibly one she wished she had herself.

"It's Film Club on Wednesday. He's a serious film buff."

"I had no idea you knew Dillon Blackstock."

"Blackstock, of course!"

He was out of sight; she turned to me. "So that's how you got so friendly? From Film Club?"

"That and he's in my Language Arts class. Besides that, Magda Hornung's been taking yoga classes with my mom for a few years. Sometimes Dillon and I bump into each other at the studio or whatever."

"Who's Magda Hornung?"

"Dillon's mother. She's been married three times. That's why I can never remember his last name. Everybody in that family has a different one."

She was giving me one of her scrutinous looks.

What's wrong with this jacket? Are the sleeves too long? Is it a dull shade of blue? "How come you don't have any trouble talking to him, Loretta?"

"I told you. He's in the film club. I talk to him all the time."

"About movies."

"No. In Film Club, we talk about reforestation."

"I was just asking." She was still looking scrutinous. "You seemed really chummy."

It was the way she said "chummy" – as if she was saying something else. "Excuse me. I may be misinterpreting here, but is it possible that you're interested in Dillon Blackstock?" Dillon is arty and very smart. Which made him a radical change of pace from the boys she usually liked.

"Only as a person, Loretta." She shifted the bag she'd managed to fill while we were shopping for me from one hand to the other. "Movie geeks aren't really my type."

"That's funny. I had the feeling that if you were a cat you'd have been purring."

Her smile was as sweet as vinegar. "There you go exaggerating again. I was just being friendly. It's not like I never saw him before. We go to the same school, remember?"

"Yeah, I remember."

File under the heading: *Watch this space.*

ZiZi

Compared to the rest of my high-school career, my junior year is a ballgown on a rack of plain shirts

I knew right from the start that my junior year was going to get five stars and rave reviews. Seriously? I knew even before it started, because the Summer after tenth grade, I got a job at the Old Clipper Inn. The town has a great diner (known for its burgers and tuna melts) where a lot of kids hang out, a couple of chain places and a handful of small restaurants and cafes, but the Old Clipper Inn is where your average celebrity eats when she's in town. Because here's the thing. Howards Walk is just a normal small town in the winter, but come June the rich summer people start to arrive from the city. The Old Clipper Inn is posh and expensive, and it caters to people with luxury boats, second homes and fancy cars. I applied spontaneously. I'd been thinking I should get a job to save for my future after high school (seeking fame and fortune under the bright lights of New York or LA). My parents were of the view that I should get a job to save for college (drudging away under a desk lamp in some state university). Anyway, I was passing the Inn, and I remembered how a lot of actors/models wait tables till they get their big break (a lot of college students wait tables, too, so it would take my parents' nagging down a notch). And I thought, *Why not? It can't hurt just to ask.*

And it didn't hurt to ask! I lucked out. They were short-handed and needed staff. Even though I didn't have any experience, Mr Schonblatt gave me a job on the spot because of my outgoing and positive personality. "Any fool can carry a tray," said Mr Schonblatt. "But not everybody can get along with the customers." He could tell that I was a natural when it comes to getting along with the customers. "And it doesn't hurt having a pretty face." That's the kind of statement that would have Loretta hissing and spitting, but I took it for the compliment it was. He gave me a big smile, and I gave it right back. Mr Schonblatt put me in the main dining room, where there were always a lot of workaholic businessmen and hedge-fund types (men who can eat and talk on their phones at the same time). They gave me the chance to really work on my charm and my flirting skills. And Mr Schonblatt was one hundred per cent right. I was a natural. Customers loved me. I got good tips, and being friendly and outgoing makes hauling plates of Yankee pot roast and clearing tables a lot more interesting than it is. I was so good that Mr Schonblatt said I was guaranteed a job next summer, too. I figured if I kept that up till I finished high school I'd have enough to move to the city of my choice the day after graduation (whether my parents liked it or not!).

Anyway, I took that as a major sign of great things to come. And I wasn't wrong about that, either.

School started and on the first day I walked into my Media class and there was Dillon Blackstock, like he'd stepped right out of one of my better dreams. I could hardly believe my luck. (Be still, my stampeding heart!) But it was true. He was sitting by the windows with his best friend Tobias Tuten. The two of them were having an intense conversation with the teacher, Mr Ethan. That's when I remembered that Dillon was in the Film Club and a movie geek and everything (everything meaning a friend of Loretta's, proving that she's right and the universe is pretty random!).

And to think I almost didn't take Media as my elective. I thought it was a good idea because of maybe being an actor someday, and I was pretty much born watching movies, but this course was a combination of theory and practice. You got to work on projects, but you also had to analyse a lot of films. So I kind of went back and forth about it in case the analysing part sucked all the joy out of the motion-picture experience. And then, on the day we had to hand in our options for the next year I went for it. Just like that. More or less on automatic. Media! Done! I reckon what swung it was all the movies I watched with Loretta (they had to give me an advantage!), but as soon as I saw Dillon in the class I knew in my heart that wasn't the reason. I'd made that last, fateful decision because my guardian angel (who takes a lot of days off) was saying "Go, girl! Go!" and shoving me in the right direction. If my heart had been a cheerleader it would've done a double cartwheel and a split.

Because here's the thing about Dillon Blackstock. On a scale of 1–10, he's a solid 9.8 (and that's just because nobody's perfect, there's always a flaw, and I don't want to be unrealistic). He is not just awesome-looking, he's part of the arty, sophisticated crowd (more sushi than pizza), and so cool being near him is like standing in front of an open fridge. In classes, he's always interesting and funny, but not show-offy. I'd been kind of into him in a general, that'll-never-happen kind of way for ages. (Not something that made me unique. He was on the wish list of half the girls in school.) But, to be really honest, the younger, less mature me was more pizza than sushi. Plus, he'd been going out with one girl for ages (we all figured she was super hot and everything but she went to some other school and no one had ever seen her). I would never go after a boy who has a girlfriend because of what Catie Coulson did to me (and that wasn't even my boyfriend she stole, it was just somebody I was interested in). So I could imagine how you'd feel about as happy as a gutted fish if your boyfriend dumped you for someone else (someone who ignored the already-taken sign).

Anyway, those are the reasons I never did anything about liking Dillon. Not even after I found out Loretta was so friendly with him (seriously, who'd have thought?).

But there he was. Fate had brought us together. I couldn't bite the hand of Fate just because Dillon Blackstock had a girlfriend. I figured the least I could do was show my gratitude by being friendly. Without thinking even once, I crossed the room and sat down next to him. Mr Ethan smiled at me. Tobias smiled at me. Dillon said, "And he's a director who never forgets the importance of music in creating mood." Tobias and Mr Ethan nodded, and I nodded too (even though I had no idea who they were talking about).

And then, not a week later, he broke up with his

girlfriend (it was the talk of the girls' toilets). *Quel new hope for the previously hopeless!*

Dillon was the star of the class. Mr Ethan loved him. And you could see why. He always knew what Mr Ethan was talking about. (And don't think I was the only one who didn't!) He always had something to contribute. (Ditto.) When you had to explain why you liked a movie, Dillon always knew. So I followed his lead. I never paid so much attention in a class as I did in that one. My mind never wandered the way it did in some lessons. I took notes. I asked questions. I had opinions. I never missed an opportunity to tell Dillon I agreed with him about whatever, even if I wasn't totally sure what it was I was agreeing with. Plus, I had a secret weapon. I had Loretta Reynolds. Not only was she someone Dillon and I had in common ("Loretta says hi," "Loretta told me about that…"), but, without Loretta, getting friendly with Dillon would've been a little like me trying to climb a mountain by myself wearing a summer dress and platform shoes and without a map. But now I had a fully equipped guide to get me up those steep and treacherous slopes! Because I'd already watched a lot of movies with her, there were plenty of times when Dillon or Mr Ethan mentioned a film and I could say, "Oh, I saw that!" Winning me points from Mr Ethan and (sometimes) a smile from Mr Blackstock (or at least a nod). And if something was said in class that I didn't understand or someone mentioned some movie or director I'd never heard of, I went straight to Loretta and got filled in so that next time, I was ready if it came up again. Here's the thing: even though I was tempted to join the film club, I decided against it. I didn't want to be too obvious. Plus, I didn't want Loretta to know what I was up to, and she was already suspicious from the time we ran into Dillon at the mall. (You can tell. You can see her thinking.) I figured she'd be negative. She'd either believe I wasn't serious about Dillon (because of the boys I'd dated in the past), or she'd try to discourage me (because of the pizza–sushi thing).

I know broken hearts take time to mend. Plus, you don't want to get somebody on the rebound, because there's a really big chance they haven't stopped bouncing yet. But that didn't mean I couldn't prepare the ground for new seeds of love. When his broken heart was mended, I wanted Dillon to turn and see me sitting next to him (or walking beside his good friend Loretta). There I'd be, a girl who shared his passion for film (as proven by how many movies I'd seen, including ones with subtitles). A girl with a talent for style, colour and design (all my Art teachers said so). A girl who knows what a McGuffin is.

(Yes, I had to ask Loretta, but I know!)

Life being the way it is, the road to love, happiness and Dillon Blackstock wasn't one that went downhill. It was straight up, steep and winding and there were things in the way. I'm really good at letting a boy know I like him without sending up flares, but I always wait for him to make the first move. Only Dillon isn't like the boys I usually dated, the Duanes of this world. They're nice guys and everything, but mainly I dated them because they're good-looking and popular. Not because I thought God could give Himself a pat on the back for making them. Something He absolutely could do for making Dillon Blackstock. Dillon's never boring (yes, Loretta, like Duane can be) and I really liked talking to him. That's another thing. Because he's so into being a filmmaker, Dillon really listens to other people. And watches what's going on like he's mentally taking notes. But because he was different from my usual, I wasn't sure I knew how to read him. He didn't flirt like normal guys. There was no showing off or being super nice with Dillon; he was the same with everybody (except Mr Ethan – Mr Ethan he called "sir"). If I saw Dillon when I was with another boy, Dillon never looked like he wondered what was going on, or like he wished it was him I was with. So if he was making any moves or dropping any hints, they were so subtle that I totally missed them. Even though I was looking for them like a detective looking for clues.

Media was pretty chill. We were more a crew than a class (helping each other with projects and sitting around discussing stuff), so it was all very friendly. But, like I said, there was no sign that Dillon was friendlier to me than to anyone else (he was even friendly to Miles Kinko, who was obsessed with alien invasion movies and could empty a room faster than a fire drill). And Dillon always had a bunch of people around him. So although I felt like I was making progress as the year went on (lots of smiles and nods and walking from class with him – and at least four other people and Tobias) there was no offer of "You want to come over and watch that Norwegian film we were talking about?" or anything like that.

And then, one Friday towards the end of the year, a few of us went for a coffee after school like we sometimes did. That's when Dillon said he had this great idea for a movie. He was going to spend the summer in Howards Walk working on a documentary about his brother's wedding.

I've always loved weddings, so that really grabbed my attention. "Is it going to be one of those big, romantic, fairy-tale weddings?"

"Oh, it'll be big. But fairy-tale depends on what kind you're thinking of." Dillon laughed. "Me, I'm pretty sure it'll be dark and scary, and everybody'll wish someone had put a spell on them so they slept through it. Because if anybody's going to turn into a bridezilla, it's going to be my future sister-in-law. She's a total princess. You'd think she'd be dizzy all the time, having the world revolve around her the way it does."

I figured sympathy was the best response here. "Your poor brother."

"What can you do? It's his life. And she's the kind of high-maintenance girl he likes. All moods and drama and demands." Dillon shrugged. "About the only thing my brother and I really have in common is our mother."

Dillon already had a pretty good idea of what he wanted from the movie. He was going to do behind-the-scenes interviews and record as much of the planning process as someone who didn't live with the bride's family could. "At least I'll be able to film the fights between her and my brother." (I swear his smile could bring about nuclear disarmament!) From the house to the church to the reception and beyond, Dillon and his camera would capture every second.

"It's not just about the bride and groom," said Dillon. "The guests are important characters, too. What they say.

What they think. What they get up to." He winked (possibly at me – at the very least, close to me).

I smiled back. Conspiratorially. But enthusiasm for his idea wasn't what you'd call universal. Looks were exchanged. Brows furrowed. A couple of people suggested that everybody does wedding videos nowadays.

"No way is it going to be your normal wedding video," said Dillon. "The potential for high drama is enormous. I want the tantrums and the fights. I want everything from her father bossing everyone around to the last guest passing out in his dessert. But what I'd really love is a shot of when her old man gets the bill. This guy's a real case study. Mega rich and mega greedy. He'll drop three hundred dollars on a shirt and then go into meltdown if someone short-changes him a nickel. If I could get him throwing a fit like that, it would make for awesome social commentary. It could be a YouTube sensation."

Tobias shook his head. "I don't know, man. I mean, everybody's family is pretty dysfunctional. You'd need something really out there. You know, if somebody got shot. Or if it turned out the bride and groom are related. Or if one of them rode off into the sunset with some dude on a Harley. Then maybe you'd have some awesome social commentary."

"Or if Mars attacked the reception," said Miles.

"That'd make it spectacularly vivid."

Tobias ignored him. "Otherwise, all you do have is another wedding video. Bride. Groom. Rice. Boring speeches."

Everybody else at the table nodded. Just another wedding video.

Dillon was used to looking down at the page he was on and seeing Tobias right beside him. You could tell he was disappointed.

I couldn't bear that. So even though I'm less confrontational than washing instructions, I had to disagree with Tobias about it being ho-hum (even if I was disagreeing with Dillon's best bud). "I think you're all wrong." I said I thought it was a really terrific idea. And I didn't see why they thought it would be just the same old same old. No two mascaras are exactly the same, so it was pretty obvious that no two wedding videos are, either. "Yeah, sure, it'd be absolutely awesome if the bride's father does have a meltdown while the camera's going and maybe punches the groom. Something really memorable and dramatic like that." I looked right at Dillon. "But even without that, I bet you could get enough interesting stuff to make a significant statement about modern life."

"Maybe if the bride's old man declares his undying

loathing for his new son-in-law," argued Tobias. "But not if all that happens is that one of the bridesmaids gets drunk and throws up on the table."

"Oh, come on..." It's important to smile when you're disagreeing with someone, so they know you're not mad. "It's the editing that's really important." The footage you shoot is the material, but the editing gives it shape and form. "We all know that a documentary isn't the true story of what happened. It's just one version of the true story of what happened." Didn't I say I pay a lot of attention in Media? "So no matter what happens, or doesn't happen, it could still be funny and revealing. A real picture of the insanity of modern life." And sometimes I pay attention to Loretta, too! "Maybe I haven't been to a trillion weddings myself, but, let's face it, something interesting always happens. A wedding's like a microcosm of human behaviour. It's all there – the people, the emotions, the craziness – it's like a living allegory."

There were some murmurs of agreement when I was done. And I could tell Dillon was impressed because he'd never looked at me that way before. You know, like we were the only people in the room who spoke the same language.

"That's true," said Dillon. He was nodding away and

looking thoughtful (a very good look for him). "That's totally what it is. It has everything. It's a living allegory."

Then I told them how at my cousin's wedding her ring bearer was her pet wolf and the best man and the groom were both women. It wasn't really dramatic, maybe, but it was pretty novel. Especially when the wolf decided he liked cake.

Dillon said, "Really? Are you serious? A wolf?"

I said yes. I don't have the imagination to make something like that up. "My family's a lot more interesting than you'd think from seeing my parents."

"That is wild." Dillon grinned. "A wolf! Did it eat the little bride and groom on top of the cake?" Everybody laughed at that. "I really wish I'd been there."

So did I.

That's when I got really bold and said that if he wanted I could help him with his movie. "I'm around all Summer," I said. "I'd love to work on it with you. It's a lot more interesting than going to the beach."

He looked thoughtful again. "You know, you may have something there." He was kind of looking at me and not looking at me at the same time. "You might understand the bride a lot better than I do. And you have a real female viewpoint, don't you?"

I said I absolutely had a real female viewpoint. "I'm

all girl!"

"Yeah, you are." He nodded. "That could be really important and dimensional."

If I was sure I didn't have any other big plans for the Summer.

Seriously? Maybe if I'd been booked on a flight to Paris I might have hesitated, but anything else I would've cancelled faster than you can kick off a shoe. I mean, let's be real. If you get to heaven and the angel at the gates invites you in, you don't say you'll think about it. I said to count me in.

Because here's the thing: even though I knew Dillon liked me okay, and we were friendly and everything, sometimes I kind of had the feeling he didn't take me totally seriously. Not seriously like he took Tobias or Mr Ethan. I don't want to sound like Loretta here (I mean, really, God forbid!) but I figured this was my big chance to show Dillon that I wasn't just a pretty face (even though a pretty face is important). And as for working together, it wouldn't be just for the Summer, would it? Once we shot everything, there'd be the rushes, the editing and all that other stuff. Plus, there's this thing called propinquity. It means that people who see each other a lot have a good chance of forming a relationship. I figured that with propinquity on my side, there was no way Dillon and I wouldn't be dating by the middle of July. And chances were I'd be going to the wedding, too, since he couldn't possibly film it all by himself. Weddings are known for bringing people together. So if we weren't already dating before his brother got married, we would definitely be dating afterwards. I saw the future and right at the centre of it was Dillon Blackstock. I was rolling on the River of Love.

But there was a waterfall I hadn't counted on.

Loretta

My balloon of hope starts to drift away

I was really enjoying my junior year. I had some great classes and great teachers (especially Ms Wallenstein for History, who was nothing short of empowering and inspirational) and I was doing well in all of them – even for me. I was also getting a lot from my extracurricular activities – the school paper, and the Film and Astronomy Clubs – especially the Astronomy Club. Given all that, I should have been as pleased as a person who just had a planet named after her. I was less pleased than that by a light year or two, and the reason why can be summed up in two words: Gabriel Schwartz.

Gabriel and I had worked closely all sophomore year on projects and events for the astronomy club. It was Gabriel's idea that we fulfil our community service requirements by giving talks on the universe to primary schools – which was both innovative and a remarkable success. It was my idea that we show screenings of the *Wonders of the Solar System* and *Wonders of the Universe* series to raise money towards buying the school a serious telescope – which was both innovative and a small triumph. Together, we were planning a club outing in the August between our junior and senior years to view the Perseids – another first. Best of all, Gabriel was elected president of the club for our senior year, and I was vice president. Which for definite was a significant bond.

All of this meant that we saw a lot of each other – in an official sort of way – and would be working together even more closely come September. There was only one thing that could have made me happier, of course, and that was if Gabriel and I saw a lot of each other in an unofficial way. We got on really well – he's easy-going and smart and funny – and we have a lot more in common than the universe. Neither of us has any trouble giving a talk or speaking up in class, but we're both socially shy – if not actually completely inept. Yet, though ZiZi was right about my trouble talking to boys, I had no trouble talking to Gabe – and he had no trouble talking to me. The new top I'd worn at the club dinner at the end of our sophomore year hadn't had the effect I'd wanted – it hadn't had any effect at all if you want the truth – but all wasn't lost. Sometimes, after a meeting, he'd give me a ride home; and sometimes we texted or talked on the phone – usually about club business or something like the latest Mars probe. On one memorable afternoon we talked for over an hour, parked outside my house, about the Higgs boson. For the first time, I actually could see myself going on a date … having a boyfriend … being kissed. I used to think that if those things ever happened to me, it wouldn't be until graduate school – when the popular girls were all taken – but now I wasn't so certain. Although I didn't know how much Gabriel liked me or in what way, I knew that he did like me. Realistically, you don't sit in a car in a snowstorm talking about the Higgs boson with someone you don't like, do you? I really don't think so. When I finally got out of the car and went into the house my heart was filled with hope, floating above me like a balloon filled with helium.

The problem was that, after that memorable afternoon, nothing changed. I can't flirt, and Gabriel's about as flirtatious as a monk who's taken a vow of silence. ZiZi flirts the way most people breathe. She can let a boy know that she'd say yes if he asked her out simply by the way she asks to borrow his pen; and she can tell if he thought she'd say yes simply by the way he offers to loan her a pen. I've more than watched her, I've studied her, trying to get a handle on how she does it. I've decided that it's a talent that you're born with, which can't be learned any more than the ability to add six-digit figures in your head.

I was about to put hope back in its box for a few years when Gabriel and I had the idea for making a club event out of the summer meteor showers. We were so excited about it that he suggested we make fliers to put around school and the town, inviting anyone who was interested to join us. We worked on the wording together one Friday after school – our heads almost touching as we sat side by side at the computer. He has a state-of-the-art graphics programme on his own laptop and took it home to work on the layout and design. That night he called and invited himself over the next day to get my approval before he printed them out.

I hung up in a daze. That had to mean something, didn't it? He invited himself over. It was April, the Perseids were in August. He could have waited until Monday to show me; he could have waited until June.

Yoga instructors and psychotherapists don't work regular hours or days, which can be irritating when you're little and want them to do things with you on the weekend, but which, when you're older and want the house to yourself on a Saturday so you can be alone with Gabriel Schwartz, is a godsend.

I was determined to act as if it was a regular Saturday. I didn't spend hours getting dressed and staring at myself in the mirror. I got up, washed and put on my usual outfit – T-shirt and jeans – but the T-shirt was my Albert Einstein one for good luck. After I fed the cats and had my breakfast, I sat down to do some homework. I have a strong will and forced myself not to look at the time every two minutes, but I could feel it crawling by in a trough of setting cement, weights tied to its ankles.

Gabe and I had never been completely alone before – not unless you counted the time spent in his car, which I didn't count because he was usually driving. When we were in his car and he wasn't driving – like that afternoon in the snow – there were always people around who could see us and we could see them. Especially Mrs Shaunnessey, who is a one-woman neighbourhood watch, looking out of her living-room window as if she's expecting trouble. It was the idea of being completely alone with him that made it difficult to concentrate on my homework; I couldn't stop thinking about what might happen later. I'd offer Gabe a snack and something to drink. Because I didn't know if he'd want something hot or something cold, I'd double-washed two glasses and two mugs. We'd sit in the kitchen discussing his design and checking over the copy again. After we'd exhausted that as a topic of conversation, we'd just be sitting in the kitchen talking – the two of us, all by ourselves with the refrigerator gently humming behind us. Would I get up the courage to ask him out? Would he get up the courage to ask me? I could imagine myself asking him if the moment was right. If we were both laughing at something, or if he smiled at me that way he did the afternoon the club watched the Curiosity rover on NASA TV. I could just about imagine him asking me, clearing his throat the way he does when he's anxious, saying my name as if it was a question. I was nervous, but in a good way. My hope-filled balloon was bouncing against the ceiling.

When the doorbell rang, my strong will stopped me from running to answer it; my heart began running instead. I was smiling before I reached the door, practising what I'd say, *Gabe, hi! Come on in! Gabe, hi! Come on in...*

I opened the door. "Ga—" but it wasn't Gabriel Schwartz standing on the porch. "Oh. Zi. It's you."

"You don't have to sound so glad to see me."

"I wasn't expecting you. This guy from astronomy club's dropping something by."

"Oh, right." She breezed past me. "I just had to get out of the house. I had this massive fight with my mom and I need to vent."

I followed her into the kitchen. I wanted to tell her she had to go, but I couldn't. Massive fights with her mother weren't as rare as a blue moon, but that didn't mean she wasn't upset. She was practically sending off sparks. ZiZi helped herself to water from the fridge, threw herself into the chair Gabriel was supposed to sit in and launched into what had happened with her mom and how unreasonable Gina was.

I don't know why, but I wasn't ready to tell her about Gabriel yet. With hindsight – which is so much more accurate than foresight – I reckon I probably should have. She'd have understood the situation and would have left us alone or at least gone to my room to wait for him to leave. I should have told her, but I didn't. This time when the bell rang, ZiZi broke off in the middle of a sentence. "Aren't you going to get that? It must be your star friend."

"Yeah." I jumped up. "That'll be him."

The other thing I should probably have said was to Gabriel when I answered the door. I should have told him that my friend ZiZi was inside; that she'd dropped by unexpectedly. I didn't say that either. I said, "Hi. Come on in." He followed me down the hallway, talking the whole time, but I have no idea about what. All I could think of was ZiZi, sitting at the table with her glass of water, waiting to resume her story.

Gabriel shut up the second he stepped into the kitchen and saw her.

I started to say, "You know ZiZi," but I didn't get any further than "You".

I don't know if he tripped because he was so surprised to see ZiZi, or if he tripped because it was turning out to be that kind of day, but he did trip – and catapulted past me and into the fridge. The impact of him hitting the refrigerator caused the cereal boxes that live there to topple; in trying to avoid the avalanche of cornflakes and muesli, Gabriel landed in Gertie and Alice's food dishes.

"That's quite an entrance," said ZiZi.

She was the only one who laughed.

Gabriel helped me clean up the mess – clearing his throat and apologizing the whole time – and then he said he had to go, he had somewhere to be. He left the flier in its envelope on the table for me to look at later.

I watched him hurry down the front path as if someone was chasing him, and above him my balloon of hope drifted off into the clouds. Possibly never to be seen again.

ZiZi

Loretta could make a pig's ear out of a silk purse

Loretta and I were both in Ms Wallenstein's American History class in our junior year. Most people picked the usual topics for their term paper – the Civil War, Manifest Destiny, the American Revolution, the Colonial Period, the Civil Rights Movement. Stuff like that. Here's the thing. Ms Wallenstein is a feminist (when we did the Declaration of Independence she made really sure we understood who the Founding Fathers meant by "all men are created equal"). Naturally, Ms Wallenstein loves Loretta. Me not so much. So when Loretta decided to do her paper on women in American society (in Loretta's case, the radicals, the abolitionists, the suffragettes and the anarchists), I decided to do mine on women too (in my case, pioneers, who, if you ask me, have a much higher profile). I figured I was killing two women's-righters with one stone. It would win me points with Ms Wallenstein and make Loretta happy (one less thing for her to gripe about).

It was after Easter when Loretta called one night and asked if I wanted to go into the city with her at the weekend to do some research for our History papers.

"This weekend?" It was pretty short notice for Ms Plan Every Detail Months in Advance.

"What city?"

"Reykjavik."

"What?" It sounded like some kind of weird cheese. Probably mouldy.

"Oh, for God's sake, Zi." Loretta sighed. "What city do you think? We're a lot closer to New York than we are to Barcelona."

"Really? Are you serious?" New York! Even though we weren't exactly thousands of miles away, New York wasn't somewhere we went very often. If ever. I was so excited I nearly knocked over the nail polish. "We're going to New York on the weekend?" And then I pictured being in the car with her parents, and then walking around the city with them. Don't get me wrong, I like Loretta's parents a lot, but they can be a challenge. (They are related to her, after all!) I had a flash of hours and hours of her father going on and on about every incomprehensible topic he could come up with until even my eyebrows were numb and her mother telling me (over and over) how I had to eat more or a good wind would break me in two. (There's no chance Loretta was adopted, she's so much like them you'd think she'd been cloned.) "You mean with Stew and Odelia?"

"They can come if they want to, but I was thinking it would be just you and me."

"Just us? Seriously?" Usually, there was no way my parents would let me go into New York without an adult, just to wander around and possibly get into some kind of trouble. But this was different. This was for school. My parents would've let me kayak to Connecticut if I was doing it for school.

"Completely seriously. I want to check a couple of things at the Women's History Museum. And I figured you'd want to come, too. They're bound to have a lot of material on pioneer women."

I couldn't believe what I was hearing, and I don't mean about going to New York by ourselves (incredible as that was). It was the museum part that threw me. I knew things like paintings and aeroplanes and bottles have their own museums but when did women get one?

"What's in it?" I asked. "Quilts and corsets and knitting needles? Cosmetics through the ages?"

"I'm going to assume you're joking, ZiZi," said Loretta. "Don't disillusion me."

I said of course I was joking. And didn't add, "But not about the cosmetics."

"It just so happens that they have some fantastic exhibits and photographs. They also have a terrific library, including original papers and documents."

Would the excitement never end?

"You think we'll have time to do anything besides the museum?"

"Like what?"

You see what I'm up against here, right? I mean, only Loretta would have to ask what else you could do in New York besides visit a museum. If you gave her ten minutes in a department store to choose anything she wanted, the only thing she'd walk out with would be a pair of wellies.

"Manhattan may not be a gaseous planet or anything awesomely exciting like that, Lo, but there is a rumour that it's a pretty fascinating city. People come from all over the world to walk its streets and see its lights. I was thinking maybe we could just do a little exploring. Have a meal. Check out a couple of stores. You know, things that normal people do."

"We'll see what we can fit in," said Loretta. "But for definite we'll have supper there. I read about this incredible vegan restaurant I want to try."

Of course she did. That's what the Big Apple's known for: tofu.

"Well? What do you say?" asked Loretta. "You in?"

Like there was even a chance as big as a blackhead that I'd say no, right? Not that I really needed to do any more research. I'd got tons of information already and was pretty set. Plus, I'd seen enough TV shows and movies, and I'd even read *Little House on the Prairie* in middle school, so I knew a lot about female pioneers. Make your own soap, kill your own chicken, shoot your own gun. But the only times I'd ever been to New York were once on a class trip (to look at dinosaur bones and stuff like that), and twice with my parents and their other children (once to a Broadway musical and once to the Rockefeller Center at Christmas). Going without either my fourth-grade class or my family was an opportunity not to be missed. I didn't care if she was planning to spend the day with her nose in a book, I'd still rather go to New York with just Loretta than walk on the moon (even if she'd probably rather walk on the moon).

"Are you kidding? Of course I'm in."

To Loretta this was a chance to read some suffragette's diary (*chained myself to railings, got arrested*, that kind of thing), but for me it was a chance for Fate to open her arms and embrace me. New York is the kind of place where a girl with potential can be discovered just walking down the street (you wouldn't believe how many famous models were spotted by agencies when they were just going about their normal teenage lives). Being discovered before my parents sent me off to college was my dream. You could bet your last lip gloss that was something that was never going to happen in Howards Walk – which is the kind of place where a trunk full of magazines from 1900 might be discovered, but not the next face of Clairol. And if I was discovered, I wouldn't have to spend four more years in school. Not even my parents could argue with Clairol.

Loretta

None so blind as she who will not see

I didn't begin with the idea of taking ZiZi with me to the Women's History Museum. Initially, the only person I was thinking about was myself. I'd always wanted to visit it, and now I had the perfect reason for going; there would be information there that I couldn't get anywhere else. As soon as I decided to go, I knew that I wanted ZiZi to see it, too. ZiZi, of course, has as much interest in museums – no matter what's in them – as she has in the internal combustion engine. Possibly less; she does like riding in cars. Which means that if the museum weren't in New York City my chances of convincing her to accompany me would have been less than zero. Fortunately, it is in New York; there was no convincing necessary.

I knew even before we left Howards Walk that it was possible that I had unrealistic expectations of ZiZi. As I said, she's not a museumophile no matter how much you stretch your imagination, but I sincerely believed that seeing the Women's History Museum would be good for her. That it would open her big blue eyes. That it might even change her life – or at least her attitude. After all, we'd only had the enlightened Ms Wallenstein for this year so it wasn't exactly ZiZi's fault that she thought that all the great thinkers, innovators, philosophers, artists, writers, leaders, etcetera of the world have always been men. As if women had done nothing for millennia but change diapers and make soup. The sad fact – as they say – is that history is written by the winners, and throughout the centuries, the winners usually have that Y chromosome. Even though the Y chromosome was discovered by a woman. File under the heading: *Truly ironic*.

That's why I thought getting ZiZi to the museum was important. Not only is Nettie Stevens, the geneticist who first linked the Y chromosome to sex determination, there – in spirit if not in body – hundreds of other women are there, too. For the first time, ZiZi would see for herself all the women who had gone against convention, society and all those Y chromosomes to be their own people – and change the world.

Of course, before ZiZi could have her eureka moment about women, we had to get to the city. And because ZiZi was involved, we almost missed the train.

I wanted to get an early start in order to have the most time possible in the museum. It's not the kind of place you want to rush through. That is, it's not the kind of place I want to rush through. It should be studied; absorbed; savoured. The trouble was it was a Saturday. My parents were both working and couldn't take us to the station, and ZiZi's parents would only complain about being treated like a taxi service and not being able to sleep late on a day off if we'd asked them to drive us. We agreed to walk into town, and save the parental ride for our return.

I got up as soon as my alarm went off, dressed, had some breakfast, made lunch, packed a day bag and was at ZiZi's even earlier than we'd agreed – which is the only way you stand a chance of getting anywhere on time with her. Because I didn't want to wake her parents, I texted her that I was outside. ZiZi came to the door; she wasn't ready. It's a wonder I didn't faint from the shock.

She just stood there for a few seconds, eyeing me as if I had on socks with sandals, which, apparently, is a felony in the world of fashion. "Is that what you're wearing?" This wasn't a question or a statement; it was a disappointment.

No, of course it wasn't what I was wearing. I had a ballgown and heels in my backpack.

"It is what I have on, ZiZi."

"And I have on a robe, but it's not what I'm wearing." She was still looking at me as if I was a dress-sense criminal. "I just thought you might make a little effort to go to one of the fashion capitals of the world."

And I would do that *why*?

"We're not going to the Easter Parade. We're going to a museum." I held up my phone so she could see the time. "You better get moving. The next train's at twenty-five past, and, if we miss that, there's an hour till the next one."

"I'm nearly ready." She waved me in. "There's coffee in the kitchen. Why don't you have a cup while I finish getting dressed."

I marched past her. "Hurry."

Ten minutes later, I was tapping on the bathroom door. I had to whisper so as not to wake everyone else in the house, but I whispered urgently. "For God's sake, what's taking you so long?"

"I wanted to finish reading *War and Peace* before we go."

"ZiZi!"

"I'll be right there."

Ten minutes later I was back at the bathroom door. "ZiZi! For God's sake, the idea was to leave early this morning. Not early tomorrow morning. Why can't you do this on the train?"

"Because train toilets are small and part of a speeding vehicle, that's why. I'd be lucky not to blind myself. Go wait outside. I'll be with you in a minute."

I went outside and sat on the bumper of Mrs Abruzzio's car. I had a book with me – experts recommend having something to read while waiting for ZiZi – but I was too agitated about not making the train to concentrate on it. I spent the wait – which was longer than a minute by at least another ten – staring at the house, willing ZiZi to come out, and checking my phone to make sure that time hadn't come to a dead stop. When she did finally emerge, I nearly fell off the car. She had a wheelie case and was dressed for a party, probably in a penthouse with lots of famous people.

"Look at you!" I may have wailed slightly. "I'm not going to mention the dress." We would've been there bickering for another hour if I'd mentioned that her dress was never made to see daylight. "But those shoes! Are you insane? You can't walk around all day in those." They were the twenty-first-century equivalent of foot-binding. "They're practically stilts."

ZiZi groaned. "You're exaggerating again, Loretta. They're nothing like stilts." It was astounding that she could stand on one leg and swing out the other foot without falling. She should have been a gymnast. Or a ballerina. "Stilts don't have bows." Apparently unaffected by the laws of balance and movement – and with an impressive burst of speed – she swept past me and started down the street.

I fell in beside her. "We're never going to make the train." She was already slowing down. "Not with an average speed of three yards an hour."

"You're always so damn negative." ZiZi sighed loudly, to remind me that she'd said that almost as often as she'd said that I exaggerate. "How many times do I have to tell you, Lo? Things always work out okay. You just have to believe that they will."

I would have argued with that; I read papers and watch the news, I know it isn't true. But that's in the real world, not in the world of Giselle Abruzzio – which exists in a parallel, and much better, universe. Which explains why, before I could even open my mouth to disagree, a car pulled up in front of us. A smiling boy leaned his head out the window. It wasn't a head I recognized. "Yo! ZiZi! You need a ride?"

"Who is that?" I grabbed her elbow. "Do you know him?" The mere fact that he knew her name was no guarantee.

"Of course I know him." She shook me off, smiling straight ahead. "That's Jeremiah Hakilah. He's in my French class." To him she said, "We're going to the train, and we'd love a ride. But we don't want to put you out."

"I'm heading into town anyway." The passenger door opened. "Hop in!"

"Oh ye of little faith," whispered ZiZi – and then she climbed in next to Jeremiah. I got in the back with the burger boxes and the sweat socks.

You could tell that Jeremiah Hakilah was pretty happy to have ZiZi sitting beside him. He kept grinning at her when he should have had his eyes on the road, and he talked when he should have been concentrating on steering. That aside, if there'd been a minimum speed limit, he'd have been under it. I leaned forward so my head was between them. "What time's the train again, ZiZi?" I asked.

"I totally didn't get that piece we had to translate last week," said Jeremiah. "Was the guy who wrote it on drugs, or what? It really did my head in."

"Mine, too," said ZiZi. "After a while I just gave up and let the internet do it for me."

Jeremiah slapped the steering wheel. "Me, too!"

A meeting of minds.

The train was in the platform and the last passengers

were boarding when we finally pulled up in front of the station. Very slowly. It was all I could do not to jump out the window.

"Uh-oh," laughed ZiZi. "We better hurry. Thanks for the ride."

"Yeah." I opened my door. "Thanks for the ride."

"You're welcome." Jeremiah waved. "Now run!"

It defied all the laws of physics but she did run – up metal stairs – in those stupid shoes. Yet another example of the Giselle Abruzzio parallel universe.

"We're not going to make it," I said as we staggered onto the platform. I could see that the conductor was about to shut the doors. "I told you we weren't going to make it."

ZiZi raised one arm. "Wait, please, sir!" she called. "Please wait!"

Her voice has the effect on men that high frequency whistles have on dogs. The conductor looked over.

ZiZi smiled and waved. "We're coming! Please wait!"

The conductor waited and we hurried on board.

"Whew!" ZiZi laughed as we sat down. "That was close."

"Oh, do you think so? You mean because, if we'd been a minute later, you'd have been waving the train goodbye, not Jeremiah What'shisname?"

"Hakilah," said ZiZi.

I leaned back in my seat. "You know, I really can't believe that, just this once, you couldn't get up, get dressed and be ready to go on time. If we'd missed this train, we would've lost most of the morning."

"I was as fast as I could be."

"Yeah right. You could've painted an SUV in the time it took you to do your make-up."

"Only a toy one. And anyway, I don't see why you're making a federal case out of it. Maybe you didn't notice, Loretta, but we didn't miss the train." She gestured to the trees and houses flashing past the windows. "Here we are! Safe and sound, and New York bound!"

"We made it by mere seconds, ZiZi. If the conductor had closed the doors—"

"But he didn't. He saw us and waited."

"You mean he saw you."

"We're together, Lo." Her voice was taut with patience. "If he saw me, he saw you."

"He didn't help me on board."

"You don't need help. All you have is that miniature backpack."

"Because all I brought is my iPad – so I can take notes – my phone and my lunch. What do you have in there? We're not staying for a week but you're practically dragging a trunk with you."

"God, there you go again with the exaggerating. It's nothing like a trunk. It's not even a suitcase really. It's more like a really large handbag. We're going to be out all day, remember. I have to bring everything I might need."

"For what? Ending up on a desert island instead of in the city?"

"For if something unexpected happens."

She had a change of clothes in case of an emergency – an unspecified emergency. Change of shoes, for the same reason. Make-up. Hairbrush. Phone charger. Toothbrush. Water. Breath mints. Extra eyelashes in case a sandstorm blew off the ones she was wearing.

"You don't think that's a little excessive?" I argued. "You couldn't even get your bag up on the rack by yourself. What if that man hadn't helped you?"

"Loretta…" She patted my shoulder. "That's what you don't seem to get. There's always some man who'll offer to help. That's the beauty of being a girl."

My sigh probably registered as an Earth tremor in Utah. "You mean that's the beauty of being a girl like you."

ZiZi

Despite everything, I stay cheerful and optimistic

For once, Loretta hadn't planned for everything.

It was a sunny Spring day when we left Howards Walk, but it started raining while we were on the train. What a weather expert would call unexpected showers. I figured they'd stop by the time we got to the city. I really wanted them to, and not just because I didn't want to get wet. My New York fantasy was that, when we came out of the station, we would walk right into a shoot for a commercial, and that the director would take one look at me and shout, "That's her! That's the girl I've been looking for!" (You have to admit that, even if it was improbable or at least unlikely, it wasn't totally impossible. Stuff like that happens all the time.) What we walked into was a deluge, like God was planning to flood the Earth again (but hadn't told anybody his plans this time). I watched my dreams run down the sewer with the rain.

We'd bought MetroCards so we could use the subway and buses, but we didn't have an umbrella. Loretta had a jacket (because the weather forecast had mentioned dropping temperatures), but I didn't even have that. I thought I'd packed everything I might possibly need (back-up clothes, shoes, make-up and all that stuff, plus a small hairdryer, because you never can tell when something like that will come in handy). Unfortunately, neither I nor the weather bureau had thought it might rain. And walking in a cloudburst was not an option, not for me. My shoes would disintegrate. God knows what would have happened to my dress.

Loretta stood beside me, sighing. "We're going to be drenched just getting to the cross-town bus." (As if it would make any difference if her hair or clothes got wet.) We were on the west side of midtown and had to get to the Lower East Side. "And then we'll have to get another bus downtown…" Two buses. Or a gondola if one happened to be passing. "Maybe if we get some plastic bags—"

"Plastic bags?" She expected me to cover myself in plastic bags? That would get me noticed by agency scouts. *There's Garbage Girl! She's just what I've been looking for!* "What exactly are you planning to do with plastic bags?"

"We could wear them instead of boots. At least our feet would stay dry."

You have to know her to really believe her.

"Loretta," I said, "I am not putting plastic bags on my feet." For God's sake, in New York even the dogs wear designer boots. "We'll have to take a cab."

"Oh, sure," said Loretta. "We and everybody else on this street."

I asked her if she had a better idea.

For once in her life, she didn't.

I shivered ever so slightly. "Heads or tails to see who goes?"

"God forbid you should ruin your hair. I'll do it. But I'm putting on my hat."

It's not really a hat. Loretta always carries one of those plastic rain bonnets, the kind not usually worn by anyone under fifty. (Sometimes I think she goes out of her way to be unfashionable if not totally nerdy.) Normally, I would rather have hives than be seen with Loretta in that thing, especially in the world's capital of sophistication, but I didn't argue. Already my feet felt damp. Maybe no one would notice her with all the rain.

In case you've forgotten, Loretta isn't exactly shy and retiring or easily pushed around. Every time an empty cab appeared, she charged at it like a young hippo. But New York is a jungle. The other hippos were bigger. Determined. Experts. Elbows and shoulders blocked her.

Computer bags, briefcases and shopping buffered them. These hippos took no prisoners.

I stood in the shelter of the entrance, watching Loretta dash to the kerb, try to wedge her way to the taxi door, get shoved away or out-wedged and come dashing back. At the rate she was going, we'd be spending the whole day in front of the station.

"This is when you want to be Wonder Woman," she said after her fourth attempt, through gritted teeth.

It seemed to me that what we wanted wasn't Wonder Woman but her prettier, more charming and personable sister. So the next time an empty cab turned the corner, I pulled Loretta back, held my handbag over my head and went for it myself.

Loretta claims that men invented high heels so women can't keep up with or run away from them, but I can run when I have to, even in heels. (It's a skill you learn, like defusing a bomb.) I put my hand on the door handle at the same time as a man in a classic Burberry raincoat. He was forty if he was a day, but still handsome (clean-shaven, black hair just starting to grey at the temples, the *Wall Street Journal* over his head).

I widened my eyes. "Oh, please..." There was noise all around us but I kept my voice soft and coaxing (I'd just seen an old Marilyn Monroe film with my dad and was channelling her). "I know it's a lot to ask and I'm sure you have somewhere important you're going, but my friend…" I pointed to Loretta, a wet, defeated young hippo with what was pretty much a plastic bag on her head. "This is her first time in New York and everything's going wrong." I gave him my best smile (and my best smile is really good; if it could be bottled I'd make a fortune). "It would be so kind of you."

He smiled back (his smile was pretty good, too). "No problem. We can't have you standing out in this rain, can we? That's no way to welcome you to New York."

I couldn't thank him enough.

Loretta, who should have been grateful for my intervention, didn't thank me at all. She was all askew because I got us a cab in less than sixty seconds and she "nearly drowned" trying. (My fault, obviously. You had to wonder who she'd blamed for everything before she met me.)

As we climbed in, she said, "So how did you manage to do that, Zi? Have you been practicing white magic again?"

"I don't need magic." I snapped the seat belt over me. "I have a positive personality."

"Yeah," said Loretta. "That and a tight, short dress."

* * *

Imagine the most exciting, awesome and wonderful thing that could ever happen to you. For example, let's say that you lived in the suburbs of some fourth-rate city and shared a room with your little sisters and their pet gerbils, and then one day you found out you're really a princess and should have been living in a palace with an entire wing to yourself and someone to put the toothpaste on the brush for you and tell you if it was raining or not. Would you be happy? Yes, you would be. You would be way-over-Mars happy. Well, that's how happy Loretta was to be in the Women's History Museum. She said it was "a dream come true" (the rest of us just want to be on the cover of *Vogue*). And that's even though it isn't a real museum that takes up a whole block and looks like the Romans built it. It's two old houses knocked together, and the only windows are at the front and the back. (My first time in New York City without a chaperone and I couldn't even see daylight!)

I wasn't super impressed. Not that I expected to be. I figured it would be pretty dreary and boring, and, no matter what Loretta said, a lot about mops and childbirth. But I had a couple of surprises.

Nobody was going to miss New York Fashion Week to visit this museum, but I was still amazed at how many women (sans mops and infants) were featured in the main exhibition. Maybe, like me, you thought that for most of history men were out in the world doing things and women were indoors taking care of the house and stuff like that. Here's the thing. A lot of them did get out of the house. Way more than you'd ever guess. Doctors … lawyers … spies … farmers … soldiers … musicians … painters … abolitionists … suffragists … writers … explorers … journalists … war correspondents…

They were all there. What wasn't there, was men. And I don't just mean in the exhibits themselves. There wasn't a single man wandering through the rooms as a visitor, or hovering in a doorway keeping an eye on things. You'd think at least one might have come in to get out of the rain. It was like they'd all been moved to another planet. Or we had.

"Don't you think it's weird?" I asked Loretta. "The only time we're anywhere that's just girls is gym."

"It's just another example of the way things work," said Loretta. "From sports to books, things about men are meant to be interesting to everybody. But things about women are assumed to only be interesting to them."

"Either that, or the guys are too busy out running the world," I joked.

Loretta didn't laugh.

So here's the other thing I totally hadn't planned for.

Being in the museum brought out the professor in Loretta. Lecturing's something Loretta's prone to anyway, but as soon as we stopped at the first display case, she was off. How, historically, women were patronized and marginalized. How hard they had to fight to get into professions. To be taken seriously. To be acknowledged and given the credit they deserved. I said that if all these women were out there writing symphonies and making medical discoveries, you'd think I would've heard of some of them. Loretta humphed. The reason I'd never heard of any of these women, she informed me, was because men were the ones who usually wrote history.

I must've been nodding off standing up, because she suddenly said there was something she knew I'd like, and marched me upstairs to the section on women's fashions through the ages. Fashion is my thing, so I was all set to be interested. And I would've been interested, if I'd been by myself. (The exhibit pretty much started with grass skirts and worked its way up.) But Professor Loretta sucked all the joy right out of it like drawing fat from a thigh. According to her, women's clothes have always been designed either to restrict them so they can't possibly do the things men say they can't do, or to expose their bodies so they're nothing more than a sex toy. Or possibly to do both. (And I'd always thought fashion was about beauty and fun!) We went from one exhibit to the next, with her pointing out everything that was wrong with each era. I can't tell you what a relief it was when she decided she was hungry.

At lunch in the cafeteria (a couple of vending machines and some tables and chairs), she gave me an earful about skipping meals and the carcinogens in diet sodas while she chomped on her sandwiches. After Loretta's alternative History class, the dungeon in the basement where the library was located felt like an oasis in the desert. At least she couldn't talk in the library.

Loretta recommended a book about the "real West" she thought I should look at (God knows how she knew about it). She was always recommending books to me, and normally I ignored her, but it was easier to take that off the shelf than to find something myself, so I did. I knew all about the brave pioneer women who stood shoulder to shoulder with their men and skinned bison while in labour and stuff like that. And about women like Calamity Jane and Annie Oakley (there weren't as many of them!). But this book had a lot about the women who didn't climb into a Conestoga wagon with their husband and their children and a barrel of flour. These were women who had no choice but to be mail-order brides – or prostitutes (there were quite a few of them).

And women who disguised themselves as men so they didn't have to get married or join a brothel. I actually checked on the spine to make sure Loretta hadn't written it, it sounded so much like one of her lectures about what the choices for women used to be (marriage, prostitution or charity). I'm not saying it wasn't interesting, but it was pretty depressing. I flipped through it, and took some notes, but by then I was feeling pretty done. "I'm going to go get a coffee," I whispered to Loretta. "I'm leaving my bag here." Loretta was so stuck into her research that she wouldn't have noticed if everybody in the library was suddenly changed into a box of salt. She nodded without looking up.

Someone (a woman, of course!) was walking through the front door as I came up the stairs to the ground-floor hallway. Outside, the rain had stopped and the sun was shining. I'd been in the museum for so long that I'd forgotten I was in New York City. Before I knew what I was doing, I was on the street.

Quel liberation!

Loretta

ZiZi continues to dash my hopes against the frilly but treacherous cliffs that loom over her bubbly pink sea

The library was even better than I'd thought it would be. Which means that I was so absorbed in my research that I didn't realize ZiZi had left the building until the museum was closing for the night. We'd both been working for a while when she said she was going for a coffee. I assumed she'd be back after she finished her drink. When she wasn't, I used the wrong type of logic to work out where she was. I used deductive: we're in the museum, the museum has an impressive exhibit on the history of women's fashion, ZiZi loves fashion, therefore ZiZi has gone back to that exhibit. I should have used inductive: ZiZi's a lot more excited about being in New York than about being in the museum, therefore ZiZi has decided to get her coffee from a café on the street and not the machine in the museum.

When they announced that they'd be closing in twenty

minutes, I finished what I was doing and put the book I was reading back on the shelf. I'd half expected ZiZi to materialize to get her things but there was still no sign of her. I picked up my bag and hers, checked in the snack bar in case she was in there on her phone and time had melted away like the last patches of snow at the end of winter, and then I went upstairs. I waited in the foyer entrance till I was asked to leave. The door was locked behind me.

There were a lot of people on the street, of course, but none of them were Giselle Abruzzio. She knew when the museum closed – wherever she'd gone, she had to be on her way back. I sat on the steps and called; her phone wasn't on. I left a message. Unless she'd stopped off at the Whirlpool Galaxy, she was taking her own sweet time. I had my book, but I couldn't read and watch out for ZiZi; watching out for ZiZi took priority. The museum staff left, which is when I started to worry. ZiZi thinks she's seriously sophisticated because she can tell the brand of a handbag without seeing the label, but in my opinion she isn't always that good at judging guys. This was New York – a city absolutely teeming with men – and a lot of those men were not going to be the salt-of-the-earth, trustworthy type. Something could have happened to her. Given the statistics, that something could easily be murder, rape, robbery or abduction. If male aggression was taking the day off, she could have been hit by a car or crushed by something falling out of a window. The best-case scenario was that she was lost and wandering the unfamiliar streets with no idea of where she was. Where was she? Chinatown? Brooklyn? Greenwich Village? Harlem? The Upper West Side? Was there any chance she'd found her way to Queens? How would she ever find her way back?

I sent another text; I called again. I didn't know what to do. It seemed a little premature to involve the police, but my worry was increasing by the minute. Besides which, I imagined arriving back home without her. Questions would be asked; tears would be shed. I'd be known for ever as the girl who lost her best friend. Crippled by guilt, I'd abandon my career plans and take a job selling womenswear at a major department store, convinced that one day ZiZi – alive but suffering from amnesia – would come in to shop. She would never forget how to shop. Her disappearance would haunt me the rest of my life. I was just about to phone my mom to ask her what she thought I should do when I caught a flutter of colour at the end of the street, and there was ZiZi. She started running as soon as she saw me. I was so relieved that if I hadn't had my bag and her suitcase I would have met her halfway.

I got to my feet. "For God's sake, Zi. Where the hell have you been?"

"I'm sorry! I'm really, really sorry! It wasn't on purpose!"

I was so happy to see her that I immediately began explaining about not realizing she'd left the museum. "When I got outside and you weren't here, I started to think that something ha—" I began. Which was when I saw the shopping. "Oh for God's sake. I should've known!"

"It's not what you think," said ZiZi. "And anyway, you can't be mad at me if you didn't even know I was gone. You didn't even miss me. Some best friend you are. I'm the one who should be annoyed."

"I didn't miss you because I was *working*!" Relief was being elbowed out of the way by my usual ZiZi-based frustration. "Not shopping. I thought you were going to get more out of today than new clothes."

"That's what's wrong, isn't it? It's the shopping. That's what you're really mad about. There you are, learning all about the oppression of women, and I'm out buying instruments of torture." She held up the bags. "Socks, Loretta. Tops. A jumper. Trousers. I'm practically shrieking in pain already."

I didn't want to, but she made me laugh.

"That doesn't change the fact that something could have happened to you."

"But it didn't." Of course not. She lives in ZiZi's universe, where everything always turns out fine. "And anyway, I am really, really sorry, Lo. You know me."

"Never one to over-think a situation?"

"That wasn't what I meant. I meant self-absorbed. It was just that I was so excited to be here… Let's not ruin everything by fighting. We both had a great day."

She was right. We had both had a great day; even if it wasn't together.

"Point taken," I conceded. "Let's not ruin the rest of the day by arguing. I did what I came to do." I gave her shopping a meaningful look. "And you obviously did what you came to do. So let's forget it." Besides which, if we were going to eat before our train, we couldn't hang around arguing. "Let's go get supper. I'm starving."

The restaurant I'd read about was called Blue Moon. Which seemed appropriate, since it's once in a blue moon that you get ZiZi to a museum. It was on the west side, which meant that we'd be able to get a subway to the train station. We strolled across town – ZiZi with her shopping bags and me carrying everything else – talking and laughing and trying to take everything in at once. It was a really nice evening, and after spending the afternoon indoors it felt good to be out in the unfresh air and all the noise and people. ZiZi's right that there's an excitement in New York that you don't get in Howards Walk – similar to the difference between being on a space station and watching it pass overhead. I'd completely recovered from worrying about ZiZi – and from being irked by her – and was really enjoying myself.

Blue Moon was small and very busy.

ZiZi couldn't believe there were so many vegans in one place. "It's like walking into a party and everybody else has red hair."

There was at least a twenty-minute wait for a table.

"Damn!" For the second time in less than an hour, I didn't know what to do. "I'm not sure we can wait that long if we're going to make our train. By the time we order and everything…"

"So we'll go somewhere else," said ZiZi. "It's not like it's the only restaurant in the city. I mean, my God, there must be thousands."

"I know. It's just that I kind of had my heart set on this one." I'd never been to a completely vegan restaurant before. In Howards Walk, if you want vegan, you're talking baked potato, pizza without cheese, or a stir-fry. "I really wanted to see what it's like."

"Maybe they do takeaway," suggested ZiZi. "Then we can eat it on the train, and you get your full-vegan experience and we get home when we said we would and everybody's happy."

I was about to say that wasn't a bad idea when one of the two guys at the table nearest us said, "If you don't mind sharing, you ladies can sit with us."

We both looked over. For definite, they were college guys. Good-looking college guys. Especially the one who was grinning at ZiZi as if he hadn't eaten for a week and she was a beanburger.

ZiZi leaned her head against mine. "I didn't think boys who look like that ate tofu," she whispered.

No, only girls who look like me eat it.

I butted her with my hip to let her know that I thought sitting with the attractive tofu-eaters was a bad idea. It's already been well established that I'm not good at talking to boys. I'm okay if we have something to talk about – mathematical formulas or theories of creation or torque wrenches, for example. I can talk to Gabriel Schwartz for hours just about the exploration of Mars. But when it comes to pointless conversation, I'm lost; my small talk is so small it's not there. Especially if I don't know the boys – and especially if they're older ones who obviously wouldn't have seen me if I'd been by myself. Talking to

– and flirting with – strange men, however, is, of course, the sort of thing ZiZi excels at.

ZiZi didn't think the hip-butt meant, *Let's leave now.* She decided it meant, *Why look a gorgeous vegan gift horse in the mouth?* and returned his smile with interest. "Oh, we couldn't impose."

"Not an imposition." He pushed the chair beside him towards her. He winked. "More like a favour."

"And an honour," added his friend.

And an honour? Did he really say that? Who says a dumb thing like that, especially in public? This is an example of why I can't flirt and probably wouldn't if I could. It's so embarrassing that if they played a tape of you flirting at your funeral, you'd come back to life just to turn it off.

This time I squeezed ZiZi's elbow. But it was too late – she was already sliding into the chair. "Well, if you insist," she laughed.

"I'm Darius," said the better-looking of the two. "And this here's Vass."

"I'm Giselle and this—" ZiZi pointed to me. They were all looking at me expectantly as I stood there, making me feel like everyone in the restaurant was waiting for me to sit down. I didn't seem to have a choice; I moved over to the other empty chair. No one pushed it out for me. "This is Loretta."

Darius and Vass both told me how nice it was to meet me.

Which was the first and last thing either of them ever said to me directly.

Darius asked ZiZi if we lived in the city. ZiZi explained that we'd only come in for the day to do research at the Women's History Museum.

"Really?" Vass grinned. If his teeth were lights we'd have been blinded. "You're much too pretty to be a feminist."

"It was research," laughed ZiZi. "Not a commitment."

I knocked my fork off the table.

Then, having established that ZiZi was only visiting and was too pretty to be a feminist, Darius and Vass started telling her all about themselves. They were at NYU. They were both in pre-law. They were both from somewhere else. They loved New York. There were so many cool clubs and things to do. They both had like a trillion other interests and hobbies. Marathon running. Climbing. Kayaking. Windsurfing. Gaming. Sailing. Golf.

In a pause while they took in air and food, I said, "So I'm guessing you both want to do corporate law."

They must have heard me, because they got all enthused about what an exciting and opportunity-filled field corporate law is – and how lucrative – but they were talking to ZiZi.

ZiZi, the pro; she smiled and nodded and made positive comments now and then ("Wow!"; "That's amazing!" "Jeez; I never knew that.").

Unhampered by the demands of conversation, I finished my meal, and checked my phone. It was getting late. We had to get going or this time we really would miss the train. I tried to get her attention, but she hates to be rude to boys – even strangers – and she ignored me. Too.

After a few more futile attempts to get ZiZi to stop bobbing and smiling and to look at me, I waved to the waiter for our bill. Interrupting a story about some lawyer friend of Vass's father who owned his own island, I said, very loudly, "ZiZi, we have to go. Look at the time. If we don't hurry, we're going to miss our train."

"So miss it," said Darius. "There's a party in Brooklyn. You could come with us. It'll be serious fun."

"We'd love to," said ZiZi. "Really. I'm sure it'll be better than anything we've gone to at home. But if I miss the train to go to a party in Brooklyn, my parents will go total nuclear war on me, and it'll be my last party till I'm fifty-eight."

They must have thought she was joking; they both laughed.

"But you guys have been great," ZiZi went on. "You're our saviours, letting us share your table and everything. We can't thank you enough."

Darius said how they should be thanking us, but I didn't hear the rest because by then I was out the door.

I was halfway down the block when ZiZi caught up with me. "Are you mad at me again?"

"I don't want to talk about it, Zi." Up until that moment, I'd been more tired and anxious than angry, but as soon as she asked me if I was mad I was furious. I'd really hoped ZiZi would get more from the day than two bags of shopping. Besides that, I'm the daughter of a psychologist. Which means that, if I'm being completely honest, I was a little fed up with being the plain sidekick. Knowing that if ZiZi and I were being attacked by two-headed monsters from a distant galaxy no one was going to be risking his life to save me.

"Look, I'm a million times sorry. I only sat down because you said you really wanted to try that restaurant. I thought—"

"Not now," I ordered. "We really are cutting it close. Let's just get to the station, okay?" I thumped down the steps to the subway.

There was a train at the platform when we got to the turnstiles. Zizi swiped her MetroCard through the machine and raced towards it. The doors were about to close. "Wait!" she shouted, flapping her shopping bags. "Wait!"

A man standing next to the door held it for her and she gracefully jumped on board.

Back on the platform, I watched the train pull away.

File under the heading: *It can't be merely coincidence or luck.*

ZiZi

Loretta makes up for how quiet she was at supper

So this time Loretta was really mad at me. (It's about the only time her face has any colour.)

"Just once, it'd be nice not to have to run for a train." She was fuming. We were running for the train and she was practically producing steam. "You know," she puffed and huffed, "like regular people who just turn up on time and stroll on board and don't spend the first five minutes of the ride trying to get their breath back?"

I said that was glaringly unfair. Not only was she doing a really good job of talking for somebody who couldn't breathe, she was also forgetting exactly how many trains we'd ever run for together in our whole lives. Two. That's not exactly a history. It's not even a footnote.

"That's because we've only taken two trains together," snarked Loretta. "If we'd taken two hundred, it'd be two hundred."

I wasn't sure which made me feel more guilty, the snarling or the silence.

"You don't know that. It might only have been one hundred and ninety nine."

"In your dreams."

But for all Loretta's negativity, we did make the train. (Not with hours to spare, maybe, but we got on before it pulled out!) And to me the important part is what did happen, not what could have happened. I ruined a good pair of tights because I had to take off my shoes or risk being permanently crippled, and because I was shoeless I stubbed my toe, but we made it. We collapsed in the first empty seats.

My toe was turning an unnatural shade of magenta.

"It's your own fault," said Loretta. "That wouldn't have happened if you wore sensible shoes."

I said next time I'd make sure I brought my skates. "At least you can't blame me for nearly missing the train."

Loretta said, "That's where you're wrong, Giselle. I blame you completely. Among other things, you left me on the subway platform."

"I didn't leave you. I thought you were right behind me. It's not my fault the scientific genius couldn't swipe her MetroCard."

"Maybe." She really hates to admit she's wrong. "But

ignoring me in the restaurant when I said we had to get going absolutely was your fault. You just sat there like a mindless idiot listening to them drone on for hours."

I'm sure I don't have to point out the enormous exaggerations here. It wasn't hours that we were in the restaurant. It wasn't even two.

"I wasn't sitting there like a mindless idiot, I was being a good listener, like women are. Except for you."

"They weren't interested in listening to you, though. They were being the way guys are around you. They were showing off and talking about themselves like peacocks waving their feathers all over the place." She made a face like she'd just bitten into a lemon. "Thank God you're too pretty to be a feminist or they'd have had nothing to say."

"Oh for God's sake, Lo, he wasn't serious. He was just flirting with me." One subject Loretta is not an expert on. "Plus, they weren't waving their feathers. They were being sociable. We were having a conversation."

"That wasn't a conversation. That was a series of monologues. When there's a conversation, both sides get to say more than the occasional exclamation of admiration or awe."

"Give me a break, will you?" For someone who's so smart, she really is out of touch with reality sometimes.

"It's not like college men are going to want to listen to me explain how to make your lashes look longer. And, for sure, they don't want to hear you explain that women shouldn't shave their legs because that was started a hundred years ago by Gillette to sell razors to women."

"You don't think those topics are at least as interesting as running and the biggest law firms in the city?"

"Not to them they aren't."

"And vice versa. But, for some reason, guys think that what they do and think is important to everybody and what women do and think is only important to them." She sighed the way I figure the planet would sigh if it could. You know, hopeless and weary. "And so do you."

"No, I don't. It's just that I'm outgoing and friendly."

The sound Loretta made when I said that, I was surprised everyone else in the carriage didn't look around to see who'd brought the horse on board.

"You're more than outgoing and friendly, Zi. You have this girl thing going on."

"*Girl thing?* You mean like getting your period?"

"I mean like you'd rather be a girl than a person."

"I don't want to be the one to break the news and turn your world upside down, Loretta, but, in case you didn't notice, I am a girl. That's one of the reasons my parents called me Giselle and not George."

"And, in case this has escaped *your* attention, I'm a girl, too."

"Yeah, but you like to keep that a secret."

"I just don't happen to believe being a girl means I need help to set up a garden umbrella."

When she wants to, she has a photographic memory. "That was one time, Loretta. And I didn't act like I didn't know how to put it up. Duane just assumed that it was something he'd be better at and I didn't want to hurt his feelings."

"The only thing Duane Tolvar's better at than you is peeing standing up."

"That's so not true. He's a much better wrestler than I am, too. And anyway, he didn't think I could put it up by myself, and I didn't see any reason to disillusion him. Guys can be sensitive about stuff like that."

"That's what I mean. You defer to guys."

"No, I don't. I'm just not always competing with them or trying to prove I'm smarter than they are."

"Is that what you think I do?"

Do models watch their weight?

"What you don't get, Loretta, is that men and women are different. That's a fact."

"Actually, the scientific fact is that the male and female brain are the same. Which means that any differences –

aside from size, strength and who gets pregnant – are learned. Males are taught to be boys, and females are taught to be girls."

If she hadn't looked so serious, I would've laughed. "You're saying I learned to be a girl?"

"Yes. That's exactly what I'm saying. From the first time they put you in a pink onesie and gave you a doll. "

"Oh, please … I'm me. And the me I am has always liked being a girl. Girls don't get blamed for everything that goes wrong in the world the way men do."

"That would be because women don't run the world," snapped Loretta.

Arguing with Loretta can be like trying to find the end of a circle.

"Here's the thing," I said. "I happen to like being attractive. I don't see what's wrong with that."

"It depends what you think is attractive. What most women think is attractive is what men have decided is attractive for women."

I couldn't help myself. That time I did laugh. "What? They take a vote?"

She let that pass. "You know that programme you watch? The talent contest? Why do you think the male presenters wear jeans and ordinary shirts while the women all dress like they're going on some hot date?"

"Because women like to look nice."

"Dream on," said Loretta. "It's because they're on TV, which means they're sexual objects first and presenters second."

"Oh, come on, they don't look like sexual objects, they look feminine. And if you ask me, women who aren't into their femininity are just wannabe guys."

"Maybe they're just wannabe people. Like I am. I don't see why I should have to conform to our society's gender stereotypes to be a girl."

"And I don't see why I can't be how I want to be."

"You limit yourself," said Loretta.

"You think you don't?" I sure thought she did. "Plus, maybe you don't conform to society's. stereotypes, but you conform to yours. Like nobody will ever take you seriously if you look too girly. You think it's a sign of weakness to look pretty."

"I never said that. What I'm saying is that you don't have to obey the conventional rules of what a girl or a woman looks like to be one. Clothes and ideas of female behaviour have been used to control women for centuries. To make them objects, not people."

I pretended to yawn. "So that's why you think you shouldn't wear a dress or make-up or anything."

"Yes. Because everybody makes assumptions based

on appearance. I want to be judged for what I am, not for what I look like."

"But you're still judged on how you look. And anyway, you make judgments. You're afraid people won't think you're smart if you look too feminine. So you use how you look just as much as I use how I look. Maybe you think you wouldn't be you if you wore a dress."

"That's ridiculous. Of course I would. You're the one who'd be lost if you couldn't rely on your über girlness."

"I could do it, no problem. You're the one who couldn't change."

"Are you kidding? You don't go into the backyard without make-up on."

"And you haven't worn a dress since primary school."

And that's when Loretta had her big idea.

"You want to bet?"

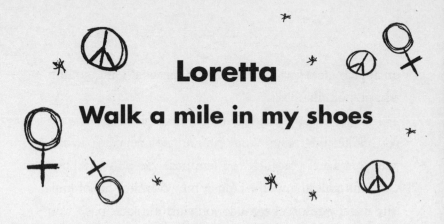

Loretta

Walk a mile in my shoes

"You want to bet?" I didn't plan to say that, it was a flash of pure inspiration. Not as brilliant as inventing the wheel, maybe, but as brilliant as putting the wheel on a wagon. Just like that: "You want to bet?"

ZiZi's first reaction was to laugh. Shriek with laughter might be a more accurate description.

"Bet? Are you serious? You mean we switch around? You're going to wear make-up and dresses and I'm going to look like someone who will never get a date? Is that what you mean?"

That about covered it.

"Yes. I'll go for the girly, look-at-me image, and you'll go for the androgynous, talk-to-me one. And we'll see who cracks first."

ZiZi and I both like to be right, which means that we'd made plenty of bets before. How far ZiZi could walk in her new heels. How long I could go without starting an argument. I bet her that she couldn't be on time two days in a row. She bet me that I couldn't go shopping with her for an entire afternoon and not complain once. As far as winning went, the judges agreed that we broke even.

This time she was gazing at me with the sort of look she usually reserves for a serious fashion faux pas. "You know, sometimes I really don't know why you think you're such a logical person. This is totally crazy."

"You don't think I can do it?"

"Can bears tango?"

"You're wrong." She was for definite wrong. With our previous bets, ZiZi always won if it was her idea, and I always won if it was mine. This was my idea. How could I lose? "You're the one who can't go more than ten minutes without checking how she looks in the nearest reflective surface."

"And you're the one with all the principles. If some guy paid you a compliment, you'd probably hit him."

I knew it might not be easy, but I would treat it as sociological research. Almost a scientific study. Writers and journalists do that sort of thing all the time. Dressing all girly might not be exactly the same as Barbara Ehrenreich working in Walmart or Gloria Steinem being a Playboy bunny, but it was still an interesting experiment.

"I can leave my principles at the back of my closet with my work boots. The question is, can you leave your obsession with how you look in the drawer with your make-up?"

"It's not an obsession, Loretta. It's a lifestyle choice. I can unchoose it as easily as changing my earrings." She smiled. "The only trouble is that your idea won't work."

"Why not?"

"Think about it, Lo. We couldn't possibly pull it off. Not in Howards Walk. Everyone knows us. They'd catch on that it wasn't for real. They'd think we were just messing around."

That's the problem with flashes of inspiration: you don't always think them through. I hated to admit it, but ZiZi was right. I couldn't just appear at school one day in a miniskirt and a blonde wig; no one would take it seriously. There was a good chance they'd laugh until they couldn't breathe. And if ZiZi showed up looking gender-neutral … as soon as the Earth started turning again, they'd be searching her locker for drugs. Realistically, the only way it would work would be if our families agreed to move to a place where no one knew us – Montana, for example, or the Outer Hebrides. Unless, of course, Montana and the Outer Hebrides moved to us.

"Wait a minute. We're not thinking laterally. We can

make it work. It's almost Summer. We could get away with it easily in the Summer. No school to go to, we'll both be working and the town will be filled with strangers who never saw us before." Come June, the Summer people start to arrive. None of them know ZiZi and me, and even if they had seen us before they wouldn't remember. Which meant we'd have maximum time to conduct the experiment and minimum hassle and lifestyle impact. "That's pretty much perfect."

"Summer?" It's rare that you actually hear someone gasp. "Now I know for sure you've totally lost your mind. We can't possibly do it in the Summer. I'd rather wear bellbottoms. And I wouldn't wear bellbottoms in my grave."

"But why not? You broke up with Duane again months ago, so you don't have to worry about what he thinks." Which was probably the first time I used the words "Duane" and "think" in the same sentence.

"I do have other friends, you know."

"Yeah, but if you told them about the bet they'd probably go along with it, wouldn't they? I don't see the problem."

"You wouldn't, Loretta. You don't wait all year for bikini weather like I do. But, for normal people, Summer is fun-in-the-sun time. Beach days. Barbecues. Pool parties. And there is no way I'm wearing a one-piece like my mother. I mean, seriously? I might as well just skip the precious years of my youth and go straight to middle age. Maybe I should start saving for a mobility scooter."

"It wouldn't have to be the whole Summer. You'll probably cave in on day one."

"You mean, you will. And no. You're incredibly stubborn. I'm not taking the chance that you'd hang on just to spite me."

"What if we say no more than one month? Surely you can put your busy fun-in-the-sun social life on hold for just one month."

"No."

"July? Just for July. August is always the best month for the beach, anyway."

"How would you know? You only go to the beach in the winter when it's empty." Her mouth was a blockade. "And absolutely no."

"You know you'd lose, that's why you won't do it."

"No, I would win. But it's impossible. Not this Summer. I have plans."

"A barbecue is not a plan, ZiZi."

"Besides that stuff. I have something to do for school."

"In the Summer? You're going to miss beach days to do something for school?" This was an event far less frequent than the passing of Halley's Comet.

"It's for Media." She was staring at some point behind my head. "One of the guys is making a movie and I said I'd help out."

Since I know ZiZi so well – she is not a girl to do schoolwork when she doesn't have to – I was immediately suspicious. "One of the guys?"

"Yeah." She nodded, her eyes not quite connecting with mine. "One of the guys in my class."

She was being evasive, but I decided not to push her. "Well, I don't see how that makes any difference. What does it matter what you wear if you're not in front of the camera?"

"No, Loretta. I'm not changing my image in midstream."

File under the heading: *Something is going on.*

ZiZi

A girl has a right to change her mind

Here's the thing. Even though Summer is the only time Howards Walk is more exciting than a weather report for the desert, I kind of wanted to do the bet. It would be worth missing a couple of pool parties and barbecues just to see Loretta looking like a girl.

Plus, I was sure I'd win. And, because I'd win, I figured it would shut her up once and for all about gender this and gender that and the beauty myth and the tyranny of fashion and the objectification of women and all the other things she yammers on about till you want to put cement in your ears. And I know Loretta. She thought it was going to be easy as opening a compact to beat me because she thinks I have no self-discipline. In the Loretta Reynolds universe, it was only people who study all the time and can name every woman who ever won a Nobel Prize or burned a bra who knew what self-discipline is. Like looking good doesn't take enormous amounts of self-discipline. Your hair just styles itself. Your make-up just appears on your face by magic. Your body doesn't need you to exercise or pass up the chocolate cake and French fries to look great. Did she have any idea how long it takes just to do your nails? To put on eyelashes? To wax your legs? And what about shopping? You don't just walk into any old store you come to and grab the first thing you see. Shopping requires knowledge, self-control, stamina and skill. (If there was any justice in the world, they'd make it an Olympic event. It's a lot more demanding than beach volleyball.) Compared to all that, what's wearing a T-shirt, jeans and trainers? Nothing! I mean, seriously? If my brothers can do it, anyone can.

But seeing Loretta in make-up and a skirt (even a really short, pink skirt with ruffles) wasn't worth missing even ten minutes of working with Dillon Blackstock on his documentary, and there was no way I was working with Dillon Blackstock while I was dressing like my brothers.

And then my guardian angel went on one of her unscheduled vacations and Fate marched in, trampling all over my expectations and changing everything.

The first thing that happened was that I found out no one was going to be around that Summer. No one I ever hung out with, at least. All my normal friends were leaving town for one thing or another. *Quel social wasteland!* So that meant no beach days, no pool parties, no barbecues, and less fun than sunburn. It wasn't the worst thing that could happen, but it was a blow. And then the worst thing happened.

Some people think I pay too much attention to unimportant trivia (like looks), but the sad truth is that, if you ask me, human beings are way less reliable than a good foundation.

We got closer and closer to saying our goodbyes to Howards Walk High for the Summer, and still Dillon hadn't said anything more about his movie. Everybody was pretty busy in the last few weeks of school with tests and papers and everything, so I never had a chance to ask him about it privately. In class, he sat with Tobias (and came in with Tobias and left with Tobias). Outside of class, the one time I saw Dillon by himself was when Mitchell Crause and I were putting up the paintings for the Art Department show. I was holding the ladder and Mitchell was asking, "Is it straight now?" so I couldn't very well say anything to Dillon right then. Plus, I didn't want Dillon to think I was pushy. After what he'd said about his future sister-in-law (the princess), I figured he wasn't the kind of guy who responds well to pushy (even if he is pretty friendly with Loretta!).

Cal Kupfer and I were on the school's Community Committee, and once a month we delivered the food-bank donations to the Methodist church in the next town. Cal's one of those guys who can't do enough for you, so on that afternoon, when we stopped at Johnson's for petrol on the way back, he jumped out to do the pumping without me having to ask. (I was happy to let him do it because I once ruined a pair of fabric shoes dripping petrol on them and I was wearing new sandals.) Since my parents won't trust me with my own credit card, I had to go inside to pay. And who do you think was ahead of me at the counter? Dillon Blackstock! Even better, there was nobody with him.

I said, "Hey Dillon!"

He turned around. "Oh, hi." He sounded like a service station was the last place he ever expected to see me. "How's it going?"

I said it was going fine. And then we kind of stood there for a few seconds smiling at each other. I don't really use the sledge-hammer approach favoured by Loretta, but my summer happiness was on the line. So I just came out and asked him what was going on.

I said, "I was wondering when you want to get together to talk about the documentary."

His smile is really great, even when it looks confused. "What?"

I said, "You know, the movie you're making of your brother's wedding? The hilarious, behind-the-scenes social commentary and living allegory? I'm ready when you are."

And Dillon said, "Oh God, the documentary. I'm afraid that idea's been axed."

I had a little trouble taking in that information. You know, because it wasn't what I was expecting to hear. "Axed? You mean you're not going to do it? But I was planning on helping you with it. Remember?"

"I know we talked about it," said Dillon. "But it was only an idea."

Maybe to him, it was. To me, it was a promise.

"It was a really great idea."

"Yeah. It seemed like it was." His smile was still fantastic but rueful. "Only it kind of turned into a passing thought."

I was trying super hard not to let my soul-crushing disappointment show. "Right. A passing thought."

"I'm really sorry. I guess I should've told you, but everything's been so crazy at home I totally forgot."

I nodded as if I was sympathetic with how crazy it must be at home for him to totally forget about me.

"So," I said, "why'd you decide not to do it?" I pitched my voice so he'd know I was unhappy about this but without sounding annoyed. "I really did think it was an awesome idea."

Dillon said it wasn't that he cancelled the film. His brother's fiancée cancelled the wedding.

"Really? She called it off?" I couldn't believe what I was hearing. How could she do a thing like that? Seriously. And not just because she'd torpedoed my Summer. Cancelling a wedding's not like cancelling a dental appointment. A wedding is one of the most major things you can do unless you're an astronaut or something like that. You might as well cancel your life.

"You know what girls can be like," said Dillon. "She had a big fight with my brother. It was all ten-thousand-mile-high drama, and, the next thing you knew, the whole thing'd been thrown in the garbage with the engagement ring."

"She threw away her ring?" This girl wasn't a princess, she was psychotic. Who throws away her engagement ring? It's like throwing away your fiancé's heart.

"It's okay, he got it back."

I said maybe it wasn't really that serious. Everybody knows how stressful weddings are. There's so much to do, and you want everything to be totally perfect. People about to get married always get jittery and have second thoughts and want to back out, but then they realize it's just nerves and worrying about fitting into the bridal gown or something like that and it's all on again. It's practically part of the ritual.

Dillon said, "Not this time. She smashed his windscreen with a golf club." Dillon laughed. "And then she tried to run him over. Even her dad stays out of her way when she's in one of her moods, and her dad makes your average ruthless dictator look like a puppy. She's a real emotional girl."

I was starting to feel like a real emotional girl myself. I said well, maybe we could come up with a different idea for a documentary that'd be just as good.

"We've already solved that problem. We leave next week, the day after school ends."

"We" didn't mean him and me (perish the thought!). It meant him and Tobias. (I should've known!)

Tobias's cousin was living in a tent in the woods in the back of beyond. The idea was that he wouldn't spend any money for at least a year. He had to live really simply (that's why he was in a tent), forage for food, barter and do stuff like that. So Dillon and Tobias were going to do a movie about him.

"What he's doing's called freeconomics," said Dillon.

(It sounded more like freakonomics to me!) "It's really wild. But he's having a terrific time, and so far he hasn't spent a dime."

"Well," I said, "that really sounds awesome."

Dillon thought so, too. Mega social commentary. Scathing criticism of our consumer society. He and Tobias figured it had a lot of potential.

I could only hope that potential was for having their camera eaten by a bear.

As we came out of the store, I was trying to concentrate on not crying in front of him when I noticed that my mom's car wasn't where I'd left it.

"Over here!" called Cal. He and the car were by the air machine. "I figured I might as well do the tyres, too, while I was waiting for you."

Dillon muttered something that sounded like, *Come the hour, come the boy.*

I said, "What?"

"Nothing. I have to get going." He gave Cal a wave. "See you around, ZiZi."

Not unless I got lost in the wilderness.

"Yeah," I said, "see you around."

I couldn't have been more crushed if a tractor had rolled over me. Dillon Blackstock was spending the whole vacation in some place without air conditioning being a responsible filmmaker with a political agenda. It's the kind of thing that shakes your faith in humanity. Right then, standing in the forecourt of Johnson's service station, I decided that I might as well go ahead with the bet with Loretta. I mean, why not? Realistically, what did I have to lose? Nothing. I wasn't going to be doing anything over the Summer except working at the Inn. At least the bet would be something to do so I wasn't bored out of my brain. And it would distract me from my bruised and aching heart. Plus, I had a lot to gain. Beating Loretta. Beating Loretta wouldn't make up for missing out on months of propinquity with Dillon Blackstock, but it would make up for a lot of parties and games of beach volleyball that never happened.

I took out my phone as I walked over to the car and texted Loretta: *You're on!*

Loretta
Let the show begin

By the time I got ZiZi's text saying the bet was on after all, I'd more or less put the whole thing out of my mind in all the turmoil and activity of the end of year. I was so astonished at this turnaround – she's known for her obstinacy as much as her dress sense – that I actually looked out of the window in case some other extraordinary phenomenon was occurring – fish raining from the sky or a faint blue moon appearing over the ocean.

That same night I went over to keep her company because her parents were out and she had to stay with Obi to do damage control.

"What made you change your mind?" I asked as we settled ourselves in the living room.

ZiZi put the DVD in the machine. "You know what Ms Wallenstein was talking about the other day?"

I scooped up a handful of chips. "You mean Harriet Tubman?"

"No, not her. When she was talking about challenging yourself and getting out of your comfort zone?" I was surprised ZiZi even heard that. She usually turned off incoming when Ms Wallenstein started one of her life lectures. ZiZi plopped down beside me on the sofa. "So, anyway, I was thinking that maybe she has a point."

"You were?" The Abruzzios' very ordinary living room with its family photographs on the mantelpiece and its souvenirs from family trips on the bookshelves suddenly seemed almost dreamlike and surreal, as if the normal rules that govern our world no longer applied and the boundaries between dimensions had dissolved. Where was I? Who was this girl? What was she saying? What did it mean?

"Uh-huh." She picked up the remote. "Like Ms Wallenstein said, we're on the brink of adulthood. Now is when we should be exploring ourselves and expanding our limits. You know, before we're so old we can't even remember being young."

Did she actually think I'd believe that? I'd never known ZiZi to have any real desire to explore much more than the mall. "No, be honest here. What brought this on? Are all your other friends going away to be counsellors at Summer camp? Or is the Mob after you and you want to lie low?"

"You're too young to be so cynical." It was the wrong remote. She picked up another. "A girl can change her mind, can't she? And anyway, I just told you. I've been thinking it over. I feel it'll help me grow as a person, and this is the time to do it. While I'm young and all my options lie ahead of me." She tried a third remote. "It's now or never."

"Your pool-party friends are all going away, aren't they? That has to be it."

"You're the one who's always at me to broaden my horizons and rush out and grab my potential." She dug remote number four out of the side of the sofa. "I didn't expect you to be so suspicious."

I was looking right at her. "That is it, isn't it?"

ZiZi was looking at the TV. "Okay, so maybe Shona, Marilee and Isla are going to be out of town for the duration. That doesn't mean I don't really want to grow as a person. I could find other people to hang out with if I really wanted to, you know."

Sometimes ZiZi acts as if we've never been introduced; as if I have no idea what she's like or how her mind works.

"Oh, wait a minute." I put my hand out to stop her pressing play. "It's Dillon, isn't it?" She might be able to replace Shona, Marilee and Isla; Dillon would be a lot more difficult. "What happened to the movie you were going to be working on with him?"

It hadn't taken me long after our conversation about the bet – approximately one hour and twelve minutes – to realize that the "one of the guys" she was talking about doing a film with had to be Dillon Blackstock. There was no way in the universe that she would agree to the bet if she was spending time with him. She had never said so in so many words, but I knew she had a serious crush on him. Not only did she talk about him a lot – Dillon said this and Dillon said that – but she was always asking me questions about the sorts of films she never used to watch, as well. This was the first time ZiZi had been interested in a boy who was actually worthy of her, but, so far, he'd shown a lot less interest in her than in Japanese samurai movies. The serious but unrequited crush was something I could identify with completely. Ever since he fell into the cat food, Gabriel Schwartz hadn't been quite as friendly as he'd been before – as if I'd seen him in his underwear or something equally embarrassing. Which put ZiZi and me in the same black hole of despair. She'd thought the movie would bring her and Dillon together; I'd thought the stars would do the same for me and Gabriel. So far, we both were wrong.

"He's not doing it," said ZiZi. "Apparently, he's had a better idea." Dillon was going to the wilderness to make a documentary about living without money. "So, to be honest…? There's nothing to stop me going for the minimal effort, unisex look."

I felt bad for her – I could tell she was really disappointed and I, for definite, know what that's like. On the other hand, I couldn't help feeling pretty pleased that the bet was going ahead after all. I couldn't imagine a scenario in which I didn't win. Unlucky in love, lucky in personal contests of will.

I said, "We'll have to have some ground rules."

ZiZi made a face as if we'd been through this a dozen times before. "I know. No make-up. No girly clothes. No flashy femininity."

I was mulling. I'm probably the only non-family member who has ever seen ZiZi before she gets ready to leave the house; I wasn't sure she looked that radically different. "You need to make a fundamental change."

"I'm not binding my breasts, Loretta. That's two hundred per cent not happening."

"I was thinking more of cutting your hair. That should do it."

She didn't say anything for a few seconds, possibly weighing up the pros and cons of short hair versus a flat chest. "Okay, but then you have to make a fundamental change, too. I think you should colour your hair. At least put in highlights or streaks. It'll make a real difference."

"Okay, I can live with that." I was pretty certain I could get something that would wash out. "However, I am not going to flirt or act useless."

"I wouldn't ask you to flirt, you'd only mess it up and it'd be totally counterproductive. But you have to listen better to guys. And even if they say something really dumb, don't get that look on your face like the emperor doesn't have any clothes on. Just try to remember that you get more flies with honey than you do by whacking them with the nearest heavy object."

"No fear. I can do that." I held out my hand. "Then I guess we have a deal."

"I think it's only fair to warn you, Lo," said ZiZi as she took my hand. "You are so going to wish you never started this, because there's no way I'm not going to win."

Which is an example of the optimism of someone who thinks that if she uses moisturizer every day she'll never get old.

We agreed to begin our transformations as soon as school ended. ZiZi lent me some things that fit me despite the slight difference in our heights and builds, and the more than slight difference in our bra size. There was an awful lot of pink: pink jeans, pink skirt, pink dress, pink tops. I said I felt like I was drowning in Pepto Bismol.

"Pink is feminine," said ZiZi. "It's gentle and warm."

No it isn't; it's insipid and indecisive.

"You know there isn't any scientific connection between girls and pink, don't you? It's not as if you have a gene for pink the way you have a gene for blue eyes."

ZiZi said that was my opinion. "Some things are just naturally feminine, Loretta. And the colour pink is one of them."

I said she was too old not to know the difference between opinion and fact. Opinions being what she has, and facts being on my team.

"And that's another matter of opinion," said ZiZi.

In return for the glut of pinkness, I lent her some things for her new persona – ZiZi Lite. T-shirts mainly, my favourite dungarees, a hooded sweatshirt – she does have one hoody but you'll never guess what colour it is – and a long black skirt for special occasions.

"You mean special occasions like a funeral," said ZiZi.

We figured we could get anything else we needed in the way of clothes from a charity shop.

I thought I'd be able to use ZiZi's make-up but apparently that was a hilarious example of how uneducated I am in the feminine arts.

"No way," said ZiZi. "I'm basically a blonde."

God help me, and all this time I'd thought she was a redhead.

"And?"

"And our skin tones are totally different. We need different palettes."

"It's not like it's a big deal. I just need a lipstick and some eyeliner."

"No, you don't." The Oracle of Howards Walk had spoken. "There's more to this than you think. You need the whole package, not just a swipe of lipstick and a smear of liner, or the bet's off. I'll go with you to the store or you'll get all the wrong stuff. We can get the highlighter for your hair at the same time."

It truly is an ill wind that blows no good.

On Friday we went to buy my make-up, and what I think of as my make-up enablers – all the things that aren't cosmetics per se but without which, it seems, the glosses and liners are next to useless. ZiZi was right, there was a Hell of a lot more to it than I'd thought – which is like saying there's more to cosmology than "Twinkle, Twinkle, Little Star". There were tweezers, lash curlers, cuticle nippers, cotton pads, brushes, fixing spray, moisturizer, primer, concealer, foundation, bronzer, blush, shadow base, eyeshadow, liner, mascara, lip pencil, gloss, nail varnish, cuticle softener, cuticle cream… It was like the magician's handkerchief trick where it keeps on coming and coming and coming – only, in reverse. We were putting things into the basket and they kept on coming. Every time I thought we must be done, ZiZi reached for something else. And to think I'd spent so many years being happy with soap and water.

Obviously, I knew ZiZi's morning routine was more complicated than just slapping on some lipstick and eye shadow – and that her evening routine was more complicated than just washing it off – but I hadn't really appreciated how much more complicated. It gave me a new respect for both her discipline and her intelligence; the workings of the universe pale into insignificance beside her beauty routine.

"Are you really sure I need all this junk?"

"Yes, I'm sure. And it's not junk. These are the essentials." ZiZi tossed another bottle into my basket. "There's no point in doing this unless you do it right. You want the whole experience, don't you?"

Did I? I stared at the laden basket; it looked like we were emptying the store. She seemed to think I wanted my whole experience and someone else's, too.

We lugged it all back to my house, and ZiZi laid

everything out and explained how to use each item. This is for this; that is for that. Do this first; do that last. Don't ever...; don't forget...; don't do them together. The more she explained, the more I understood that the wonder wasn't that she was late so often; the wonder was that she ever showed up at all.

Then we locked ourselves in the bathroom while she did my hair.

I'd wanted to get henna or something gentle like that, but ZiZi insisted that wouldn't work for what we wanted. What we wanted was to make my hair almost sparkle; an effect that required a form of medieval torture to bring it about – and that wasn't going to wash out in any hurry. She put a plastic cap filled with tiny holes on my head and pulled hair through the holes with a hook.

"Are you sure you've done this before? You're digging into my scalp."

"It isn't brain surgery, Loretta." Although it definitely felt like it. "I just have to follow the directions."

She mixed a chemical potion that could probably double as weedkiller; the smell alone would do the trick.

I kept my eyes shut tight until she finally finished and tried to think of something pleasant. The pleasant thing I focused on was Gabriel Schwartz. Maybe the problem wasn't him, maybe the problem was me. Maybe, because we shared so many interests, he could only think of me as another future physicist. I know it went against all my principles – and I know Gabriel is intelligent and evolved and isn't one of those guys who only cares about looks – but I started wondering if the make-up and the hair and the clothes might make him see me differently. See me not simply as someone he could discuss quantum physics with but as a girl, as well. Do the trick the top I bought for the Astronomy Club dinner failed to do.

While we waited for the dye to work, ZiZi kept busy on her phone, and I kept busy thinking of reasons to arrange a meeting with Gabriel so I could introduce him to the renovated me. The meteor showers were weeks away, but he might agree to going together to find the perfect spot to watch from. I was imagining us walking along the shore in moonlight, discussing which would be the best vantage point, when I finally realized that ZiZi was shouting, "Earth calling Loretta! Earth calling Loretta! Time's up." I opened my eyes, blinking; it took me a few seconds to realize what she was talking about.

After ZiZi rinsed out the dye and washed my hair, she did my face.

If the highlighting was torture, the making-up was like an operation – minus the blood, but not minus the pain.

ZiZi wished we had a chair. She wished I were shorter.

She wished the light were better. She wished the window weren't so small.

"Stop flinching," ZiZi ordered. "This is hard enough without you moving around like you're trying to get out of the way."

"I can't help it. I am trying to get out of the way. I'm not used to having things mashed into my skin."

"I mean it, Loretta. If you don't stop flinching, you're going to wind up with mascara in your nostrils."

When she was done making my face feel like it was caked in mud and my eyelashes feel like they were glued together, she turned me towards the mirror. ZiZi stood behind me, head to one side, studying her work with professional scrutiny. "What do you think?" she finally asked.

Think? I didn't know what to think. Staring back at me was someone I'd never seen before; I hadn't even been aware of her existence. I wasn't even sure we were related. Forget that, I wasn't even sure we belonged to the same species.

"Loretta." ZiZi gave me a poke. "What do you think?"

"I look so different."

She clapped her hands together. "I know! Isn't it awesome? Nobody'd ever guess you read non-fiction books for fun."

They might not even think I could read.

I'd expected to look like me but with a lot of crap on my face. But I didn't; I looked so different that if I'd met myself on the street, I would have thought I was someone else. I was girlier, yes, for definite – there was no mistaking me for anything but a girl. It was more than that, though. I'd have been girlier if I'd clipped a bow in my hair. I looked like a girl who went on dates and waxed her bikini line; the kind of girl who'd been planning her wedding, not her career, since she was twelve. I was sexy. Pretty. Hot. A babe. Even still wearing my old black jeans and a T-shirt. I, Loretta Reynolds, was a babe. I'd been a feminist since I was eight. How could I be a babe? A babe who was probably a fantastically good listener, too.

"I think I may be having an allergic reaction."

"For God's sake, Lo!" ZiZi made the same sigh she's been making since we first became friends. As in, if she were a foot I'd be a blister. "Is that all you can say? You might be allergic? You don't think you look absolutely amazing?"

"I do. I look amazing." Which I did. Only whether you were defining "amazing" as terrifying or wonderful was open to debate.

"Thank you, ZiZi, for making me look so totally, spectacularly awesome." She curtsied. There was no debate as far as she was concerned. Amazing could only be good. "Just call me any time you want to stop traffic."

What I wanted right then was to practise the part where I removed everything from my face, but ZiZi insisted that I show my parents the new me. "Unless you're planning to come and go in a burka, they're going to see you eventually," she argued. "So why not now?"

Because I hadn't told my parents what we were planning to do, that's why not now. My parents have always encouraged me to be a person. And they've always been very ambitious for me – academically and for my future. I did have a doll when I was little – I took her apart to see how her eyes worked – but I also had trains, a toolbox, a pedal car and a lot of non-gender-specific toys and games. I never had one of those just-like-mommy's strollers – my mother didn't have one either (she strapped me to her) – a princess dress, fairy wings or pretend high heels. My mother helped me build a tree house, she was the labourer; my grandfather was a tailor, so it was my dad who taught me how to sew. I was on a mixed softball team in elementary school. I got my first telescope when I was seven. They'd never given any indication that they felt I'd deprived them of the most interesting years of my adolescence because I never showed any interest in fashion, make-up or being a model. Too late, I realized that I should have warned them so they'd know what to expect. I didn't want to bring on a stroke or anything like that because the shock of seeing me painted up like a chorus girl proved too much for them. They're liberal, but everybody has limits.

They were watching the news.

"Ta-dah!" called out ZiZi.

They both looked up.

There were a few seconds of the sort of silence you'd expect if you opened the front door and found an alien on the doorstep asking for directions to the mall.

My dad recovered first. "Well, bless my soul, Mom," said my dad. "It's a girl!"

ZiZi

Like a sheep to the shearer

Even if I have to say so myself (and I do, because Loretta's not going to), I did a fabulously amazing job on her make-over. It was like one of those Before and After magazine features where a dowdy housewife is transformed into eye candy. I did such a fabulously amazing job that I'd consider being a make-up artist if the model/actor thing doesn't work out. And that's not all. I had this awesome revelation while I was doing it. For the first time in my life, I understood what it must feel like to be some kind of genius artist. There you are, with an empty canvas in front of you. You pick up your brush. You make a line here and a shape there. You splash on colours and dab on shades. You add shadows and highlights. And when you step back, you've created something totally mind-blowing out of nothing. Life from emptiness. Beauty from blank. Not that I expected Loretta to appreciate what I'd done. Grouse, groan, grump. Her face felt stiff. Her eye-lashes felt like they'd been cemented together. What was that smell? What colour was that supposed to be? Was I trying to blind her? You can bet the Mona Lisa didn't carry on like that when she was being painted. Can you imagine? *What in Heaven's name do you think you're doing, Leonardo? Do you call that a smile?*

But if Loretta's reaction could be described as under-whelmed, you should've seen Stew and Odelia when she walked into the room looking like that. You could've knocked both of them out of their chairs with a cotton ball. And I mean literally.

You probably think that, since they're the parents of an obsessive overachiever who thinks glamour is a dirty word, the Reynolds parents would find me a challenge. Not like some enormous mountain to climb; more like you went to dinner expecting nut cutlets and quinoa (these are the Reynoldses we're talking about) but what you got was steak and cake. And I admit, I was a little nervous the first time I met them. Loretta couldn't understand why. She said, "Nervous about what? They're just regular par-ents." Which seemed pretty unlikely to me. You don't get hats from a shoe store. I said I figured they wouldn't be expecting someone like me – because Loretta and I are so different. Girl and geek. "They're not judgmental," said

Loretta. I said, "So who is it you take after, then?"

But here's the thing. Mr and Mrs Reynolds liked me from day one. And they are pretty normal really. Way more normal than I'd thought they'd be. Stew's some kind of therapist but he doesn't have a beard or anything like that. And Mrs Reynolds teaches yoga but she wears lipstick, nail polish and dresses, and you can tell from her hair that she knows what the inside of a beauty salon looks like. Anyway, the first time I met them they were in the kitchen. Mr Reynolds was yelling at the radio and Mrs Reynolds was frowning at her computer. (I could totally relate to that. My dad does a lot of yelling at the TV and my mom frowns a lot.) They both seemed happy to meet me. Mr Reynolds even stood up and shook my hand. Mrs Reynolds wanted to know if my hair is naturally curly. I said no, I owe it all to chemicals. That made her laugh. Loretta wandered away to get a snack. (It was hours since lunch, God knows how she made it home.) So I was left standing by the table with her parents making the usual *How's school...? You have a nice house... What are the cats' names...?* small talk. Then Mr Reynolds went back to yelling at the radio. Mrs Reynolds said, "You look like a girl with an eye for design, ZiZi. You want to come over here and see what you think about these?" She was choosing the colour for the new living-room curtains. "Moonglow… Misty Dream… Summer Lace…" chanted Mrs Reynolds. "It all looks like white to me." I said she should go for the Summer Lace. "It's soft but not bland. It has a little yellow in it." She beamed. "I knew you'd be helpful. It's no use asking Loretta. She wouldn't care if I hung sheets on the windows." (She got the Summer Lace and has never stopped thanking me!) It was all smooth sailing after that. They told Loretta I'm refreshing, so I figured that, despite the yoga and the counselling, I gave them hope that, deep down, Loretta is a normal girl and not just a wannabe boy. When I saw their faces at the sight of their born-again daughter, I knew I was right.

I can't say that I was as enthusiastic about my own transformation as I was about the miracle I'd performed on Loretta. On Saturday, she was going with me to have my hair cut. She said it was for moral support, but I figured it was more to make sure I went. The night before, I lay awake with anticipation. Not anticipation like when you're little and it's Christmas Eve and you can't wait to get a Little Princess Beauty Salon or the night before a big family vacation and you're dying to have your picture taken with Cinderella. This was the bad kind of anticipation. I hadn't had short hair since the nit epidemic in Year One. Your hair's supposed to be your crowning glory, not the dot over an *i*. I finally managed to get to sleep by counting all the famous movie stars and models I could think of who had had short hair. Ever. Even if it was only for a specific part or ad campaign. You could call it a test. In eighth grade, Porsha Chevron had a Halloween party and I went as a mermaid with a tail covered in green sequins (I won best costume *and* got asked out by Link Smitts, the biggest catch in our year, whose conversation starter was "I don't usually like fish"). Desperate for sleep, I wound up digging through my memory like someone sifting through a bag of sequins for just the green ones. *Wasn't there that movie about time travellers? Wasn't there that ad for Hugo Boss? What about what's her name who played the robot that fell in love with a computer?*

When I finally fell asleep, I had my favourite dream. I was gliding down a catwalk (maybe in Milan, maybe in Paris) with my head up and my expression blank but sultry. Lights flashed. Videos hummed. I didn't need a mirror to see how fantastic I looked, I could see it in the faces all around me. Even the air felt admiring. I knew that after the show I'd be whisked away in a silver limo to a party where men who would have been princes if we were in a fairy tale lined up to meet me. But then the dream stopped being the one I always had (at that point it would fade out, and I'd wake up smiling). Instead, just as I reached the end of the catwalk, up popped Loretta. She was wearing a black lab coat and goggles, and was holding a pair of scissors you could have used to give a woolly mammoth a trim. *What are you doing?* shrieked Loretta. *You're not supposed to be here, acting like a living doll. You're supposed to be at Harvard, studying Environmental Law and reaching your potential!* It was my scream that woke me. When I opened my eyes I was already sitting up, and breathing hard.

We went to Roma's Salon, the best Howards Walk has to offer. I'd been going there since I realized there was a difference between haircuts, just like there's a difference between shoes from Shoe City and Jimmy Choos. (Before that, I'd had my hair cut like my mother did, by her friend Silvia in Silvia's sun porch.) I felt like I grew up in Roma's. It was there that I started bringing my hair to the colour it should always have been. There that I'd had my first perm, my first manicure and my first wax. The staff all knew me really well.

Loretta had never been in a beauty parlour before and looked around with all the wonder of someone who's never before been inside a torture chamber. *What's this? What's that?* She read the list of services posted by the register like it was in a language she'd only been learning for a month. Which at least took attention from me. Everyone was watching her.

"Your friend's not from around here, is she?" asked Roma.

No, she's from Mars.

I poked Loretta in the side. "Get yourself a coffee and a cookie," I whispered, "and stop gawping like your spaceship just landed."

I sat down in front of a mirror, staring at my reflection like a girl waving goodbye to the lover who is going off to war and may never come back. I studied every detail. The long, softly curling hair, the dangling earrings, the carefully outlined eyes, the silky halter-top. This was not just my last day with hair, it was my last day looking like me. The day joy died. My miracle was that I didn't burst into tears and wind up spending my last hours in make-up looking like a raccoon.

"You want what?" Roma stared at me in the mirror, her expression the definition of disbelief. "You want it cut short?" Those were words she never thought she'd hear from my lips.

Roma has been in charge of my hair since my first appointment, and (except for when I had a perm) it was always the same. Trim, lighten and shape.

I felt like a doctor ordering an amputation on herself. "That's right. Cut it. Short."

"How short?"

"Short as mine," chimed in Loretta.

Roma didn't turn around; she moved her eyes across the mirror to Loretta and then back to me. I could tell from the way she winced that, even with the highlights, she knew Loretta cut her own hair. Possibly with pinking shears. "You sure?"

I nodded. "But, you know, styled, not just chopped off." I lowered my voice. "Something that makes a statement that isn't *I don't care*."

"Ummm," said Roma. "What about the colour?"

"I thought I'd let it grow out."

"You did? Clipped like a hedge and back to dirty blonde?" She smooshed her lips together the way she does when she's trying to decide if one side is a sixteenth of an inch longer than the other. "So what happened, ZiZi? You lose the bet?"

From behind us, Loretta said, "Not yet."

Loretta said I was exaggerating how different I looked. (Well, she would, wouldn't she?)

"No, I'm not." Now I knew exactly how Truly Silverado felt in eighth grade when she got a haircut that

163

made her look like a squirrel (and missed the school trip to DC because she wouldn't be seen in public for over a week). "I'm in shock."

"For Christ's sake, Zi. All you did was have your hair cut. You do know it'll grow back, don't you?"

I held my phone in front of me. The dark screen didn't make me look any better.

"Tell me the truth," I ordered. "Do my ears look big in this?"

"That's the spirit," said Loretta. "Laugh, and the world laughs with you."

Cry, and you cry alone.

Loretta offered to come home with me but I wanted to be by myself. I needed time to adjust.

I was counting on the fact that, since it was a Saturday, there wouldn't be anyone there (unless Nate or Obi were still asleep, and, if they were, I could have herded elephants past their doors without waking them). I stepped inside, and into the peace and quiet that only exist in our house when it's either three a.m. or there's no one in it. Bliss.

I went straight into the bathroom and took off my make-up and earrings so I could judge the full effect. The full effect was horrific. Except for the dress I was wearing, I looked like an extra in one of those World

War II movies where the resistance fighters live in the forest and forage for food. *Get used to it*, I told myself. *It isn't that bad*, I told myself. *You're still you.* If you take the cover off a book, it doesn't change what's inside. And anyway, I wasn't going to look like this for that long. Loretta wouldn't last a week. I'd already had to forbid her to wear a hat or any kind of jacket unless it was raining (and it had to be raining really hard). It wouldn't be long before her principles mutinied and made her quit. That cheered me up enough to go into the kitchen for a drink. I should've stayed in the bathroom. Nate was there with Marsh. They were fixing themselves a snack (that's the other time that peace and quiet can exist in our house, when the guys have their mouths full of food). I checked the urge to turn around and make a mad dash for my room before they saw me. I was in my own home. Among friends (at least, in theory!). This was as easy as it would get.

"Hi, guys," I said.

Nate and Marsh looked around.

Marsh is a big fan of mine. He knows I'd never go out with him (even if he wasn't my brother's best friend, we'd have to be the last two people on the planet before I'd consider it, and then I'd say no), but he admires me from afar. I always get a dopey grin and a flirty, "Hey, there,

Giselle. How's it going?" Today he just nodded. Without much enthusiasm.

Nate showed more emotion. "What happened to you?" asked my brother. "Did someone die?"

You'd think an alarm had gone off alerting the neighbourhood because right then the back door opened and Dad and Obi walked in from the yard. Even if they weren't carrying a bat and a catcher's mitt, you'd know what they'd been doing. They were both sweaty, bruised and grass-stained (baseball's not something either of them is good at).

"What phase is this now?" asked my dad. "Don't tell me you've joined some cult."

"Cool!" screamed Obi. "You're like the living dead!"

Marsh looked from me to Nate. "Oh, man," said Marsh. "Is that ZiZi?"

I never had the chance to answer any of them. Right on cue, my mother came in behind me. "What's going on?"

I turned around. Say what you will about Gina (and I say plenty), she didn't twitch a single eyelash.

"Let me take a wild guess," said my mother. "You and Loretta made a bet."

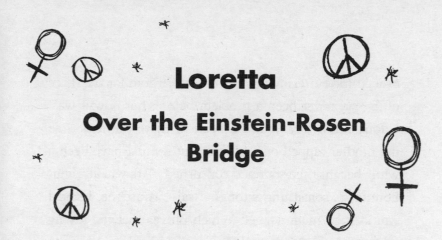

Loretta
Over the Einstein-Rosen Bridge

The Sunday before the official start of the bet, ZiZi and I walked into town to have lunch. This was our test run. You don't simply climb into a space shuttle and head for the stars, you have to practise beforehand: simulate the experience; learn the drill; prepare for the pitfalls.

As a testament to how seriously she was taking the bet and what it entailed, ZiZi wrote and printed out two pages of notes so I could make myself up the way she'd shown me. "I know you like to be thorough," said ZiZi.

It takes her a long time to get herself ready for public appearances, but it took me longer. I put on too much eye shadow and not enough blush, and in the process of fixing those mistakes, discovered how much easier it is to put make-up on than to take it off. My liner was crooked and I poked myself in the eye with the mascara wand three separate times, making my eyes water and everything run. Having only one bathroom for the three of us had never been a problem before, but now it was. I don't know how long I'd been in there the first time my mother rapped on the door, but it must have been a while because she sounded concerned. "Are you all right, Loretta? Is something wrong?" I said I was fine. I said I wouldn't be much longer. Which proves that the saying "Hope dies last" is true, because the next knock on the door was my father's. "What are you doing in there?" he demanded. "Retiling around the tub?" I said yes, but that I was almost finished. The next time my mother came to the door she jiggled the knob so much I thought it was going to fall off. "You know, your dad can always go in the bushes," she shouted. "But that isn't an option all of us have." After that, every few minutes, one or the other of them would let me know the aggregate time that I'd "been in there" so far. I kept shouting back that I wouldn't be much longer, I was being as fast as I could, but of course the pressure of having them baying and pawing the ground in the hall made it all that much worse. I became confused. I dropped things. I got lipstick on my teeth, and then put so much on my mouth that I looked like I was running away to join the circus. Which was beginning to seem like it might not be such a bad idea. When I was finally as done as I was going to get, I yelled,

"Bathroom free!" and raced to my room before either of them saw me. I put on one of ZiZi's sundresses. She'd loaned me three pairs of shoes – sandals that kept your feet a good four inches out of the sand, pumps and flats. The pumps fit best; I stuck them in my bag to change into when I got to her house and wore my trainers on the walk there.

By the time I was ready to leave, my parents had returned to the kitchen and were finishing brunch and reading the papers. Alice and Gertie were curled up in the sunshine on the windowsill behind them. Everyone looked over when I came into the room. Only Alice and Gertie didn't seem a little surprised; but they rely more on smell and sound than sight and I'd drawn the line at fragrance.

"Do we know you?" My mother peered over the top of her glasses. "You do look familiar. Maybe you were at that fundraiser for the hospital last year?" My mother may be a yoga teacher but she mistakenly thinks she's a comedian as well. "Didn't you sing a song? What was it?" She pursed her lips around an invisible straw, a gesture that apparently helps her think. "Was it something from Rodgers and Hammerstein?"

I'm not actually familiar with the Rodgers and Hammerstein songbook but, knowing my mother, she was thinking of a song that was a paradigm of sexism. I said, "You should stick to your asanas and leave the jokes to the professionals."

"So, this is serious," said my father. "You and ZiZi are really going to change places? Is it because you always wanted siblings? Is that what this is about?"

"We're not changing places, Dad. We're merely swapping images. In a general sort of way."

"Swapping images," he repeated. "We used to swap baseball cards when I was a boy. Of course, those were simpler times." He laid his paper on the table. "And you're doing this why?"

Do everyone's parents make them sigh the way mine make me sigh? "Because it's Summer and we'll be bored with no classes to go to. We could do drugs or steal cars, but we figured this would be amusing *and* keep us out of jail."

My father pretended to laugh. "What's the real reason?"

"I told you, Dad. Because I think ZiZi limits herself by being too girly, and she thinks I limit myself by not being girly enough. It's an experiment."

"Interesting…" My father nodded. "Very interesting. I was reading an article on gender studies recently that you might want to take a look at."

"Maybe later," I said. "When our results are in."

"Of course. That makes sense." My father has a work smile and a family smile; he gave me the work one. "I have to admit that I never expected to see you look like…"

My father's paid to talk; it's not often that he can't find a word.

"Like what?" I prompted.

"Like you look. It's a big change." He picked up his paper and shook it out. "I'd say you're lucky you have ZiZi to advise you."

Which seemed to me the same as saying you're lucky it was a doctor who ran you over.

"I wouldn't be doing it if I didn't have ZiZi."

"Well, she's done a good job," judged my mother.

My father said, "She certainly has." He said it with enthusiasm.

"Maybe she should be a stylist to the stars," said my mother. "Or a make-up artist. She obviously has a real talent."

"Indeed she does," said my father. "What you have here is a very expert makeover."

Stylist to the stars… Expert makeover… This was all completely bizarre and out of character for my parents. They're professional people whose tastes tend more towards serious drama than celebrity reality shows.

When did they stop reading specialist journals and start reading gossip magazines?

I gazed at their smiling faces. My parents liked ZiZi and had always encouraged our friendship. I'd thought that was because they saw in her what I saw; a girl with a lot of potential who just needed someone to shove her in the right direction. Or drag her, kicking and screaming, if necessary. This was the first time it occurred to me that I might have been wrong. That they'd hoped ZiZi would influence me; that even though they'd be proud when I became a theoretical physicist, they'd be happier if I was a theoretical physicist who looked like a girl.

When I got to the Abruzzios' it was Obi who answered the door. He was eating a bagel with cream cheese and jam. Grape jam, at a wild guess. Chewing slowly, he stared at me for a few thoughtful seconds, as if he'd never seen me before. "Yeah?" I asked for ZiZi. He looked into the house and hollered, "ZiZi! There's some girl here for you!"

From the kitchen, ZiZi shouted back, "Oh, for God's sake, Obi. That's not some girl, that's Loretta. I told you she was coming. Shut up and let her in."

Obi turned to me, and stared as if he was an astronomer and I was a new planet. "Wow," said Obi. "You look really different."

I stepped inside. "You look different, too. I'm not used to seeing you with cream cheese and jam all over your face."

The Abruzzios were sitting around the kitchen table. ZiZi's family has few things in common with mine, but Sunday brunch is one of them. They obviously had been briefed about today's venture because Gina and Frank smiled and said hello in a casual, normal way. Nate said, "Hi," but didn't look up from the crossword he was doing.

"I won't be long, Lo." ZiZi held up her mug. "I'm just fortifying myself with caffeine before we go."

"Maybe Loretta would like a coffee," said Gina.

All his attention on filling in Seven Down, Nate said, "Maybe Loretta'd rather have a tea." He finally looked up. "You know she—" He couldn't have looked more surprised if I'd been dressed in an army uniform with a rifle slung over my shoulder. His pencil clattered to the floor.

Clearly, this was a day for people acting very bizarrely; first my parents and now Nate. Nate and I always got on well. If anything, I thought of him as the big brother I'd never had. We both loved motorcycles, Kurt Vonnegut and sourdough pretzels.

Nate resurfaced with his pencil.

"You okay?" I asked.

"Yeah, yeah." He nodded. "It's just, you know…" He

laughed. "I guess I didn't know you had legs."

ZiZi's mug banged onto the table. "You'll have to excuse my brothers, Loretta. I'm afraid they're both idiots." She stood up. She was wearing an old pair of jeans and one of my T-shirts. It was kind of like looking in a mirror, except that her eyes aren't brown, her nose is smaller and her eyebrows are unusually straight – and she has more chest. "Come on, let's get out of here before they say something else to embarrass their parents."

I changed my shoes on the porch and we set off into our brave new world.

The pumps had been a bad idea. They made it difficult to walk. Not impossible, but difficult. I wasn't actually staggering or partially crippled – which for definite was good news – but I was pitched slightly forward and couldn't seem to stand completely straight. This, I thought, is how you develop curvature of the spine. I was acutely aware of every step I took. They were so unsteady you'd think I knew nothing about balance. I know a lot about balance, I've been doing yoga since I was three. But standing like a tree is a lot different than walking on sticks.

"Don't start, Lo," warned ZiZi. "Those heels aren't that high. And anyway, you picked them. You could've worn the sandals. Or the ballet flats. The choice was yours."

It wasn't that much of a choice. The sandals and the flats were both a little tight, and I'd reasoned that since we were doing a significant amount of walking, it would be better to go with the shoes that actually fit. File under the heading: *Wrong again.*

"I'm definitely swaying. I feel as if I'm on a boat in rough seas."

"You're supposed to sway. That's why you have hips."

And all these years, I'd thought I had hips for child-birth – that or for carrying baskets.

I'd been so traumatized by the ordeal of putting on my make-up and the bathroom lockdown that I hadn't felt any different on my way to pick up ZiZi, but now I began to feel enormously self-conscious. As if I were on display. Suddenly, the dress I was wearing seemed really short and my legs seemed really long.

ZiZi let out one of her steam-engine sighs. "Oh, for God's sake, Loretta. Stop fidgeting. Now what's wrong?"

"I feel really exposed."

She stopped abruptly, put her hands on my shoulders and looked me up and down. "No, you're not exposed. All private parts are covered. You have my word."

"You know what I mean." I tugged at the skirt. "It seems really short."

"It is short." She started walking again. "It's Summer,

Loretta. In Summer everybody but you wears short skirts. Unless they skip the skirt part and just wear shorts."

The closer we got to town, the stronger the impression grew that I was on show. Was it my imagination, or were people looking at me? Were heads turning in my direction? Were curtains twitching as I passed? ZiZi and I are roughly the same height, but she was wearing high-tops and I was wearing her stupid pumps, which made me feel like I was about six feet tall and looming over her.

We turned onto the main road and it immediately became clear beyond even the shadow of doubt's shadow that it wasn't my imagination; people really were looking at me.

"Of course they're looking at you," said ZiZi. "That's the whole idea, isn't it? To get attention. To show off how good you look. They're admiring you."

Admiring or judging. I felt as if I was a contestant in a beauty pageant. Or a pedigree poodle in a dog show. Any minute, someone was going to tell me to heel.

"They're admiring me because I have legs and breasts? Everybody has legs and breasts. Chickens have them."

"They're admiring you because you look great. You're like the goodwill ambassador from a planet where all the girls are young and pretty. You cheer people up. You make everything seem better than it is."

Philosopher Barbie speaks. The preening and prep-
ping were all about altruism, not vanity – that was nice
to know.

"I thought I was just showing off, and here I am
saving the world with a short skirt."

The man smoking a cigarette in front of the deli
smiled.

"Trust me," said ZiZi as I swayed dangerously close to
a lamppost. "You'll get used to it."

Maybe. If I lived that long.

On this early summer Sunday afternoon, Howards
Walk was already more like a bustling metropolis than a
small, sleepy town. The marina was packed, the streets
were crowded, the stores were all busy and there were
tables outside every café and restaurant that had room.
Most of the time when you walk past stores with ZiZi
she's checking herself out in the windows, as if some sar-
torial or cosmetic disaster might have occured between
the World of Cheese and Kradinkski's Hardware – her
collar was askew or something had gone wrong with her
eyelashes. I thought that now she wasn't obsessing about
how she looked, she'd stop doing that, but apparently old
habits really do die hard. Every three seconds she was
glancing in a window at herself. Everybody else seemed
to be looking at me. *Spotlight on Loretta…* Which was

extremely discomfiting for someone who never actually got on the stage before.

Most of the shoppers and diners were summer people, but not all. I recognized two girls from school. I didn't know them or anything – they were a year ahead of us and super popular types who had never given any indication that they were aware of my existence – but, though they didn't stop their conversation, they both nodded and smiled in my direction as they passed. I turned around to see who was behind me; it was a middle-aged man in a captain's hat, his eyes on his phone. They had to be smiling and nodding at me. Nor were they the only ones to suddenly decide we were acquainted. A boy I also recognized from school and a couple of college guys who looked vaguely familiar all greeted me, too. More bizarreness. I wasn't used to being noticed, never mind being beamed at by strangers, and I found it unnerving. It's just as well I'm not interested in being a celebrity; I wouldn't be able to take the stress – no wonder so many of them drink or do drugs. I couldn't wait to get inside to sit with a table shielding my legs and my back to the door. As we reached the bistro, a young man in a panama hat was coming out, but he stepped back when he saw us and held the door open with a flourish. "Check out the black-bean burrito bowl," he advised me. "It's really good."

I thanked him. I wasn't used to getting menu tips, either.

We grabbed a table at the back, and I sat so I was facing the wall and could pretend that, behind me, the town had disappeared.

"Fine by me," said ZiZi. "Unless I drape myself in lights nobody's going to be looking at me anyway."

Safe in our corner, I began to relax and feel like myself again. My legs were under the table, my back was to the room, there was nothing in front of me but ZiZi and a *Day of the Dead* poster – nothing that I could see my reflection in.

The waiter brought water and menus – and a smile for me.

"I know it's the point of the whole exercise, but I still think it's amazing how differently everyone's acting towards us." I hadn't expected it to be quite so blatant. Or so quick.

"What have I been trying to tell you all this time?" ZiZi took a drink of water. "Clothes make the girl."

"Clothes make the image, not the girl." I picked up a menu. "We're still the same people."

"Sure we are." ZiZi winked. "But try telling that to your new friend the waiter. Or my family, even. Seriously? I mean, we have the ongoing college saga, but apart from that I always thought they were pretty happy with me.

Now I'm not so sure."

"Same here. My folks have already shown signs of a previously hidden dissatisfaction with their only child."

We started swapping shocking but true stories about the reactions we'd had so far.

"Talk about adding insult to injury," I confided. "I actually overheard my mother saying she thought my makeover must be because I have a boyfriend I wasn't telling them about. I was totally shocked."

"I can beat that," said ZiZi. "Gina thinks I'm doing this because I'm taking the last break-up with Duane harder than usual." She made a can-you-believe-it? face. "I mean, duh. Breaking up with Duane is like stopping banging your head against the wall. Even she has to know that usual is like not at all."

I told her how my dad had to pretend he was looking for beetles when Mrs Shaunnessey next door came out of her back door while he was peeing in the bushes because he couldn't get into the bathroom. "Dr Reynolds with his trousers down, can you imagine? For definite, I'm never going to hear the end of that."

Nate's best friend Marsh – who's always had a not-so-secret thing for ZiZi – thought she was me the first time he saw the new her. "You should've seen his face when he realized," gasped ZiZi. "It was like he thought he'd been flirting with a girl all this time only to find out he'd really been chatting up a broom!"

"You think that's something?" I practically shrieked. "My father offered me money to go shopping. Can you believe that? The man who thinks you only buy clothes at the start of school and maybe in the winter if you need a new coat, because that's what they did when he was a boy!" And my mother asked if I wanted to go with her to her hairdresser next time she went. "Can you imagine?" I was nearly choking with laughter. "Me and my mum side by side under the dryers? Chanting and meditation are one thing, but this is a level of bonding I wasn't expecting and absolutely don't want."

ZiZi said her parents kept telling her how nice she looks and how it's a sign of maturity. "That's what makes me think they're not as happy with me as I thought," said ZiZi. "And like that's not bad enough, Frank wanted to know if I'm taking up a different hobby from shopping now. I said, 'Like what?' and he said that was up to me. So I said I was thinking of racing elephants."

We had each other in stitches.

By the time we left the restaurant, I think we both felt so much like our usual selves that we'd almost forgotten how we looked. We were still laughing as we walked back up the street. And then Gabriel Schwartz came out of the bookstore, walking towards us.

I swear, I felt my heart hit my feet and bounce back up again. How would he react? Would I be able to tell what he was thinking? What would he say? I checked the impulse to see how I looked in the nearest window. Would this be the moment he discovered that there is more to me than a highly intelligent mind?

He was practically on top of us when I realized he wasn't going to say anything; he was just going to walk right past us. Forget him finally noticing that I'm a girl; he didn't notice me at all.

"Gabe!" I put a hand on his arm. "Hey, hi!"

I've emptied the trash with more enthusiasm than his "Hi" in return. He looked as nonplussed as Nate had. And then he laughed. "Loretta?" His laugh was like a prisoner waiting to be sentenced. "Sorry. I didn't – I…" He cleared his throat. "You look…"

Looked what? Different? Better? Like a girl he'd want to date?

"What'd you do to your hair?" His smile was clinging to his face with a certain amount of desperation. "It kind of looks like a night sky."

Did it? No one else had noticed the similarity.

"It's highlights."

"Highlights." He was looking at me as if he wasn't

sure what he was seeing. An impact crater on the surface of Mars or proof that there once was a sea? "And a dress." I willed him not to say he didn't know I had legs. "You going someplace special?"

"No. We're just – you know – walking around."

He cleared his throat again. "So, how you doin'?"

I said I was doing fine. I said I was looking forward to the Perseids. "It's going to be the best part of the Summer. I can hardly wait."

He nodded, but it wasn't a nod of agreement, it was the way you nod when you have no idea what the other person is talking about and don't really care. You'd think he'd never heard of the Perseids; that we hadn't been planning this outing since April.

"The Perseids," I repeated. "Remember? You wrote the flier?"

"Oh, yeah, yeah. Of course. The Perseids." Even though he was standing still, he seemed to be moving. "I'm sorry. I guess I was thinking of something else."

"You're still up for it, aren't you?"

"Yeah. Sure. Yeah. We'll talk before. There's plenty of time." He'd hadn't so much as glanced at ZiZi up until then, but he suddenly turned to her as if he was lost in space and she was the rescue party. "We haven't been introduced…" This wasn't strictly true. I doubted he'd ever actually spoken to her – he certainly didn't speak to her the day he fell into the fridge – but he knew who she was. I introduced them anyway. *ZiZi, Gabe; Gabe, ZiZi.* He shook her hand. "You should come, too. They can be really spectacular. It'll be fun." ZiZi was so surprised that for once she had nothing to say. "Well, I better get going," said Gabriel. "I don't want to be late."

Late for what? I wondered. It was Sunday afternoon. Where was he hurrying to? He wasn't, of course; he was hurrying *from*, hurrying away from me. We watched him disappear down the street; he turned at the corner – and didn't glance back.

ZiZi couldn't believe Gabe didn't know who she was; I couldn't believe that he was happier to talk to her than to me.

The Einstein-Rosen bridge is another name for the wormhole theory. Which is the idea that there may be shortcuts through space-time. I've always fantasized about being able to open a door – or step through a mirror like Alice – and find myself in a different place and time. When I was little, I'd go around the house, pressing on every mirror and door, hoping one of them would give. I spent hours standing in front of the full-length mirror in my parents' bedroom, imagining the world on the other side – where everything looked the same but wasn't. What with all the unusual attention I'd been getting from people I didn't know – and all the attention I wasn't getting from a person I did know – I was beginning to wonder if my wish had come true.

ZiZi

The invisible girl

Maybe instead of trading looks, Loretta and I should have traded families. I could really have used a new one. Take my brothers, for example. (And don't worry about bringing them back.) *There's some girl here to see you…* Seriously? Like Obi'd never met Loretta before? How many games of *Troll Invasion* (or whatever dumb thing he's obsessed with) did she play with him before he stopped asking her because she always won? (Probably thousands!) Okay, she did look different (about a hundred times better), but she didn't look *that* different. No reconstructive surgery was involved. And then there's the other one: *I didn't know you had legs…* Sometimes I can't even believe I'm related to either of them. What was that supposed to mean, "I didn't know you had legs"? Plus, you should've seen Nate's face when he finally looked at her. (You never have your camera handy when you really need it, do you?) You'd think she'd walked in naked. And it's not like they had no warning. I'd explained what we were doing very clearly. I was painstaking. You have to be. Loretta isn't the only one who thinks boys never hear what you say. My mother's always complaining that the male Abruzzios don't listen to her. She tells them she's going to be out for the night and then one of them calls to find out where she is. She asks my father or Nate to pick up milk on his way home, and then they complain that there isn't any milk. And I've had my own personal experiences, too, so that sometimes even I think that when women talk all they hear (and by "they" I mean male humans) is white noise.

My parents, however, did listen to me (even Frank). They thought the bet was a great idea. If anything, they were too enthusiastic. *What a clever plan. What an interesting experiment.* "Maybe you should consider studying psychology or sociology at college," suggested my mother. (This had obviously given her new hope that I wasn't going to try to get out of further education.) My dad said Loretta and I should do a blog. That would be really interesting. You never knew where it might lead. I said I could guess. (Straight to a dead end!) Girls want to hear about make-up and clothes, not the lack of them. Here's the thing. My family are all onions except for me.

I'm the only rose. So you'd think they'd be a little upset to see their rose's beauty fade into the plainness of a root vegetable pretty much overnight. But unless they were hiding how they really felt to spare me, they weren't upset at all. What they were was pretty jubilant! Gina said this was a wonderful opportunity for me to finally learn that I have more to offer the world than a pretty face. (But after she saw Loretta, Gina wouldn't shut up about how great she looked. *Quel hypocritical* is that?) Frank wanted to know if this meant it was his chance to send his credit card to rehab since I wouldn't be shopping for a while. (Like I don't pay for a lot of my stuff myself!) That's when I started to wonder if they secretly think I'm shallow and superficial. If they'd gotten a rose, but what they really wanted was a baking potato.

Anyway, I told them the same thing I told Loretta. This wasn't going to change *me*. I might look different, but, inside, I was the same person I'd always been. Only with less hair and wearing more (and more boring) clothes.

I admit I was pretty traumatized by the haircut at first, but I sincerely believed I'd managed to recover from my initial shock. I'd spent a long time looking at myself in the bathroom mirror getting used to it (two and a half hours according to my father, the family timekeeper).

I told myself that it wasn't that bad, not really. Roma had done a good job. It was sophisticated. With make-up and the right clothes and accessories, it would make a statement: *I am a model for a bold, futuristic designer who laughs in the face of conformity and convention.* (I know I didn't have make-up and the right clothes and accessories, but you could see the intention was there.)

Plus, what I said before was totally true. It didn't make me a different person. For God's sake, a rose with faded petals and no body spray is still a rose.

For Loretta's and my first journey into the real world together, I was wearing my grossest old jeans (usually reserved for major art projects or painting my room) and a T-shirt. I was cool and calm as Loretta and I strolled into town, but to tell you the truth, I was putting on a brave face. Super brave. Inside, I was really nervous – bordering on ready to have a breakdown. Every step we took made it clearer that I'd been kidding myself about being okay with the new me. Because here's the thing. Intentions aren't visible. Girls are. Without all the trappings and trimmings, I looked more like I was enlisting in the army than I looked like a pioneer of fearless fashion and originality. People were going to see me. (I know my family had already seen me, but they so don't count.) And it wasn't just strangers who were going to see me. Kidding myself? I'd been seriously delusional. I mean, okay, so Isla, Marilee, Shona and Dillon Blackstock (whose opinions mattered most, especially his) were all safely out of the way, but they're not the only people I know. Or who know me. School is full of them. Plus, hard though it may be to believe, my brothers do have multiple friends. My parents have friends. I've been in the school system a long time, so there were literally dozens of teachers roaming around who know who I am. It was a really long nightmare waiting to happen. One of those really unpleasant nightmares where you go to the prom dressed in the old bathrobe your mother uses when she touches up the grey and the sheep slippers you had when you were three, and your date is that fat English king who killed all his wives.

Loretta managed to distract me from my own problems for a while by griping and groaning the whole way into town. You'd think she was really suffering, the way she was carrying on. Tugging at her skirt, complaining about how the shoes made her walk. Then we swung onto the main street where most of the stores and cafés and stuff like that are and she developed a major case of paranoia. Loretta, the girl who couldn't give a used tissue what people think of her, was suddenly convinced that everybody was looking at her. And? People always look at her (because she's weird and says odd things and wears mismatched socks), but that never bothered her. The difference was that now they were looking at her in a good way. They were thinking, *Wow, she's hot!* Not, *Wow, she's peculiar!* So she should've been happy. But no, Loretta always has to be contrary. She wasn't at all happy. She said she felt like a dog. (*Quel ironic*, right? If either of us looked like a dog, it wasn't Loretta!)

We weren't in town more than fifty-six seconds when who do I see sashaying towards us but Lissa Jamison (that year's prom queen) and Suzanne Migas (almost that year's prom queen). Lissa was texting and Suzanne was talking. The three of us weren't in the same circle, but we were in circles that overlapped and rubbed up against each other now and then. Friendly, if not exactly friends. (Okay, not super friendly, but friendly enough. Lissa once asked me where I got my blue cashmere top.) I held my breath and waited for their reactions. They glanced at us the way you do when you know someone's ahead of you and you don't want to bump into them, then they smiled and nodded at Loretta. And sailed past me like ships passing a monotonous landscape.

I wasn't sure if I was more relieved or annoyed that Lissa and Suzanne saw Loretta but didn't see me. More relieved, probably. At least they weren't going to get online and blab to the world and its relatives and friends that I'd gone geek. *Wait'll you see ZiZi Abruzzio! She looks like a guy...* And then it happened again. And again. People (male people, mostly) looked twice at Loretta, they smiled at Loretta, but they didn't see or smile at me. Like I was a shadow beside her. A very faint shadow. So I didn't have to worry about being seen – all I had to worry about was being trampled to death by people who didn't know I was there!

"Oh, for God's sake," Loretta grumbled. "What is wrong with you? Even now, you can't stop looking at yourself in any reflective surface."

"You mean even now that I'm so nondescript I could rob a crowded bank and get away with it – since no one would remember what I look like?"

Loretta sighed like she's the only person on the planet who is ever reasonable. "I thought you were all worked up because you thought someone would see you. Now you're worked up because no one has."

"I'm human. I'm inconsistent." I glanced over at the deli. Shimmering over the jars of artichokes and sun-dried tomatoes was my own ghost. If you looked closely, you could just about see the girl I once was, but was no more. No wonder no one saw me. Even the guy in the bait and tackle shop who always calls me honey stood in the doorway and watched me go by like I was made of air. "And anyway the only reason I'm looking in windows is to make sure I'm still here."

"Pinch yourself," said Loretta. "If you don't feel it, you are somewhere else."

"You know," I said as we walked along. "I think we've already proved that I'm right. If you dress plain, you are plain. The most important thing is how you look."

"No, it isn't," argued Loretta. "We already know that boys have better eyesight than brains. What you've proved is that those girls we saw who you think are so great are better at recognizing clothes than faces. It's all the same superficial garbage. It's who you are that matters for anything important, not whether or not you have blonde hair and blue eyes and wear a short dress."

"But how you look changes how you're seen." I swear, if Loretta was a wall, even Superman wouldn't be able to knock her down. "You know that's true! People aren't looking at you because you're really smart and are worried about the fate of the planet. They're looking at you because you're pretty."

"I get that, Zi. But my point is that they're never going to know how smart or how worried about the degradation of the planet I am if all they care about are my breasts. That's why we should dress the way we want, not conform to some warped cultural ideal."

We got to the café and this kind of hip-looking guy held the door open for Loretta, and she sailed through. Then he practically knocked me over coming out while I was trying to follow her in.

We agreed not to argue over lunch. It's bad for digestion. Loretta said she heard the black-bean burrito bowl was really good. Where did she hear that? When? Neither of us had ever been there before. Loretta said someone mentioned it. So we both got that (and it was really good), and I was so disoriented with all the stress that I ate the whole thing without once wondering how many calories were in it. But lunch was cool. We both relaxed and felt normal. Plus, it wasn't even Day One really and already we both had funny stories. The laughing made me feel better about everything. I figure that so long as you can laugh at something, it can't really be that bad. It's when people don't laugh that they start throwing themselves or other people off rooftops and stuff like that. We were still laughing when we left the restaurant.

And then Loretta stopped laughing. Her face turned red under the make-up and this look came onto her face. Like it was Christmas and she got everything she wanted. I followed her eyes. One of Loretta's geeky science friends was coming towards us. The tall and weedy-looking one, with too-long hair and a silver star in one ear. We do go to the same school, and he and Loretta are space freaks and stargazers together, so I kind of knew him. We'd even had one or two classes together. Not that he'd ever spoken to me or anything like that. (I am so not his type of person, never mind type of girl.) He didn't even speak to me that time he came over when I was at Loretta's. I don't know if he was surprised to see me there or what, but he tripped over the hooked rug, ricocheted off the fridge, got hit in the head by falling boxes of cereal and landed in the cat food. I tried not to crack up because Loretta looked as embarrassed as he did, but it wasn't really possible. Seriously. *Quel hilarious or what?* He only stayed long enough to leave, so I never knew why he was there in the first place. Anyway, it wasn't until I saw the Christmas look on Loretta's face that the light went on in the attic of my brain. Loretta Reynolds had a crush on whatever he's called! Maybe she was a lot more of a girl than I'd thought.

He was going to walk right past us, but she grabbed his arm. Boldly. So then I remembered his name. It's Gabriel (like the angel, but really he looks more like an ostrich). They started talking about the Astronomy Club (that's what I mean about space freaks!) – at least Loretta did, he was mainly nodding. I stood there, waiting for them to finish, warily scoping the street, but though I saw several people I knew, no one started waving frantically at me or calling my name. The way they would've a couple of days ago.

And then I heard Star Boy say, "We haven't been introduced…"

I refocused. Since it was just the three of us standing there, he had to be talking to me. Was he serious? I mean, maybe no one had done formal introductions (we were in high school, not the government) but we'd been in the same school for three years. How could he think he'd never seen me before? Even Loretta was surprised. There was a pause long enough to tie a shoelace before she said, "Oh, I'm sorry. Where are my manners? ZiZi, this is Gabe. Gabe, ZiZi."

He actually grabbed my hand and shook it like an old man would. "You should come, too," said Gabe. "It's the best meteor showers. It'll be fun."

Of course it would be. Staring up at the sky looking for shooting stars practically defines the concept of fun.

Gee thanks. I was smiling at a mad man. *I'll put that on my calendar.*

Loretta laughed as we started walking again. "Was that amazing, or what, Zi? He's seen you like a million times and he didn't know who you are."

"My only consolation is that he didn't seem to know you, either."

But it wasn't much of a consolation. It wasn't just that I was in the background, it was like I wasn't even in the picture. The invisible girl. Which is kind of funny since, when I was little, I thought it would be totally cool to be able to make myself invisible. That would've been my superpower of choice. Now you see her, now you don't. I figured it was way better than being able to fly or jump over buildings or whatever. Think of all the advantages! You could go and come as you pleased. You could never be grounded. Forget that. You'd never get in any trouble because you'd never get caught. You could pretty much do what you wanted. Always. Petty thefts. Exclusive parties. Gala openings. Nobody could stop you. Plus, when Catie Coulson and I were best friends, I used to fantasize about being invisible so I could follow her around without her knowing and see what she was up to. (And hear what she was saying about me. It would have saved me a lot of time and mortification.) *Quel naive!* Because now that I was invisible, I wasn't sure that I was liking it at all.

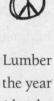

Loretta

For the first time in my life I'm late for work, and that's only the beginning

I had a full-time job at Chelusky's Hardware and Lumber that Summer. I'd begun working there part-time the year before. At first, I was just a sales assistant, but besides the hardware and the lumber Mr Chelusky offers a handyman service for people like my parents who can't change a doorknob, and eventually he made me part of that, too – as a helper, to begin with, and then, when I'd proved myself, for small jobs on my own. But, towards the end of June, Leroy Pine fell off his kitchen table changing a light bulb – evidence that most accidents really do happen at home. Leroy ended up in traction. Summer is a busy time in the lumber world, and, with one man down, Mr Chelusky needed someone temporary to take his place. He offered me Leroy's position till school started again, and I didn't waste a second thinking it over; it was just what I needed to beef up my savings for college.

My usual work clothes – whether I was at Chelusky's or doing odd jobs in the neighbourhood – were dungarees or a pair of old jeans and a flannel and a T-shirt – unless it was really hot and then it was just the T-shirt. If I was starting first thing in the morning, I got up, washed, pulled on my clothes, had a good breakfast and left the house. That was usual. But now that I was on the other side of the Einstein-Rosen bridge, my routine had changed drastically.

On that momentous Monday – Day One of the bet – I set my alarm an hour early so I had enough time and didn't have to rush. I couldn't get in the bathroom. Yoga teachers don't work nine to five; my mother teaches a class for people who want to twist themselves into complicated positions before they go to their jobs, and she was already in there. I decided I might as well dress before I washed and put on somebody else's face. I'd already picked out a pink skirt ZiZi found in the charity shop and a wrap-around top of hers that also contained a great deal of pink; a colour not previously associated with me. When I went back to the bathroom, my father had taken possession. I had to be grateful that I don't have any siblings or I might never get in.

When the bathroom was finally free, I taped ZiZi's instructions on the wall next to the mirror and lined up my collection of bottles and tubes and pencils on the sink in the order they went on – to save me confusion and time. At last, I was ready to begin. There was no more splashing some soap and water on my face. I had scrubs and gels and moisturizers. *Apply liberally … apply sparingly … rinse well … pat dry … don't rub*, said the instructions. I applied, I rinsed, I patted, I didn't rub. That was just the preparation; then came the make-up itself. After every application I peered at my reflection. Was that straight? Was that too little? Was that too much? I wished the light were better. Previously, in my life, I hadn't needed any special illumination to get myself ready – as long as it wasn't dark as a cave, I was good to go – but now I did. Already, I was wondering if I should get a make-up mirror like ZiZi's. I made a mental note that if she didn't give up by the end of the week I'd seriously consider buying one. Mercifully, I didn't have inches of hair that needed to be plaited or twisted or carefully brushed; but I did have to mousse it and shape it – God forbid it should just sit on my head the way it grows naturally. When I was finally finished with all that, I had exactly enough time to have a mug of tea and a slice of toast. Which was the least I'd had for breakfast since the week I was ill with the flu.

Yet, despite my best efforts, I was still late for work. Not hours late, but late enough that the grille was up, the door was open, the lights were on and Mr Chelusky was at the register. He looked over when he heard me come in. I guess he was expecting to see a builder on his way to a job and not me – sweaty and limp from pedalling so fast I could have won the yellow jersey in the Tour de France – because he looked surprised. "Can I help you, Miss?"

Mr Chelusky never called me "Miss". He called me Lou.

"It's me, Mr Chelusky, Loretta."

"Loretta." He didn't sound certain, as if he was thinking, *Which Loretta? Loretta Who?*

"I'm sorry I'm late, Mr Chelusky." The Loretta who works for you, that's which Loretta. "It's been an unusual morning. I promise it won't happen again."

"Loretta," he said again. He smiled as if I'd caught him having a secret smoke out back. "I didn't recognize you at first. Did you do something to your hair?"

I said yes. "I thought I'd lighten it a little for the Summer."

"It looks good." He nodded, agreeing with himself. "Different." He wasn't actually looking at my hair. He was having a taking-it-all-in look – like the first time you see pictures of Mars from a NASA rover, and can hardly believe what you're seeing. "You're all dressed up.

You look very nice." He actually chuckled – which was another thing he'd never done before. "You know, I don't think I've ever seen you in a skirt before."

Which translated meant that what he'd never seen before were my legs. What did these guys imagine I walked on?

"If you think this is dressed up, just wait till I show up in a ball gown."

Mr Chelusky usually likes my jokes, but this one didn't make him laugh. Still stuck on the skirt, he nodded again. "Well… So… What's the special occasion? Is it your birthday?" I figured it was all the pink that had him befuddled; I'm more a shades-of-black kind of girl.

"No. No occasion. You know… I just felt like a change."

He nodded. "That's women for you. You're like my wife. Always doing something different with her hair or moving the furniture around. Sometimes when I walk in the door, I think I'm in the wrong house."

I hadn't stopped smiling since I got there, but now I smiled even more. "Change is the nature of the universe, you know."

"Is it?" said Mr Chelusky. "I didn't know that. So I guess the universe is female, too." He came from behind the counter. "Now you're here, I'll put the things out front."

At night, the things that are displayed outside the

store – wheelbarrows, ladders, rubbish bins, etcetera; and at that time of year, lawn mowers, garden furniture and paddling pools as well – were moved inside. I grabbed two bins.

"Loretta! What are you doing?" He sounded as if we were on a mountain and I was too close to the edge and about to fall.

"I'm helping you."

"No, no. I won't hear of it. You get behind the counter. I'll move everything out."

"But we always do it together."

"Not today." Mr Chelusky winked. Yet one more Chelusky first. "You don't want to mess up your good clothes. Besides, we'll have a lot more happy customers if the first person they see is a pretty girl and not a balding old codger like me." He'd never before called me a pretty girl, either.

"But—"

"No more buts. Maybe you could rearrange the counter a little. Make it look more attractive."

Attractive? The counter in a hardware store? Exactly how attractive can you make displays of torches, key-rings, measuring tapes and Stanley knives?

"You want me to go get some flowers to decorate the box of builders' pencils?"

He didn't hear me; he was already hauling things outside.

Mr Chelusky was propping ladders against the front of the building when Vinnie Polo came in the back way. He glanced at me long enough to see that I wasn't who he was looking for and then spotted Mr Chelusky outside. "Oi, Charlie!" he called. "Nobody here yet? That shipment of tiles's come in. I need some help unloading."

"I'm here, Vinnie." I practically vaulted over the counter – or would have if I'd been wearing jeans. "I'll give you a hand."

"Loretta?" He laughed. "I didn't— Well … will you look at you." Which, of course, was what he was doing – apparently never having seen me before. "But it's okay. You're all dressed up. I'll wait till one of the guys is free."

I reminded him that I am one of the guys.

"Yeah," said Vinnie. "But the other guys don't wear skirts and polish their nails." Then he gave me a wink, too; which was yet another groundbreaking event for the morning. "So how come you're dressed up? You got a date after work?"

I didn't want to complicate things. The shortest distance between two points is a straight line, and it's also the quickest way to tell a story. I said yes.

Vinnie grinned as if he'd just had a piece of incredibly

good news. "Well, what do you know? Ain't that great."

He sounded like he meant it. For the first time, it occurred to me that my workmates, like my best friend – and, possibly, my mother – had been worried that no one would ever ask me out.

"Yeah," I agreed. "Yeah, it's great."

It also had never occurred to me to wonder how the men I worked with would fit into my sociological experiment. I hadn't given much thought – or any, if I'm being honest – to how they'd react to the new me.

For instance, Mr Chelusky. Mr Chelusky was old enough to be my grandfather, and as set in his ways as a pole is set in cement. Which meant that although he was used to having me around the store, he wasn't used to having a girl around. Mr Chelusky has three daughters – one is married, one is in college and the third one, the one he calls "the big surprise", is in middle school. He always refers to them as "my girls", and jokes about the drama and the tears and the fights, but he treats them like princesses. Me he has always treated the same as everyone else who works for him. If we'd been birds, his daughters would be golden parakeets and I'd be a sparrow. He'd never expect them to help unpack boxes or unload a truck; never expect them to carry ladders or run the forklift. Now, it seemed, he didn't expect me to do those things, either. I was a sparrow no more.

The other employees at Chelusky's – besides Vinnie and the injured Leroy – are Ernie, Mick and Horst. One by one that morning, they came into the store to get something or ask Mr Chelusky a question, and one by one they did a double take when they saw me – or took a few seconds to make the synaptic connection; *Good God, that must be Lou!* Unlike our boss, they did make the connection; none of them thought I was a customer who had wandered behind the counter by mistake. Ernie said I looked very elegant. Horst said I looked ace. Mick said I really cheered the place up. "You don't expect to see a good-looking girl in a room full of drill bits and paint," said Mick. Then, realizing that that wasn't quite the compliment he'd intended, he said, "Not that you weren't pretty before, Loretta, but you know what I mean." I said I knew; for definite I was starting to know. They were all happy that I had a date – a piece of news that had spread faster than fire on a parched prairie. No one said, "God, we never thought that would happen," but I could tell that they hadn't. They kept mentioning it and joking about it. Mr Chelusky even asked if "this young man" had met my parents. I felt like saying I wasn't marrying this young man – it was only a date. But I didn't say that, either. Mr Chelusky hadn't met my parents – they're not exactly lumberyard people – so I felt safe in saying yes to that question, too. "Of course they met him. They like him a lot."

I could have told them the truth. I could have explained that the reason my hair looked like somebody spilled bleach on it, my nails were coral, my eyelashes like awnings and my legs visible for the first time since I was in primary school was not because I had a date but because I made a bet. I could have said, "You remember my friend ZiZi?" That would have made them smile a little sheepishly – because of course they remembered her. Whenever ZiZi came by to pick me up from work, every one of them would find some excuse to come into the store – grinning at her like happy jack-o'-lanterns and bumping into things – no matter how busy it was in the yard. Every so often, especially if she hadn't been by for a while, they'd ask about her. *How's that friend of yours? What's her name again? She seems like a really nice girl.* "I made a bet with her," I could have said. "That's why I look like this. Because I made a bet." Only, I didn't tell them that. I let them believe that I was the kind of girl who dressed to please guys – or, in this case, a guy. I said I had a date and let them be glad for me.

Aside from that, I did my best to act as if nothing had changed – which it had. The men I worked with were all a little different around me; sort of cautious bordering on solicitous. As if they thought I wasn't feeling well or was going through a bad time. Whenever I looked up, I was facing a smile. Whenever I got to a door, it opened. Whenever I reached for something heavy, someone else picked it up first. I figured this would pass. It was just that they weren't used to me like this. Like when you get a new saw; it takes some getting used to; you have to break it in. I thought that all they needed was a little time.

As for me, by the end of the day I was beginning to understand why ZiZi smiled so much; you more or less have to when everyone is smiling at you or doing you small favours. The other thing that had happened by the end of the day – maybe because it was mentioned so much – was that I almost believed I did have a date that night.

File under the heading: *Go figure*.

ZiZi

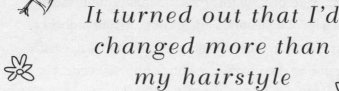

It turned out that I'd changed more than my hairstyle

Sunday night, to combat feeling kind of discombobulated because of being invisible (and because I had lots of spare time since I didn't have to spend hours deciding what I was wearing the next day or doing any preparation), I messaged Shona and Isla to see what they were up to and if they wanted to chat, but they didn't reply. (I didn't bother with Marilee because I wasn't sure what time it was for her. Plus, my father would have a heart attack and then kill me if I started texting Europe. He is so twentieth-century sometimes.) Loretta was out as a distraction because she did have to choose her outfit for the morning. And because I knew she was going to bed early so she could wake up early to get ready for work. So then I wasn't just invisible, I was also bored. I was so bored I came close as a barber's shave to asking my brothers if they wanted to play a game or something. What saved me from this humiliation was that they were deeply absorbed in some dumb movie that had a lot of helicopters and guns in it, and probably wouldn't even have heard me ask. Normally, if I had nothing else to do, I would've gone online and checked out some fashion blogs and vlogs, but now I couldn't really see much point in that. It would be like someone who had no money for food staring in the restaurant window. And anyway, I figured that I had to channel Loretta and try to get into a different mindset from my usual one (the nobody-cares-what-you-bought-at-the-mall-or-what-you're-going-to-wear-with-it mindset). So I did something I would usually never think of doing in two trillion years. I started reading a novel. It was one Loretta had loaned me, even though I never asked to borrow it. It had been sitting on the shelf in my room for a while. Maybe a year. I was wary of it because it was one of her feminist books that she was always pushing on me. Plus, from the title, it seemed to involve eating, so I was afraid it was going to be about women and dieting (one of Loretta's favourite rants, even though she totally knows that I don't go on diet after diet; I'm just careful most of the time). Here's the thing: this book was written like nearly fifty years ago and it's pretty weird, but it's also interesting (in a weird way). It's not about dieting at all. It's about this girl in Canada who, as far as I could tell, is having a kind of identity crisis. Something I could totally identify with! This girl thinks that she's being eaten. Metaphorically, not literally. (I figured that's worse than thinking you're invisible, but maybe not. I mean, being eaten was all in her head, but me being invisible was in everybody else's head.) I didn't put the book down till after midnight. That's a record for me. Usually, I don't read anything longer than a magazine article, unless it's for school.

Because I'm always running late, and because it's a meal I usually skip, I'm hardly ever in the kitchen when my brothers are having breakfast. At least, not on a weekday. But that Monday I was. The advantage of being like Loretta (if you can call it an advantage) is that it doesn't take an hour or more to get dressed, and one of the advantages of being a waitress is that you don't have much choice about what to wear (black slacks or skirt and a white shirt). So, even though I'd slept later than usual (nobody ever tells you how tired reading makes you, do they?), after I'd had a shower and caught up on all my Internet stuff, I still had over an hour to kill before I had to leave for the Inn, so I figured I might as well sit down to have my coffee. Plus, I was hungry. I blame the stress and having extra time and nothing to do in it.

Those are things that wreck your willpower.

The parents had already left for the day, but Nate and Obi and Obi's best friend Parker were all at the table. (I was pretty sure Parker had already eaten at home but that never stops him from eating with us.) Nate and Obi didn't pay any attention when I came in, but Parker stopped shovelling cornflakes into his mouth to stare at me. "Wow," said Parker. "What happened to you?"

So maybe I wasn't as invisible as I thought.

"Vampires," Obi mumbled through a mouthful of cereal. "They sucked out her blood and chewed off all her hair." At least he'd given up on the zombie idea. "She's lucky to be alive."

"Nothing happened to me." I put a slice of bread in the toaster. "I had a haircut. Like millions of people do every day."

"You kind of look like a squirrel."

I poured a cup of coffee. "You mean except for the bushy tail?"

Parker made what would've been a thoughtful face if there hadn't been milk dribbling down his chin and if he were capable of thought. "But Obi's right. You do look really pale."

"I still have blood." I put my toast on a plate and sat down. "I'm just not wearing any make-up. So all you see is my porcelain complexion, the envy of women all over the world."

Still looking almost thoughtful, and still dribbling, Parker said, "You used to be pretty."

Only a complete fool would listen to the opinion of a twelve-year-old boy who believes he saw a spaceship fly over his house.

"And you used to have a future, Parker. You know. Thirteen."

"Ouch." Nate pushed back his chair. "I think it's time for us to go."

"I'm only saying," said Parker. "Everybody said you were pretty."

I smiled extremely sweetly (especially for a really pale squirrel who'd lost her looks). "And everybody said you had a brain, Parker, but they were horribly wrong about that, too."

Nate stood up. "Okay, you guys, let's get this car in gear before blood is spilled."

"I'm still eating," protested Obi.

"No you're not. If you want a ride to day camp you have to come now or I'll be late for work."

After they left I made another piece of toast and poured another coffee. I sat there, sipping and nibbling and thinking. I wasn't thinking about anything in particular, I was just letting my mind wander around like a shopper at the mall. *Everybody said I was pretty... Now I looked like a rodent... Marriage... Book covers... Children... Frontier prostitutes... Women as food...* I was still thinking as I cleared the table of the dirty dishes, juice and milk.

When I was done cleaning up, I put on my work clothes, got my bike from the porch, and cycled into town. Usually, I'd get a friendly honk or a wave or at least, a big smile as I rode along (at the really very least I'd see guys look twice), but, of course, there was none of that now. Loretta would be thrilled. She'd single-handedly rid my life of even a hint of sexual harassment.

The Old Clipper Inn is run by Mr and Mrs Schonblatt. Mrs Schonblatt manages the hotel part of the Inn. She's the smiling, friendly person at the front desk who gets you an extra towel or tells you where to rent a boat and stuff like that. Mr Schonblatt manages the restaurant part. He's the unsmiling, unfriendly person in the office who doesn't tolerate sloppiness, mistakes or anything going wrong. Mr Schonblatt says they divided it up like that because his wife is better at dealing with beds and sheets and that kind of thing, and Mrs Schonblatt says it's because she doesn't have the head for the complexities of the restaurant. By the second day I'd worked there I'd figured out that the real reason is that Mrs Schonblatt is easygoing and good with people, and Mr Schonblatt is domineering and great with menus. As Mr Schonblatt likes to say (all the time!), the Clipper is a ship and he runs a tight one. He loves rules and giving orders, and he believes in efficiency the way other people believe in God. "This isn't some chicken shack," Mr Schonblatt also says a lot. "We have standards. Some very important people dine here."

So Mr Schonblatt isn't everybody's boss of choice. But I'd always got on okay with him. Because of my positive and pleasing personality, he liked me right from the start. And I made sure I kept being positive and pleasing. Mr Schonblatt is a control freak (the brotherhood of dictators lost a star when he decided to go into the restaurant business), but I had no problem with that. Unlike the other waitresses and the guys in the kitchen, I always agreed with Mr Schonblatt and never talked back. I listened to his endless instructions and complaints like he was explaining the meaning of life. I was the smile that always said "Yes, sir". (Loretta would have lasted about three and half minutes with Mr Schonblatt before she shut him in the walk-in fridge.) There must be someone, somewhere, who thinks Mr Schonblatt's an okay guy, but you can be sure that person never worked for him. Even he must know that if the staff had to vote on who to sacrifice to the alien invaders, he'd be the unanimous choice.

But he was pretty nice to me. He gave me the best section to work, and he didn't charge me for breakages or have a meltdown if I forgot the water glasses, like he did with everyone else. I know part of the reason he favoured me was because I was the prettiest waitress at the Inn, but there's nothing wrong with that. That's how the world works. It's not just the rich who get preferential treatment. And it's not just the squeaky wheel gets the grease.

So anyway, on that Monday morning, Mr Schonblatt had no trouble recognizing me, but he did look pretty taken aback. It could've been because I was ten minutes early, and he was used to me being a few minutes late ("Time, Giselle! Time! You know it waits for no one!"). But I figured from the way he was gazing at my legs that that wasn't the reason he looked so surprised. I'd always worn a skirt before. I could tell he was disappointed.

"Well, Giselle," said Mr Schonblatt. His eyes moved to my face. "What have we here?"

The other thing I could tell was that Mr Schonblatt also thought I used to be pretty.

"I decided to cut my hair for the Summer. You know, because it's so much cooler." My smile was still the same but it didn't have the effect it usually had on Mr Schonblatt.

He didn't smile back. "Um." You know how cats can stare like they see something no one else can? Mr Schonblatt can do that, too. "And no make-up, either? Is that because you were making an effort at punctuality and didn't have time to put it on, or is that also cooler?"

"It's my skin," I explained. "I really try to take care of it, but it's kind of sensitive right now. Because of the heat." My smile was philosophical and brave. "Sometimes you have to let it breathe."

"What about your legs? They don't have to breathe?"

I said that trousers are more comfortable, especially with all the walking we do.

"It seems to me you've decided to hide your light under a barrel," said Mr Schonblatt.

It was more like I'd turned my light off, but I didn't correct him.

He humphed. "Well, at least you look very efficient." It didn't exactly sound like the compliment you'd expect from the captain of such a tight ship.

I smiled sweetly enough to be a danger to any diabetic in the vicinity. "Thank you, Mr Schonblatt."

And what do you think he said? "Just make sure you're as efficient as you look."

I've never had this great ambition to be Miss Efficiency. I mean, why? Machines are efficient. Totalitarian governments are usually efficient. And robots can pretty much do no wrong. I didn't want to be any of those things. Plus, even if I'm not the most efficient person who ever lived, I'm a pretty good waitress. Maybe sometimes I forget things or drop a fork. And maybe I can't read minds so I don't always know when a customer wants more water or bread, or when he's done eating and not just taking a break. But I'm always friendly and helpful, and never rude or surly. Customers like me and my banter (I was known for my banter), and no one ever complained about me being disorganized or anything like that. Including Mr Schonblatt. Only now he seemed to think a nice personality wasn't enough, I should be efficient too. Robowaitress.

Quel pain in the butt!

Loretta

New me, new world

ZiZi and I made it to the end of Week Two of our bet with no indication that either of us was about to call it quits. Which isn't to say that I wasn't tempted. In my head, I'd imagined that – once I was accustomed to being physically impaired and ogled all the time – it was all going to be smooth sailing on a dead calm sea on a cloudless, sunny day. That was what I'd imagined. The reality was different. It was more as if I was lost in space, hurtling through the universe in a tiny capsule, trying not to be hit by anything and to maintain contact with mission control – and not to cry because I was homesick.

As it turned out, the clothes part was the least of my problems. Getting used to wearing uncomfortable shoes wasn't as difficult as I'd thought – they slowed me down some but I even mastered riding my bike in ZiZi's pumps. Wearing dresses limits your ability to climb too high, vault over counters or heave yourself up onto the backs of trucks without people looking up your skirt, but I easily dealt with those things, too. I made sure that when I had to do any climbing, vaulting or heaving there was no one else around.

No, what caused most of my problems were other people. I suppose that astounds no one – it's usually other people that cause all the trouble. They started treating me differently, which, of course, was something I expected. I got more looks, more smiles, more attention, more chat when I was standing in a queue. More help. I didn't have anything against help; I began to get used to it. In the past, if I had something heavy to carry, I carried it alone – opening doors with my hip and concentrating on the great cardiovascular workout I was getting. When I walked into a busy store, salesmen looked past me and waited on someone else. I learned how to change a tyre because experience had taught me that no one else was going to do it for me. Things were different now. Doors were held open, bags carried, and salesmen materialized the second I stepped inside. If the light changed while I was cross- ing a road, I didn't have to run because cars waited for me. The day the car broke down, three guys from school who'd never talked to me before pushed it to the side of the road. None of that bothered me. After all, most of these were total strangers or casual acquaintances I'm talking about; they didn't know me and probably would never see me again. I figured it was the difference between the way someone reacts to a puppy and the way someone reacts to a toad. Cute always wins. Besides which, it made the world seem like a friendly and pleasant place.

My parents quickly got used to having a girl in the house; it was other people who seemed surprised. Neighbours. Friends of my parents. The women found new topics of conversation, things they would never have brought up before – diets, clothes, the nail salon in town – and the men seemed to feel they always had to tell me how nice I looked. When I ran into kids I knew from school, they either didn't recognize me or made a big deal out of the fact that they did. No one was as weird as Gabe had been, but I could tell they they were seeing me differently. They were re-evaluating what they knew about me, what they'd assumed. But it was the guys I worked with and our regular customers that bothered me the most. I'd known things were bound to change, but I'd underestimated exactly how much.

Most of our regular customers were professional builders who came in all the time. I knew a lot of them by name, and they, of course, knew me. When I first started at Chelusky's, the regulars were surprised to see me there the way you'd be surprised if someone suddenly dumped a bucket of water on your head. Which I understood; you see a lot more women in boardrooms than on building sites. It took a while for them to accept me behind the register – even in my dungarees with a pencil stuck behind my ear. As far as they were concerned, finding a girl in the store was like finding a shelf of hair products next to the paints. *What the hell is that doing there?* They were wary, doubtful that I could do anything as simple as tell the difference between a Phillips screwdriver and a Frearson. If they had a question, they'd look around for a guy to answer it. It took a while, but eventually they accepted that I not only knew my bolts from my screws and my circular saw from my hasp, but that I also was better at math than most of them and could help with complex calculations. Once that was established, I was accepted as part of the crew and they were always friendly to me – in a businesslike way. They never called me "dear" or "honey" the way guys sometimes do to women who are serving them; our conversations largely involved measurements and tools.

Then came the fateful day when they walked in and I was wearing lipstick and a skirt – and making the displays around the register attractive. I may have been the same person I'd always been, but because I no longer looked like her they became confused. They dealt differently with a girl in a skirt than a girl wearing a tool belt. Among other things, the "h" and the "d" words began to appear. As in: *Thank you, honey* and *Where's the sandpaper, dear?*

My conversations with our customers used to be limited to supplies and orders and the weather. But no longer. By wearing lipstick, I'd automatically become a good and sympathetic listener. Which meant that I heard about illnesses, injuries, backache and indigestion. I heard about their families and their pets. Most of the time, it was a lot more interesting and more enjoyable than discussing solvents and nails. Before, I'd known them as professionals – men with houses and extensions and dormers to build. Now, I knew them as husbands and fathers and men who admitted that they didn't always understand girls – and, for some almost endearing reason, thought that I, since I was part of the enigma, did. That was good.

What was less good was that, before, they'd seen me as the junior member of Chelusky's crew. Now, they saw me as the girl at the till. You talked with the girl on the till, but you didn't ask her to help you carry paint cans to your van. You might get her advice on some problem you were having with your daughter, but you wouldn't seek her advice on a new drill.

To my surprise, however, it was the guys I worked with who were the biggest problem. They weren't passing strangers; they knew me, they were my friends. I'd thought that once they got used to the knowledge that I had legs they'd treat me the same as always – call me a hopeless optimist.

Since my metamorphosis from sparrow to golden parakeet, my co-workers acted as if they knew there was a secret camera embedded in the ceiling that recorded everything they said and did, and reported it back to their mothers. They'd always been nice to me – like big brothers or uncles or, in the case of Mr Chelusky, a grandfather – but now they were very nice. Mega, best-behaviour nice; courteous, polite and cautious. As if it was the nineteenth, not the twenty-first century, and men had to mind what they said and how they said it when there were women present. It used to be: *Out of stock? How the hell can that be out of stock?* and *For God's sake, Lou, I thought you said that was coming in today!* Now it was: *Please could you order me such and such, Loretta?* and *It's not in yet? Well, thanks for trying.* If they'd been any more well-mannered they could have written an etiquette book. It was unnerving. Holy Mother, they didn't even yell at me the way they used to – the way they yelled at each other. Were they afraid I'd cry, or swoon, or report them for harassment? As a sparrow, I'd been able to hang out with all the other sparrows and go where I wanted; as a golden parakeet, I was slammed into a cage. The easy guy-on-guy joshing and joking ended when I was around. If two of them were laughing about something and I suddenly appeared, nine times out of nine and a half, they'd stop talking so fast you'd have thought they'd swallowed their tongues. They started watching what they talked about in front of me. Started watching their language. Which isn't to say that Chelusky's had previously resembled an eighteenth-century pirate ship as far as oaths and curses went, but the stray strong expletive did get let loose every once in a while. The time Mr Chelusky dropped the power saw on his foot I heard several words I'd never heard before. Once I'd turned into a golden parakeet, there was no way I'd ever hear them again.

Besides the things they felt I could no longer hear there were now things they'd decided I couldn't do. Such as carry a ladder, or shift a load of boxes, or move the display pieces without male help. I don't think you'd ever convince anyone who's gone through pregnancy and childbirth that women are the weaker sex, but apparently the hefting and hauling were all man's work and I was a girl – as if I hadn't been one before. As if, now that I wore dresses and make-up, my nails wouldn't grow back if broken, my clothes couldn't be cleaned, my skin couldn't be washed. *No, no, Loretta, let me do that.* Which was why I skulked around like a spy, looking for heavy boxes to lift, planks to haul, large objects to carry, laden trolleys to push and trucks to unload. Checking that the coast was clear; that they were all too busy to notice me lugging tins of paint across the store. Not that that always worked. If I wasn't fast enough, I'd suddenly find one of them scurrying towards me, calling, "Hang on, Loretta! Let me help!"

I reminded myself that this was a sociological experiment – possibly an important sociological experiment. I was going to learn from it, and use what I learned to help others. On really bad days, when they were driving me so crazy I would have been tempted to chase them with the forklift if I'd been allowed near it, I'd ask myself: *What would Barbara Ehrenreich do? What would Gloria Steinem advise?* I didn't know. I decided to talk to ZiZi.

"I don't see why you're so wound up about it," said ZiZi. "They're just being nice. I wouldn't complain if everybody wanted to be nice to me."

"You mean you didn't complain when everybody was always nice to you. You loved it."

She went over to my dresser and started looking through

the bag of things I'd bought at the mall; now that she wasn't shopping herself she had to live vicariously through me. "What's not to love? You get out of all the grunt work."

"They're treating me as if I can't do anything for myself. As if I'm helpless."

"This is cute." She held up a floral skirt. "How come you bought this? I thought you said buying new stuff was a waste of money. You know, since you're never going to wear them again after you lose the bet."

"It was on sale."

"Oh, right. On sale." She tossed the skirt onto my bed. "And anyway, they're not treating you like you're helpless. They're just being considerate."

"Considering that I'm helpless."

"My God!" She pulled something blue and silver from the bag, dangling from its thin straps. "I don't believe it! You bought sandals? Were they on sale, too?"

"It's Summer." I should have put my things away before she arrived. "Sandals are what you wear in Summer."

"You don't. Not ones like these." She waved them in front of me. "The sandals you usually wear are as stylish as a block of wood."

"They don't go with my new look. I have to consider the whole, not just the parts."

Her eyes narrowed. Contemplatively. I've been

known to complain that ZiZi doesn't think enough, but now she was thinking too much. "You could've worn the ones I loaned you."

"I told you, they didn't fit right. These are more comfortable."

She gave me another thoughtful look, and dropped the sandals on the bed. "Going back to how badly you're being treated at Chelusky's..." said ZiZi. "You're making way too much of this. You really need to chill. Remember in Miss Gregson's class when we learned how levers work? You have to think of being a cute girl as your lever. You can get a lot done with minimal effort."

"By getting them to do it."

She beamed. "Exactly!"

"Only I don't want to manipulate, Zi. I want to confront and resolve."

"Oh, come on. If they want to break their backs being big men dragging power saws and bags of sand around, let them."

"But I've always done a lot of the things they do."

"Yeah, but now you don't have to. You can concentrate on all the stuff they can't do."

"Like wearing lipstick?"

She pretended to bang her head against the wall. "You're still making the same mistake, Lo. Being a person doesn't mean you have to be a guy." Having more time to think was for definite making her philosophical. "You're ignoring the downside of being a man. They have to drive trucks and run multinational companies and beat people up and stuff like that, whether they want to or not. But we don't. We can opt out. You should take advantage of that."

"And if I want to carry power saws and bags of sand around?"

"Just be careful you don't break all your nails."

I said that my nails weren't what I was most in danger of breaking.

ZiZi gave me another contemplative look. "You know what I think's really bugging you?"

"I just told you what's really bugging me. The only thing they let me lift now is the coffee pot." Which was sad, but true. It used to be that whoever got to it first made the coffee when there was none. But since I went from sparrow to golden parakeet everyone expected me to do it. Even if I arrived after everybody else, the machine would be in its corner, no red light glowing, no happy *plop plop plop* welcoming the workers in. When we ran out, it would sit there as empty and abandoned as a wrecked car. I'm not sure why – probably because I didn't want to wait hours or even days for a cup of coffee – but I always gave in. Grudgingly.

"That's not it." ZiZi leaned against the dresser. "What's got you is that you had it all in your head how I was going to be affected by the bet, but you never thought how you'd be affected."

"Of course I did."

"Then how come you're so surprised the guys are treating you differently?"

"Because, Giselle, these are people I've worked with for ages. They know me. I can see that people who don't know me are going to make different assumptions. And believe me, they do. But I don't expect friends to act differently."

"I never thought I'd hear myself say this…" ZiZi tilted her head, studying me carefully and thinking away. "But maybe you should stop wearing skirts and dresses."

I never thought I'd hear her say that either. "Do what?"

"Just at work."

"And why would I want to do that?"

"Because, if you stopped wearing them, the others might be more normal around you?"

"You want me to concede to their prejudices?"

ZiZi groaned. "I want you to take it down a notch. For God's sake, Lo, you are on the record saying that you hate wearing skirts and dresses."

"Well, maybe now I don't hate it so much any more."

Call me stubborn, but I wasn't about to give in now. I was going to fight my corner, come what may. "Maybe I'd rather be beamed back to a life of drudgery, corsets and oppression in the nineteenth century than stop wearing skirts."

She heaved a heavy, heartfelt sigh. "Excuse me, but you're the one who's always yammering on and on about how restrictive skirts are. How you can't crawl under a car or climb a tree if you're wearing a dress?"

"There's a principle involved here."

She was patience about to snap like a dry twig under a heavy foot. "I'm sorry, Loretta, but I thought your favourite principle was not going along with gender stereotypes."

"It is. But there's more than one lane on the highway, and there's more than one way of stereotyping people."

"Oh, God, you really do like to complicate things. I just thought it'd be easier for the guys if you wore something else. You know, something more hardware-store-friendly. Not those hideous dungarees but jeans or something like that."

"You want me to compromise."

"God forbid!" She rolled her eyes. "Don't think of it as a compromise. Think of it as an adjustment."

"Why should I make it easier for them? I haven't

changed. Just my clothes have changed."

She held up her hands. "Okay, I surrender. Have it your way." She turned back to my bag of shopping and peered in. "Hey, what's this?" She took out a white box, turning it over to read the label. "OMG, Loretta!" She swung around with a big smile on her face. "Are my eyes deceiving me? Is this really a make-up mirror?" Her eyes weren't deceiving her, but they did seem to be getting larger by the second. "Loretta Reynolds, the girl who looks at her reflection less than a vampire does, bought a make-up mirror? With light, no less!" She plopped down beside me on the bed. "So are you really sure you haven't changed?"

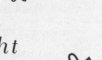

ZiZi

And Loretta thought
she had problems

You know that old saying about how every cloud has a silver lining? Well, if you turn it around, it means that every silver lining has a cloud. So while it was pretty amazing (and gratifying!) that Loretta went out and bought a skirt, sandals and a make-up mirror, it wasn't all good news. If she was investing her hard-earned money in girl things, she wasn't going to be losing the bet any time soon. Talk about food for thought. It was practically a banquet!

I would never admit it to her, but my kind-of-negative attitude was because I was starting to wonder how long I could hold out. Loretta was mad because the guys at work were being nice to her? Because they were offering her and her bike rides home when it was raining? Helping her whenever they could? Doing her favours? Seriously? Everybody should have those problems. Especially me. I wasn't exactly being killed with kindness.

Because here's the thing. Things had changed for me, too.

In the outside world, where I used to be greeted with smiles and approving looks and flirty winks and open doors, I was now being pretty much ignored. People (male people) not only walked by me without so much as a glance, they sometimes walked right into me as if I wasn't even there! "Oh, sorry," some guy on his phone or plugged into his music would mumble, "I guess I didn't see you." And I'd snap back, "I guess not. It must be because I'm wearing my invisible T-shirt!" But I wouldn't be saying it to him, because he'd already be long gone. It was pretty galling at first. After years of being treated like someone special (not like I was a celebrity, maybe, but like I should be one), I was suddenly being treated like the celebrity's maid.

And here's another thing. Things had changed where I worked, too. And the biggest change was Mr Schonblatt.

I know it's not like Mr Schonblatt was ever up for the Nice Guy of the Year award. (Maybe in some place like North Korea but not in Howards Walk.) Plus, I knew that he used to cut me more slack than he cut the others because I was pretty, but it was like overnight he'd gone from being the captain of a tight ship to being Darth Vader in a really, really bad mood.

And all of a sudden, I went from being his favourite waitress to being his favourite senseless victim. Whatever I did, I did it wrong. Every time I looked up, he was glaring at me or pointing a finger or bearing down on me like a bulldozer. *Put that there, put that here. Don't. Do. Do it again. Is that fork supposed to be clean? Where did you go to get the bread, the next town? Does that saltcellar look full? And when were you planning to clear that table, after everyone's gone home? Serviettes* (Mr Schonblatt's word for napkins) *should be folded*, not bent. I was too friendly with my customers. "They don't want to talk to you, Giselle. They want to eat." I wasn't fast enough. "I timed you, Giselle. Table six waited five minutes for their water."

Towards the end of a shift that already marked a low point in my waitressing career, Mr Schonblatt snapped at me for not serving an order that wasn't ready yet. Claire was nearby, filling water glasses, and gave me a look as he stomped off to yell at someone else. Claire was the oldest waitress and had been there longer than anybody except Mr Schonblatt. We'd never been what you'd call buddies but it seemed to be a sympathetic look, so I asked her what was wrong with him.

"There's nothing wrong with him," said Claire. "Nothing new. That's him. He's always had less charm than your average ruthless tyrant. He was probably busy measuring place settings the day they were handing it out."

"But he's being totally unreasonable. You'd think he had his period or something."

Claire sighed. "That's the beauty of being a man. You don't have to cram being irrational and bad-tempered into a few days of pain a month. You can be like that all the time."

"He's like this all the time?"

"Only when he's awake." Claire put down the pitcher. "I know he used to be nice to you, but how could you not notice?"

"It's not that I didn't notice..." I just didn't pay much attention.

The sympathetic look had morphed into one that reminded me of Loretta. "Why do you think the Inn's always short-handed and looking for staff?"

"Because people are always quitting or getting fired." It was pretty much in one door and out the other at the Inn.

"Right. And that's because...?"

"Because they don't like the job or they don't do it right?"

"Got it in one." Claire nodded. "But that's not because of them – because they're incompetent or anything. That's because the Schonblatt's impossible to work with.

Nobody's ever right but him. Fabio? The chef who left last week? The really good one? He threw his apron at Schonblatt and called him a kitchen Nazi." Claire lifted her tray. "I'm thinking of having that put on a T-shirt." She winked. Conspiratorially. "I'll wear it the day I win the lottery and quit."

One morning not long after my conversation with Claire, I was hardly through the door when Mr Schonblatt got on my case about my uniform. Had I run out of shoe polish? Had the Abruzzio iron died? Was that a stain on my trousers?

I didn't know what he was talking about. You can ask Loretta. No matter what I'm wearing, I'm not a girl to leave the house looking like I dressed in the dark. Immaculate could be my middle name.

"I'll tell you what I'm talking about." If he'd been a bear, he would've been growling. "You represent the Old Clipper Inn, not some soup kitchen in the basement of a church, Giselle. That's what I'm talking about."

Sharp, biting replies of the kind Loretta Reynolds would have made got to the tip of my tongue, but they never launched themselves from there. I was still the positive and pleasant person I always was, dumping honey all over the place and trying to get some flies. I said I was sorry.

Mr Schonblatt no longer smiled. At least not at me. "I would hope so."

Layla, the waitress I was taking over from, came up behind me. "What I hope is that he gives himself a stroke," she muttered.

I looked down at my clothes. My shoes were shined, my shirt was ironed, my slacks had just been washed. "Maybe there's something wrong with his eyes."

"There's always been something wrong with his eyes," said Layla.

I glanced over my shoulder at her. "What do you mean?"

"I mean he never hires waiters, does he? The guys are all in the kitchen."

"Well, yeah... But maybe no waiters apply."

She gave me a pitying look. "I'm so sure. And the only waitresses who apply are all of a type, right? What a coincidence. We must be the only town in the country where there aren't any waiters and the only waitresses are blondes with good figures."

"Really? You think so?"

"Yeah, really, I think so. You don't even have to be very attractive. You just have to fit his idea of how women should look."

So here was something else I hadn't paid attention to.

Layla patted my shoulder. "Welcome to the real world, Giselle."

I couldn't help wishing I'd stayed where I was in the unreal world.

And then, the day after Loretta was moaning about life at Chelusky's, Mr Schonblatt told me off for not clearing table six fast enough. Tables are supposed to be cleared as soon as they're empty. If not sooner. I said I couldn't clear it any faster, I was busy serving table nine.

"If people wanted slapdash service, they'd eat at home," snarled Mr Schonblatt. "I don't need your excuses."

"I wasn't giving you an excuse, I was giving you an explanation." Quite some time had passed by then, and with it had passed the days when I didn't talk back. What did it matter being sweet and agreeable when he was less pleasant than an abscessed tooth?

"Excuse … explanation … it all comes to the same thing, Miss Abruzzio," he thundered. "Incompetence. Sloppiness. What I want is professionalism. What I want is for you to do the job you're hired to do."

I gave him the smile that used to guarantee me forgiveness even if I messed up an order. "I guess I didn't know I was hired to be in three places at once."

Forgiveness, however, was also a thing of the past. "Well, now you do," said Mr Schonblatt.

Since I had virtually no social life these days, I'd started thinking about why Mr Schonblatt's attitude had changed so totally. I wasn't doing anything different. I was exactly the same waitress I'd been before. Why was I suddenly the scab on his life that he couldn't stop picking? Because I cut my hair? Because I was wearing slacks instead of a short skirt? Because I wasn't wearing any more make-up than he was? Even to me, that seemed pretty far-fetched. Seriously? I mean, you don't exactly need to show your legs to carry a tray. Or wear lipstick or eyeliner to take an order. It's not like I was working in a nightclub.

You remember that book I was reading, the weird one Loretta loaned me? I wasn't always sure I understood what the writer was getting at, but it made me think, too. I figured that the heroine's problem was that she wasn't sure who she was or who she should be. Everybody told her how she should act and what she should want. And so long as she did what everybody expected, they were happy because they were controlling her.

I was mulling all that over when I remembered Layla saying something about having to fit Mr Schonblatt's idea of how women should look. What he expected. Was that all part of him being in control? So it didn't matter that I still had breasts and close-to-blonde hair, I wasn't wearing skirts or make-up. And now he wasn't so sure of what to expect. His control was slipping. Things weren't the way he wanted them to be. And when anything didn't go the way he wanted it to, Mr Schonblatt yelled.

Loretta says I can be really oblivious, and I was starting to think that maybe she had a point. If I didn't want to see what was right in front of me, I guess I didn't see it. But pieces were starting to fall into place. I know this is going to sound like something Loretta would say (and it was bad enough that I was looking like her without sounding like her, too) but it finally hit me that Mr Schonblatt wasn't just a miserable old goat who liked to boss people around. Mr Schonblatt was what Loretta would call a male chauvinist pig. (And a miserable, bossy old goat, too!)

Loretta

I stick to my skirts

I think I have a pretty good imagination but it would never have occurred to me that one day ZiZi and I would be bickering about clothes and I'd be the one saying I was going to wear a skirt no matter what, and she'd be the one saying I was crazy – why didn't I just wear jeans?

As I told her, there was a principle involved here. Why shouldn't I wear a skirt if I wanted to? The guys would just have to get used to it.

Besides, I'd come too far to back down now. If I started wearing jeans at work ZiZi would think I was weakening; that I was bound to give in before she did. She'd think that all she had to do was wait a little longer and, before you could say "double standard", I'd be back in my dungarees and wiping the make-up off my face with a gauzy top. File under the heading: *Think again.*

Which isn't to say that there weren't days when I

didn't wonder if I was fighting the wrong battles. What was so awful about getting a ride home sometimes? Or with rearranging the paint cards while Mike or Horst stacked the tins? They also serve who only put on the price stickers. To be truthful, ZiZi isn't the only person to tell me that I'm stubborn. Not that stubborn's bad; stubborn means you persevere and don't give up at the first rumble of trouble. On the other side of the argument, as my father says, there is a difference between stubborn and inflexible. Was I being inflexible? Wasn't it possible that I could give in a little without actually weakening? What was the harm in that? It might even make me stronger; being comfortable in pink jeans instead of being uncomfortable in a floral skirt might make it easier to go on till the end of the Summer if I had to – if ZiZi proved to be just as stubborn – or inflexible – as I am.

I was mulling all this over when Mr Shapiro called the store to say he needed a handrail put up along his front steps.

Mr Shapiro had never used the Chelusky handyman service before; we'd been recommended by his friend Mrs Willow. Highly recommended. I'd done quite a few jobs for Mrs Willow. The first time I worked for her, she thought I was a boy. That was partly because her eyesight isn't that good, and partly because Mr Chelusky said he was sending Lou over. By the time we got my gender straight, I'd already replaced some tiles in the bathroom and put up some shelves in the bedroom. All she said when she realized I was a girl was, "Oh, of course. You remind me of the actress Audrey Hepburn." I guessed she meant because I had short hair, not because I was beautiful. After that, Mrs Willow probably forgot all about it and certainly hadn't mentioned it, because for definite Mr Shapiro wasn't expecting a girl to climb out of the car. I could tell because his first words to me were "Where's the handyman I asked for?"

I was wearing a Chelusky's coverall, which was kind of a clue if you were paying attention; I held up the toolbox. "She's right here."

Apparently, that statement needed clarification.

He eyed me suspiciously. The coverall wasn't fooling him. "You? You're the handyman?"

"Yes, me." I held up the toolbox again. "That's why I have this. It makes it easier to do the job."

"*You're* going to put up a handrail?"

"It's not against the law," I assured him.

"You," he repeated. "All by yourself?"

It didn't seem as if ZiZi's cute-girl lever was working, but I kept smiling sweetly. "How many people do you think it takes to put up a handrail?"

"One who knows what he's doing," replied Mr Shapiro.

I let that pass.

"Don't you worry," I said. "I'm much better at installing handrails than I am at baking pies."

I wondered if age had deprived Mr Shapiro of more than his hair; his facial expressions seemed to be limited to scowling and glaring.

"I don't think I can do this."

"You're not doing it," I reminded him. "I am."

He shook his head. "I can't have this anxiety." Which, apparently, was the anxiety of having a girl put up the rail. So much worse than the things that cause most people anxiety, such as being on a plane with engine trouble or not being able to pay the rent. "I have a bad heart."

He could say that again.

"You don't have anything to be anxious about, Mr Shapiro. I know CPR."

"Probably as well as you know carpentry."

"Not really. I've had more experience with carpentry than life-saving." I was rigid with reasonableness. "Look, if you're worried, why don't you call your friend Mrs Willow? She can tell you I do good work. She always asks for me." She was the reason Mr Chelusky sent me.

"Never mind her. What does she know? She's a woman, too."

"Mr Shapiro, this isn't some kind of conspiracy. Mrs Willow appreciates my workmanship."

He waved me away. "You go back and get them to send me a real handyman."

I was as rooted as a tree. "I am a real handyman."

"You know what I mean." Oh, I knew all right. "My wife, may she rest in peace, could hardly change a light bulb."

"I am not your wife. I've won awards for changing light bulbs. I am also very good at putting up handrails." If I hadn't been holding the toolbox, I would have folded my arms in front of me, ultimatum-style. "Do you really think Mr Chelusky would send me if I didn't know what I was doing?"

Mr Shapiro humphed. "Charlie Chelusky wouldn't be the first man to be bamboozled by a pretty face."

This was probably when I should have gone full-throttle on the cute-girl lever. ZiZi would have. ZiZi would have widened her eyes and burnt him with her smile, but I was too annoyed not to stick with reason. "If that's what you want, Mr Shapiro, of course I will." I hefted the toolbox, ready to go. "Only I am a little worried about the expense to you, Mr Shapiro. You know you're paying for my time, don't you? I'm already here. If they have to send someone else you'll end up paying twice."

I could see the calculator in his brain working that out. Which was going to win, prejudice or cost?

"You're sure you know what you're doing?"

"Absolutely."

He shrugged. "Well … maybe you're right. Since you're here. But you better not mess up. I'm going to be watching you. Don't think I won't."

"Oh, I don't think that."

Mr Shapiro was as good as his word. He hovered behind or beside me the whole time I was working. Fussing and fidgeting, chirping over my shoulder like a nervous bird. *What are you doing? What's that for? What's this for? Watch those bushes. Are you sure that'll hold?* I could barely move without bumping into him. If he didn't waste half his brain on being bigoted and blind, he would have realized what a good carpenter I am based solely on the fact that I didn't accidentally hit him with my hammer. If I hadn't been afraid of putting him into cardiac arrest, I would have chased him into the house.

When I was done, after he'd pulled on the rail and it didn't fall over, he refused to pay me. "I'll talk to Charlie Chelusky," said Mr Shapiro. "I'm not paying till I'm sure it's sound."

As an example of being as stubborn as Galileo, I sat down on the bottom step. With my toolbox at my feet and my arms folded. "And I'm not leaving till you pay."

Mr Shapiro stormed into the house – testing the handrail as he went. Ten minutes later, Mr Chelusky called, ordering me to go back to the store – without my money.

I was in a really bad mood by the time I got there.

And what was the first thing I saw? The empty coffee pot. Waiting for me like one of those men who sits watching the news while his wife makes the supper. It was all I could do not to smash it against the floor. Instead, I ignored it. I didn't see it, and I was never going to see it again.

I was a golden parakeet, and the cage I was in was probably pink. But I was a golden parakeet who refused to make the coffee ever again. Either they did it themselves or it didn't get done. Let them drink water.

File under the heading: *There was no turning back now.*

ZiZi

The revenge of the male chauvinist pig

It wasn't enough for Mr Schonblatt to follow me around like he was a freelance photographer and I was a Hollywood star (except instead of hearing *click click click* behind me, what I heard was *wrong wrong wrong*). To prove that I really wasn't his favourite waitress any more, he changed my section. Maybe like two hundred years ago the Inn was some millionaire's summer mansion where he brought his friends to hunt and fish and stuff like that. He must've had a lot of friends because it's so big they made it into a restaurant and a hotel. There's one entrance at the front for the hotel and another on one side for the restaurant. Downstairs, the hotel is just the reception desk and a small lounge area, and the restaurant is kind of an L-shape. I'd always worked in the main dining room (which runs along the back down one side of the building, overlooking the garden, with tables on the patio in the Summer), but, sudden as a broken zipper, the Schonblatt moved me to the dining room at the side and moved Claire to the back. Mr Schonblatt calls the back dining room the Garden Room, because even though it isn't in the garden it overlooks it, and in the Summer, there are tables on the big patio. If you're serving the room on the side, you're about as far from the kitchen as you can get without being in a different restaurant. It would make an awesome exercise programme because you practically have to run with your trays if the hot things aren't going to be cold and the cold things aren't going to be hot before you get them to the table. Or before your customers think they're never going to see you again and go home.

I know they don't have restaurants in Hell, but, if they did, waiting tables in one of them couldn't be worse than the back dining room (except that the Inn does have air conditioning, so I suppose it gets a point for that). I was sprinting back and forth from the second my shift started till the second it ended, smiling so much I thought I'd permanently damaged my jaw.

The main room is where the business meetings and people off their yachts usually ask to sit; the other room is where the families with children are put (so that the first thing you see when you walk in isn't some kid sticking fries up his nose). The main room is usually men who are into a little banter, and who are generous tippers. The businessmen and boating types can be pretty picky, but next to the families they're so laidback they're asleep. The families aren't just wide awake, they're like waitress-eating tigers. They need special chairs, more serviettes, what about a bib? There can't be anything green on Sara-jane's plate, Ben doesn't eat potatoes, Angela's allergic to bread. Glasses are constantly being knocked over, food thrown on the floor (and I mean thrown, not accidentally dropped). I timed it, and it takes five times longer for a table with children to order than it does for a table without (and that's when things are going well). Once they do order, nine times out of ten, it turns out that they didn't mean it. *Could you change that chicken to the pasta salad? Could you change the soup to the risotto? Could you make that spaghetti without any sauce?* The kids want cheese, but not that cheese. They want bread, but not that bread. They want soda but not in a glass. The ice cream's too cold, the fish is too hot. And nothing is ever brought fast enough. Adults beckon, or snap their fingers, or give you stink eye when they feel they've been waiting too long for that bottle of water. Children wail like starving wolves.

Quel exhausting! Seriously. It'd be way easier to herd

cats than serve the back room! And what made it worse, of course, was the spectre of Mr Schonblatt always watching, always waiting (ears up and nose twitching) for something to go wrong. We waitresses wondered if he had CCTV in his office or something, because he always knew when there was a problem. If there was a problem, Mr Schonblatt always knew who to blame. And it wasn't the customer. Last Summer, when I first got the job, I guess I hadn't been paying much attention to how things worked and everything. This Summer, I was paying attention. Now I realized that Mr Schonblatt doesn't much like his employees (the kitchen workers are all lazy and stupid, and the waiting staff is all stupid and lazy), but he loves people with money. Rich people are always right.

If he noticed someone looked like they were annoyed or like they were waiting for something (whether or not they looked unhappy about it), Mr Schonblatt would suddenly pop up at your elbow, hissing like a snake. *Table ten looks hungry… Table twelve hasn't ordered… Table eight wants to pay… Table fourteen needs more water.* God forbid someone should make a complaint.

But all the time I was being griped at by people who thought their children should be running the world, and racing back and forth so much it was like I was training for a marathon, I'd catch glimpses of Claire, gliding around the main dining room, smiling and chatting like I used to do. At the end of a shift, when we counted our tips, she always had more than I did. (Suddenly all my customers were tighter than Spanx waist cinchers. Tighter.) Her feet didn't hurt and she never looked like for two cents she'd dump the next plate of chicken over some child's head. Mr Schonblatt called her "dear". I started thinking maybe I should follow the advice I'd given Loretta about how she dressed for work. I could wear a skirt. I could even put on a little make-up. It wasn't like Loretta would ever find out, and I didn't really think it counted as cheating. Just enough girly stuff so Mr Schonblatt remembered how much he used to like me.

And then table nine complained.

Table nine was a couple and a small boy. I was kind of surprised they'd been seated in the back room because the three of them were expensively dressed – designer everything, gold Rolex on the father, diamonds on the mom – and the man may have been with his family but he was having a business meeting on his tablet at the same time. He only looked up once. The mother (who was on her phone most of the time but did look up every now and then) called the little boy Marlon, but it should've been Destructo. He tore up the flower that was on the table. He threw his salad on the floor. He knocked over his mother's wine. He tried to stab me with his fork. He poured his soda on his mother's bread plate. But no matter what he did, the only thing his mother said was "Oh, darling, you shouldn't do that." (And, no matter what he did, I smiled and said, "No problem.") But when I came back to their table with a new glass of soda and a new bread plate the boy wasn't there. I spotted him crawling towards the main room (like a commando, not like a baby). He was already under a table by the time I got to him. I grabbed his feet, pulled him out and marched him back to his parents.

I'd just picked up my next order and turned around to find Mr Schonblatt so close behind me the only reason I didn't scream was because my heart stopped beating.

"What's wrong with you?" He was snarling, but very softly. "I should fire you on the spot for a stunt like that."

And I was supposed to know what he was talking about?

"What stunt?"

"What stunt? For what you did to table nine, that's what stunt."

"Table nine?" They were still eating last I'd looked.

"How could you treat a customer like that?" he demanded. (He meant, how could I treat a customer *like that* like that? There was no way he'd miss the watch or the diamonds.) "What the hell do you think you're doing?" He wasn't shouting – he never shouts if there's a chance the diners might hear him – but he was red in the face from the effort of not shouting.

I said I thought I was doing my job.

"Your job? And is it your job to manhandle children?"

I said I didn't manhandle anyone. I merely removed him from under someone else's table.

"He said you shook him."

"But I didn't. I swear, Mr Schonblatt. All I did was get him off the floor. Before he hurt himself. Or someone else."

"You'll go over there five minutes ago and apologize," ordered Mr Schonblatt. "I don't know what's wrong with you lately, Giselle. Maybe it's your time of the month. Or you're going through some phase where you think it's funny to be difficult and unappealing. But I'll tell you right now that if you pull a stunt like that again, you can find another job."

He might not have to wait that long.

So I went over (with a free dessert for Destructo) and apologized profusely and insincerely.

And that's when I decided against the skirt and a little make-up. That's when I decided that the war was on. Anybody could be a pretty good waitress when she was waiting on people who were civilized. Dealing with people whose children were barely housetrained took skill. The Schonblatt wanted efficiency? I was going to be so efficient I'd practically be an android. I was going to beat that male chauvinist pig at his own game.

When it was finally time for my break I went out behind the kitchen where there's a fenced-in area so guests don't have to see the garbage or the staff sneaking cigarettes. I was fired up with righteousness and couldn't face the windowless staff room. I needed air. One of the kitchen boys was there, reading a paper. He looked up and nodded, the way you do when you're all stuck in the same Gulag. And then he looked again. "Don't I know you?" But I was still too preoccupied with what had happened to really be paying attention. I said I didn't think so. He smiled. "Yeah, I do. You're that friend of Loretta's. I'm Gabe? We met a few weeks ago? Loretta was all dressed up for something?"

Of course. It was Star Boy, Loretta's secret crush. "Astronomy Club? Meteor showers?"

"That's right. We were talking about the Perseids."

He was talking about them. "Of course. The Perseids. Only that wasn't when we met. We've had classes together."

"We have?" He peered. I bet he would've recognized me if I'd been a comet.

"Yeah. Homeroom once. And World History with Mr Hunt. But you must've seen me with Loretta, like, thousands of times. And I was at her house that time you landed in the cat food."

He was still peering. "Did you use to have curly hair?"

"That's me."

"You look really different."

I said I knew I did. I said Loretta and I thought we'd change our looks for the summer.

He nodded. Thoughtfully. "Oh, right. So that's why she— So that's why." He laughed. "I didn't recognize her at first. I thought she was going to a party or something."

"Loretta's not really the party type. Believe me, she'd rather watch shooting stars."

He said, "Me, too."

We talked for a few minutes about the meteor showers and the Astronomy Club and how smart and funny Loretta is. I was surprised I'd never run into him before at the Inn, but he usually worked nights and was filling in for someone who was sick.

"So," said Gabe, "what's a nice girl like you doing in a dump like this?"

I laughed for the first time all day. "I'm thinking of it as penance. You know, if I work here, there's no way I could ever go to Hell when I die."

Loretta

My imaginary boyfriend and other complications

If there is one thing you can say about ZiZi, it's that she's never been a complainer. Her positive personality and nature wouldn't allow it. But that was something else that had begun to change.

"You know," said ZiZi, "I have noticed that though your heart bleeds for the oppressed women and food animals of the world, it doesn't bleed for me. You're not the tiniest bit sympathetic to my plight."

"I didn't say that. All I said was I can't believe you might quit just because Schonblatt put you in a different room. I think you're overreacting."

She propped herself up on one elbow. "*Me*? *I'm* overreacting? I'm not the one who's on coffee strike."

"That's different." We were lying side by side on her bed, recovering from the many stresses of our different days. "There's a principle involved in the coffee strike. And it's not all about the coffee. Because of Sourpuss Shapiro, Chelusky's not sending me out on any handyman jobs. Which is stupid. Because I'm wearing a dress? Suddenly I forgot how to drill a hole?" I scooped up a handful of popcorn. "But you don't know why Schonblatt moved you."

"Oh, yes I do. To punish me. Because now I look efficient and he can't see my legs. He's nothing but a sexist, chauvinist creep."

She was also starting to sound like me. Which was eerie, if not actually frightening. "That could be true, but how much punishment can it really be? It's all one restaurant. Don't you think it'd make more sense to fire you if he wanted to punish you?"

"No, I don't. You haven't met him. I guarantee you he was one of those little boys who pulls the legs off insects. He wants to torture me first. When I'm totally demoralized and have lost the will to fight, then he'll fire me. That's the way his twisted mind works." She reached for the popcorn. "Hey, I almost forgot. That friend of yours said to say hi."

"What friend of mine?"

"You know. The one we met in town that time. Star Boy. What's his name?"

"You mean Gabriel? Gabriel Schwartz?" I tried not to sound too excited. "Tall? Really black hair?"

"That's the one. He's working in the kitchen at the Inn."

"He is? I didn't know that."

"Well, then, you're even. He didn't know you're working at Chelusky's."

"You talked to him?"

"Yeah. We were both taking our breaks out by the rubbish. He said he didn't even recognize you when we saw him in town that time." She chewed. Thoughtfully. "You know I kind of got the feeling that maybe he—" She broke off suddenly. "What's with that?"

I was thinking about Gabe, and how he really had been rushing off to work that day and not simply trying to get away from me. "What's with what?"

ZiZi pointed. "Your toenails. You painted them? When did you do that?"

I'd completely forgotten about them. The way you do. "Oh, I don't know…"

"You don't know? What, you were asleep when you did it?"

"The other day. I didn't actually write down the time and date, so I don't remember exactly when."

She leaned forward, studying my toes. I must have done a good job; all she said was, "And you did this because?"

"It's Summer. And I bought those new sandals. I'd like to wear them. If you're wearing sandals, it's nice to paint your toenails."

"You never did that before."

I shrugged. "I've never worn sundresses before, either."

The truth is that whereas I knew why I bought the mirror – so I could see what I was doing when I put on my make-up – I don't know why I painted my toenails. I was lying on my bed, listening to music and doing the Sudoku when I noticed my toes. Who ever looks at their toes unless they're scrubbing between them or trimming their nails? Not that many people. Podiatrists, for definite. Foot models, probably. People on the beach watching that they're not stepping on glass or sharp shells or some dead crustacean, maybe. And girls lying on their beds, plugged into their iPhones, doing an easy puzzle and thinking about what it would have been like to be the first woman to attend an all-male college: the ridicule, the condescension, the harassment, the patronizing attitudes. It made dealing with the Mr Shapiros of this world seem like a sunny afternoon reading in a hammock. You'd have had to have nerves of reinforced steel. The certainty of a saint. You'd have had to be stubborn the way the Eiffel Tower is tall. But did they disguise themselves as men? Did they reject any outward signs of their femininity – even though they knew those outward signs were the arbitrary dictates of their society? It was a hideous thought, but was ZiZi right that you didn't become a person by not being a girl? Was it possible to be both? Which was when I noticed my toes. And the next thing you knew, I was colouring them to match my fingernails.

I would have explained that to ZiZi – well, some of it, not the part about her possibly being right – but she distracted me by mentioning Gabriel Schwartz.

I'd been trying to get in touch with Gabe for weeks, but he never returned my calls and his texts only answered whatever I'd asked – which was always something about the club or the August outing – in as few words as possible. I couldn't imagine what had happened in that brief encounter in town to make him act so oddly, but now I knew. He hadn't recognized me; he'd been taken by surprise. He hadn't been in a hurry because he couldn't get away from me fast enough, he'd been in a hurry because he had to get to work – just as he'd said. That didn't explain why he wasn't answering my calls, but he had mentioned me; he told ZiZi to say hi. That had to mean something. What also meant something was the fact that Gabe and ZiZi worked in the same place. I now had more to talk about with him than the cosmos and the club. *Hey, you work at the Inn. Is it as bad as ZiZi says?* I didn't need to ask him something about the club to have an excuse for calling him; I could take the initiative. He'd said to say hi. I picked up my phone. I was going to say hi back. I got his voicemail.

I was so excited by this new turn of events and the possibilities it seemed to offer that I forgot I already had a steady boyfriend – the one nobody ever saw. Not that this was something I could ever forget for long; my co-workers constantly reminded me.

The guys at Chelusky's had always teased me a lot. Not in a mean or a flirtatious way or anything like that. Affectionately. Because they like me, but they think I'm odd. And because I was almost like a little sister – and ribbing your little sister is what guys do. They teased me about not eating meat. They teased me about the way I dressed and about liking cats more than dogs. They teased me about being better than they were at math and for being handy with a wrench and a hammer. They even teased me for getting Mick's motorcycle going when he couldn't start it. This Summer, however, they had something new to rib me about. Now they had the endlessly fascinating subject of my boyfriend.

They wanted to meet him. *How come he never picks you up here? Don't tell me he's one of these tree-huggers who won't drive a car. Are you ashamed of us, is that it? Is he a prince who won't talk to the peasants? When are we going to get to shake his hand?* They wanted to know what was wrong with him. *Does he have two heads or something, Lou? What's the problem? Is it because he's a vampire, and only comes out at night?* They wanted to make sure he was good enough for me. *We can't have our Lou going out with just anybody.* They wanted to see a picture. *Ah, come on, Loretta. Don't tell me you don't have a picture of him. You have a phone. You must have a couple of snaps.* They wanted to know where we went, what we did. If I wore something new, I got whistles and *Another hot date tonight? When's the wedding?*

There was nothing to tell, and that's what I told them. Nothing. I said it was none of their business. I said they'd meet him when they met him. *If* they met him. This discouraged them as much as waving your hands and saying "Shoo!" discourages a curious pack of dogs. They were insistent and relentless. "You know, if it was anyone but you, Loretta," said Vinnie, "I might think you were having us on." We both laughed; what an absurd idea. It was a lot of pressure to be under.

One slow afternoon, Mr Chelusky and I were alone in the store, doing a stocktake. He'd just finished counting off five-inch brushes when he suddenly said, "You're not even going to tell us his name, Loretta? Who is this guy? Rumpelstiltskin? We get ten guesses and if we're not right you repossess our cars?"

I looked up. "Whose name?"

"You know whose. This mystery boyfriend of yours. He must have a name."

Of course he didn't; he didn't exist. Not exactly a mystery, more a lie.

"We can't keep calling him 'that guy'."

And once again, when I should have said no – *I'm sorry, Mr Chelusky, but, actually, he happens to be one of those people who doesn't have a name* – or should just have kept my mouth shut tighter than a safe, I finally cracked. "Oh, for heaven's sake," I said. "It's not a big deal. His name's Dillon."

Why did I say that? Temporary insanity? Because I knew Dillon Blackstock was safely out of town? Or was it simply because ZiZi had talked about Dillon so incessantly for the last year – *Dillon said this, Dillon did that* – that his was a name etched into my mind like letters carved into a tree? Whatever the reason, it was the first name I thought of. I had to know hundreds of boys' names – most of them belonging to people I didn't go to school with and one of them belonging to someone

I actually wanted to go out with – but Dillon's was the name I came up with.

"Dillon," Mr Chelusky repeated. "Is that his given name or his last name?"

They eased up some once they had a name. Now and then, I'd get a wink and a "How's Dillon?" or a "Seeing Dillon tonight?" But that aside, I tried to forget the whole thing.

And then, a couple of days after I left the voicemail for Gabe, I looked out the front window and saw Gabriel Schwartz walking across the car park to the store. It couldn't be. What was Gabriel Schwartz doing at Chelusky's? To my shame – and horror – I actually turned around to check my reflection in the glass of one of the display cabinets behind me. Was my hair okay? Was my eyeliner smudged? I smoothed down my dress. I heard the door open and someone come in. I checked my face one last time.

"Loretta?"

I turned around.

Gabriel was standing at the counter smiling. He was smiling because this time he knew that it was me, and he wanted me to know he was glad it was. I smiled back; I was glad to see him, too. Very glad.

"Hi."

"Hi."

"I got your message. I thought… You know…" He shifted from one foot to the other. He cleared his throat. "ZiZi said you're working here. How's it going?"

"Good," I said. "And you? You surviving the Inn all right?"

He nodded. "Yeah. I'm okay." I don't know why lopsided smiles are so attractive but they really do tug at your heart. "Working under the great Schonblatt's good for learning humility, as well as Zen patience."

"ZiZi says she's developing nerves of steel."

He smiled.

I smiled.

He smiled some more.

"What's up?" I asked finally. "You building an observatory and need screws?"

Gabe laughed. "No. I–I—"

I'm painting my room? I'm looking for a special kind of light bulb? I took a wrong turn on Saskimaw and wound up here?

I was never to know what he was going to say because Vinnie suddenly came out from the back. "Hey, Loretta. You—" He didn't finish his sentence, either. He stopped beside the display of doorknobs, looking from me to Gabe and back again. Grinning like he'd just won the five-billion-dollar lottery. "Hey. I'm sorry. I didn't mean to interrupt." He held out his hand. "I'm Vinnie. You must be Dillo—"

"Gabriel!" I shouted, possibly half a nanosecond too late; possibly not. "This is Gabriel Schwartz."

"Oh. Sorry, I…" mumbled Vinnie. "Gabriel. Nice to meet you."

"Yeah. Nice to meet you."

There were a few seconds of the kind of silence you'd expect if you'd just watched an asteroid hit the moon.

"Well, I better get going or I'll be late for work." Gabe started walking backwards. "See you around, Loretta."

"So I'm guessing that wasn't him," said Vinnie as Gabriel disappeared out of the door.

Yes and no.

ZiZi

I stage my first strike but (as I'm sure Emma Goldman could've told me) they don't always work

As the days went by, I was having more and more Loretta moments. Maybe it was all the free time I had now, or maybe it was because I was in the middle of the second book she'd loaned me (that also had sat on a shelf in my room for months), but I kept hearing myself say things Loretta might say. Thinking things she might think. Noticing things I never noticed before. Loretta always droned on about the double standards, that there was one set of rules for guys and another for women, but "double standards" (like gender stereotypes and gender parity) was one of those phrases that instantly made me start thinking of something else. Until now.

Because one of the things I was noticing for the first time was that (unless you counted eating and making a mess) boys do zilch. At least the Abruzzio boys do zilch. When I was little, I had a miniature kitchen, a toy hoover, a toy washing machine, a toy iron and a baby doll, who came with her own cot and pushchair. As soon as I was old enough, I moved up to the real things (except for the baby!). I never thought about it; I just started doing things around the house. Setting and clearing the table. Learning how to wield a vacuum and a mop. Doing my own laundry and ironing my own clothes (the results are better and more predictable). I became my mom's sous chef as soon as I could use a knife without losing a finger, and quickly learned basic cooking skills. None of those abilities apply to Nate and Obi (nobody ever gave either of them a play oven, that's for sure).

Since I'd started eating breakfast with my brothers, I'd realized that if no one else cleared up, everything would be left where it was. I figured this must be pretty normal because I'd never seen any of their friends walk a plate to the sink or offer to do the dishes, either. (Unlike my friends.) They both get leaf-raking and lawn-mowing duty (if you can catch them), but indoor chores are out. They don't know where anything is in the kitchen and need help finding the peanut butter (even though it's always in the same place). The only time Nate ironed anything (because Gina had the flu), he ironed a sock (there's no knowing why) and it melted on the iron and wouldn't come off. The only time Obi used the vacuum cleaner (because he didn't want Mom to see the mess he made in the living room), he set it on fire (another of the great unsolved mysteries of Chez Abruzzio). Sometimes they manage to leave dirty socks and stuff so near the laundry basket (on the bathroom floor) it almost counts as in, but usually my mother has to shovel it out of their room. Obi once woke me up on a Saturday morning because everyone else was out, and although he knew how to make toast he didn't know how to boil an egg.

Now that I understood a lot more about how things work between men and women than I used to, I mentioned this double standard to my mother.

"So why is it," I asked her, woman to woman, "that you don't make Nate and Obi do things around the house?"

My mother stopped chopping carrots to look over at me. "Like what?"

"Like anything. They don't cook. They don't clean. They don't iron their own clothes. Pete's sake, they don't even load the dishwasher. If they manage to get a glass or a plate in the sink it's a major achievement."

"You have met your brothers, haven't you? They have no interest in cooking or housework."

Unlike me. What were my first words, *Pass me the frying pan? Where's the broom?*

I pointed out that they were pretty interested in eating and wearing clean clothes. "Doesn't that count?"

Cue maternal sigh. "You know what they're like, ZiZi. You've seen what happens if you make them do something they don't want to do." She waved her knife at me. "It's a lot easier to do everything myself than to have to clear up the mess and redo it after they've done it wrong."

"There is such a thing as a learning curve," I argued. "They'd be bound to get better eventually."

"There's also such a thing as life is too short," said my mother. "By then, I'd be too old to enjoy it."

"Well, what about Dad? He doesn't do much around the house, either."

"Your father has a job."

So does my mother. "Seriously, Mom. Dad could at least cook supper now and then."

"He does."

"He grills hamburgers on the barbecue in the Summer."

"That's the only thing he knows how to cook."

"But he could learn," I argued. "They all could."

"So you teach them." She started chopping again. "And good luck."

My mother's system worked okay normally (things got done because she made sure they did), but it fell apart the week the parents went away together to be with my aunt who just got out of hospital.

The theory was that, because he's the oldest, Nathan was in charge while they were gone.

Seriously? I know he's not technically a teenager, and he's training to be an electrician so you would kind of assume he has to be pretty intelligent and responsible and everything (or he could black-out the whole East Coast) but you'd be assuming a lot. It would've made more sense to borrow Loretta's cats Alice and Gertie and leave them in charge (they're very organized and know how to bend others to their will).

The first morning we were parentless, I automatically put the milk, the juice and the butter in the fridge after breakfast, and stacked the dishes in the machine after Nate and Obi (and the walking stomach that is Parker) left me alone with the dirty plates and debris. It wasn't until I was shutting the dishwasher that I had one of my Loretta moments. *Why?* I thought. *Why am I doing this?* Because I had a play kitchen when I was five?

That night, Nate made supper (bag of pasta, jar of sauce). I promised Gina they'd eat vegetables, so I made a salad to go with it. When I was finished eating, I brought my stuff to the sink, and when I turned around the boys had disappeared as if they'd been beamed back up into their spaceship. I looked at the mess on the counter, the mess on the stove and the mess on the table. And had Loretta Moment Number Two for the day. *Why am I the one supposed to do this?* Because I got the toy tea set for Christmas not the toy machine gun?

On the second morning, even before they could push back their chairs, I said, "Don't you dare leave this house before you clear the table." My voice was raised and hard as granite. "In case you haven't noticed, I'm not the maid."

Nate stood up. "We don't have time." If we were in a cowboy movie, you'd've said he was drawling. (Everybody thinks he's so easygoing and mellow, but, if you ask me, he does it on purpose to disguise how self-centred and annoying he is.) "I'll be late for work and the boys'll be late for camp."

And that would bring the civilized world to its knees. "What about me? What if I'm late for work?"

But I was talking to myself. The three of them had already left the room.

That night, Nate texted he had to stay late so I should start supper. I texted, *And cook what?* Like I thought he'd planned it, the way Gina would've. Nate came right back with detailed instructions: *Whatever.* He hadn't thought about it at all. There were burgers in the freezer. I got Obi to peel the potatoes by threatening to tell Mom what happened to her favourite yellow scarf (he buried a bird in it). Obi cut himself on his first potato, went to get a plaster and never came back. Nate and Obi both materialized at the table when everything was ready, like they'd been waiting behind the door for the all-clear. And when we were done eating they dematerialized quicker than you can say "do the dishes". My magic brothers.

The third day would have been exactly the same if I hadn't talked to Loretta the night before. I told her how I was fed up with doing almost everything in the house. And I was fed up with always finding the toilet seat up and with all the things that were piling up on tables, chairs and floors because my brothers think that wherever you put something is where it stays. Loretta said my brothers were pretty typical. It's a known fact that, even in the twenty-first century, and even when she has a full-time job outside the house, it's the woman who does most (if not all!) of the cooking and cleaning and everything. According to Loretta, Emma Goldman said a woman should refuse to be a servant to her family. So that's why, as I was sitting there by myself in the breakfast debris, staring at the toast crumbs on the butter and the puddle of milk on the table, I decided that Emma

Goldman was right and I wasn't going to be a servant to my family. Not any more. I was officially on strike. I left everything where it was and walked out of the house. We had a free meal at work, and I ate it. When I got home, I went to my room and I stayed there.

Day Four dawned on a scene of chaos and horror. There were two meals' worth of dishes and milk, bread and butter that hadn't been put away in the kitchen. The living room looked like it had been overturned by the cops looking for drugs. From the jars and wrappers left around, I guessed that the boys were now living mainly on snack foods and that they'd miraculously managed to find the peanut butter. I decided to abandon them completely and spend the night at Loretta's.

The Inn had a big (and awesomely expensive) wedding reception scheduled in August. Mr Schonblatt never stopped talking about it. You'd think it was Hollywood royalty (or even royal royalty), he was so wound up. To be honest, I was pretty excited about it, too. In many ways this had been a Summer of disappointment (too much Old Clipper Inn and no Dillon Blackstock), so, besides being a huge fan of weddings to begin with, I figured I could use a little glamour and romance – even if it wasn't mine. It was bound to cheer me up.

But the closer we got to the day, the more Mr

Schonblatt resembled a stress-machine in overdrive. And the more panicky Mr Schonblatt became, the more crises happened. The more crises happened, the more staff came down with near-fatal illnesses or sprained an ankle or were suddenly offered a week in the mountains that they couldn't refuse. The more staff came and went, the more panicky Mr Schonblatt got (and the uglier). *Quel vicious cycle!*

I didn't let all the trauma and hysteria get to me. I kept my head. I was resourceful, I was calm, I treated every crisis as a problem to be solved. Efficiently.

On the day that I decided to jump the good ship *Abruzzio*, something else had gone horribly wrong at the Inn that sent the Schonblatt blood pressure soaring. Even though he didn't like me any more, I was winning my war with Mr Schonblatt and was so professional and conscientious that I was now his best waitress (if not his prettiest). So that morning he called me in earlier than usual to help him out, and I was done at Gulag Old Clipper Inn with plenty of time to walk over to meet Loretta at Chelusky's. I was really looking forward to hanging out with her. Plus, it was going to be really cool to sit down without having to remove trainers and dirty socks from my chair first. And nice to have a civilized meal with people who don't think dinner conversation is pretty much limited to "Pass the ketchup" and "Is there any more?"

Since I had some time to kill before meeting Loretta at Chelusky's, I took a meditative stroll through town. It was already the beginning of August but neither of us was acting like she was going to give up any time soon. We didn't even joke about it any more. Plus, I no longer thought much about looking so different. I'm not saying I wasn't going to be glad to hit the make-up bag again (and I knew exactly which dress I was going to wear to welcome back the old me), but I wasn't desperate or anything. I was used to it. When I glanced in the window of the gift shop and saw my reflection kind of hovering over the display of papier-mâché boxes, I didn't think, *OMG, I have to find a cave to hide in ASAP!* I thought, *Does my hair already need a trim?* When some guy didn't hold a door open, or walked into me because I looked like background, it didn't ruin my day. I didn't even miss the looks or smiles or winks. I figured if a guy pays attention to one pretty girl, he probably pays attention to every pretty girl he sees. How meaningless is that? Plus, it was kind of nice not to always be wondering if I was being noticed, and if I wasn't, why. (I guess sometimes you don't even know you're under pressure until you aren't!) And when I was waiting for the light to change so I could cross and saw Lissa Jamison and a bunch of her friends on the other side, I didn't silently beg every god there had ever been to open the ground under my feet and pull me in. I just sashayed past them as if they weren't there (the way they sashayed past me!).

I had to go up Cortlandt to get to Chelusky's, which took me right past everybody's favourite diner (best burgers, awesome fries and a really good salad bowl). I hadn't been there since before school ended, and because there was still plenty of time before Loretta got off work I decided to go in for a coffee. I grabbed the booth at the back so I could read in peace, ordered a filter and a chocolate muffin (food being so scarce at my house since my mom left, and anyway, I'd been less careful lately and hadn't put on any weight so I figured I could risk it) and took out my book.

I was vaguely aware that a few people sat down in the booth behind me. Noisily. Boys, by the sound of them. They ordered burgers and Cokes and double orders of fries. Someone ordered a diet soda. Boys and a girl. The boys were loud and laughing and fooling around. (The girl kind of murmured now and then.) So, even though I wasn't listening (and was trying to concentrate on my novel), I started catching parts of their conversation. I stopped reading when I heard the words *women drivers*, followed by a lot of hooting and guffawing. And some lilting laughter from the lone girl. Not so long ago, if I'd been sitting with them, I'd've been laughing, too. Lilt-ingly. *Women drivers should have roads of their own. They can't park. They never signal. They drive too slow.* But I wasn't laughing now. I put down my book. It's Nate who gets tickets, and it's my dad who always dents the rubbish bins pulling into the driveway. *Women drivers only stop when they hit something. They back up in traffic. They get stuck at junctions.* The hilarity behind me got pretty massive. And then, in a second of silence while they caught their breath, one of them said, "Oh, dude, you know what's even worse than a woman driver? A woman mechanic!"

I recognized that voice. I don't know why I hadn't recognized it before (probably because they were talking over each other, and it was muffled by food). The world stopped turning and the day went black as the inside of a pot of kohl. Birds screamed and the wind howled. I could see my whole life flash past me, and it didn't take long, because it was really short and not exactly riveting viewing. Sitting behind me with a bunch of his friends making fun of women drivers was one of the worst driv-ers I've ever known (ever!). Duane Tolvar. What was he doing here? Of all the diners in all the towns in all the world, right? Seriously. This wasn't the only place around to get a burger. Plus, he was supposed to be working as a lifeguard (the only thing guaranteed to keep more people out of the water than jellyfish). Had they put a beach in the village or was he lost as usual? I hadn't seen Duane all Summer. Even before that, except from afar or passing in some corridor. Not since I told him I wished he'd move to Siberia (he wanted to know if that was upstate). Anyway, I didn't really want to see him now. He was bound to recognize me (eventually), and he'd have a lot to say about the change in me (all of it on the intellectual level of fart jokes). I told myself I was being really dumb. So who cared what Duane Tolvar thought? Seriously. Loretta was right about Duane. If thinking was money, he'd be begging on the streets.

And then the girl spoke clearly for the first time. "Oh, come on, you guys. You're not being fair."

I knew that voice, too. It was Alicia Smythe, captain of the cheerleaders. Known for her gravity-defying leaps and her sarky putdowns (she got a lot of practice at both). And Duane's girlfriend since the last week of school. Now I really didn't want to see Duane. (Not when he was with a girl who has more teeth than a shark.) Together they were guaranteed to ruin what up until then was a pretty okay day.

"No, man, you know what's even worse than a lady mechanic?" chipped in one of the others. "A lady dentist!"

"Nah, doctor!" said another. "Doctor's way worse than any of those. Maybe a GP giving you aspirin or something, but a surgeon? Operating on you? Sticking that knife in? Sewing you up? No way."

"Oh, hey, what about a woman pilot? That could end air travel as we know it."

"I have to go to the john," announced Duane.

There was a short hall that led to the back door right behind my booth, and the restrooms were off that. He'd have to pass me to get there. What if he looked over and did recognize me? Unlikely, maybe, but not impossible. Stranger things have happened. Like wrinkles, talking to Duane wasn't something I really wanted to think about right then. So, just to prove that women are better at quick thinking than the guys behind me thought, I was on the floor in half a second. Someone had spilled something sticky under my table, but right then that wasn't my biggest problem. I watched the legs of my biggest problem go by. Now was my chance. I figured if I walked fast and kept my head down I could get past their booth without being noticed by the boys or Alicia, and be outside before Duane came back. I was about to move when I realized that Duane hadn't. He'd stopped at the entrance to the hall. Waiting. "Hey," he called to his friends. "If you're ordering more stuff, get me some more fries and another soda." Then there was a little back and forth about whether he wanted regular, cheese or chilli fries. And some different opinions on which were better. Duane wondered if the French ate chilli fries. Opinions were divided on that question, too. *For God's sake*, I begged silently, *shut up and go to the john*. The minutes crawled by like snails dragging tanks behind them while I wondered what it was exactly that I was kneeling in. At last he started moving again. I turned, ready to jump up and scurry to the door, and nearly banged my head on the waitress's legs. She was peering down at me. Concerned. "You okay, honey?" I said I was fine. "My contact," I whispered. "I dropped it on the floor." She offered to help. Was that it to my left? Was that it by the wall? Did I want a torch – maybe that would make it easier to see? Duane returned as she finally left. I got back in my seat. The waitress brought more food and drinks to Duane and his friends. They weren't going anywhere soon. Now how was I supposed to leave?

I had no choice. I'd have to go out the back. I left money on the table, and walked slowly towards the restrooms. I couldn't risk turning around to make sure no one was watching me. I had to hope my guardian angel hadn't fallen asleep or wandered off the way she does. I took a deep breath and kept going to the end of the hall and straight through the fire door. But I wasn't out yet. There was a wire fence that ran along the back alley. So I had to be grateful I was wearing trousers and practical shoes or I'd never've been able to climb up and haul myself over to the other side.

By the time I got to Chelusky's they were about to close. The guys were getting the yard ready for the night and putting things inside. Mr Chelusky was wheeling a mower into the store. A month ago, all of them would've given me big smiles and "Hi"s even if they couldn't remember my name. Today, no one looked twice. Except Loretta. Of course.

"What the hell happened to you?"

"Nothing."

"Nothing? You're filthy." She squinted at my knees. "Is that chocolate syrup?"

"It's okay. I can get it out."

"And your shirt's torn."

"I know that, Loretta. That's okay, too. I have another one."

Loretta looked even more concerned than the waitress had. She wasn't used to seeing me stained and dishevelled. "Are you going to tell me what happened?"

I said, "It's a long story, but I kind of ran into someone I really didn't want to see."

"Not Dillon Blackstock," said Loretta.

I started to say no, Duane the Pain, but Mr Chelusky came in with a bin under each arm just then. "Blackstock!" he crowed. "So that's your fella's name. Dillon Blackstock." He was looking at Loretta.

So was I. "What?" *Loretta's fella? Dillon Blackstock's Loretta's fella?* Since I knew Dillon wasn't Loretta's fella (he was supposed to be mine!), and since I knew he was out of the state, I was pretty confused. What was Mr Chelusky talking about? "Loretta…"

"I'll see you tomorrow, Mr Chelusky." She grabbed my arm and started dragging me away. "I can explain," she whispered. "It's a long story, too."

Loretta

Maybe plans aren't always particularly useful, since you can't always predict what's going to happen

My parents were watching the news when ZiZi and I got to my house. Their smiles locked when they saw ZiZi.

"My God!" My mother inhaled sharply. "What on earth happened to you? You look like you've been in a war."

"I have," said ZiZi. "The one between the sexes."

If my mother was surprised that ZiZi knew about the war between the sexes, she didn't show it. "I'm going to assume that the other guy looks a lot worse," was all she said.

"I didn't stop to look," said ZiZi. "I have a slash-and-burn policy."

"I don't think I've ever seen you when you didn't look as if you were about to have your picture taken." My father squinted at her through his glasses. "Is that blood on your trousers?"

"Chocolate syrup," said ZiZi. "And before you ask, I ripped my shirt climbing over a fence."

"So I take it the bet's having some unexpected results," said my dad.

He was right about that. Sometimes I felt as if we'd all discovered a new level of shallow.

Possibly because of ZiZi's unkempt state, Horst had insisted on giving us a ride home from Chelusky's. Which meant there was no time for the long stories until after supper, when ZiZi and I retired to my room to discuss some of the unexpected results the bet was having.

ZiZi turned to me as soon as the door shut behind us. "Okay, Let's hear it, Loretta. How come Mr Chelusky thinks you're dating Dillon Blackstock? You're not telling me you have a thing for Dillon, too?"

"Of course not." I flopped down on the bed. Life can be really exhausting. "It's all a horrible misunderstanding." I explained about making up a boyfriend, and how the guys were always on at me about him and then Mr Chelusky pressuring me into telling him this boyfriend's name.

"Seriously? You couldn't've made up a name?" You'd think I was the one who was always exasperating and difficult. "You couldn't say Elmo or Cullen? You had to say Dillon?"

"I panicked. It just came out." I sighed sadly. "You don't know all the pressure I was under from them. It frazzled my nerves."

"And that's another thing," said ZiZi. "All I heard about was how they expect you to make the coffee. I didn't hear anything about them thinking you were dressing up because you have a boyfriend." She wasn't really upset about the Dillon mix-up, but this had her fuming. "That's a real insult. Seriously? Like a girl only looks nice if there's some guy around? Do we slouch around the rest of the time in old bathrobes and curlers? Do all the trees drop their leaves if there's no one in the woods?"

I put my face close to hers. "Who are you?"

She pushed me away. "You know what I mean. You make yourself look good because you like to look good. Guys come and go, but you're stuck with yourself twenty-four seven for ever. You're the person you need to please." She thumped the bed for emphasis. "That just shows you how self-absorbed men are. They think everything's about them!"

Was I hearing her right? She really was beginning to sound like me. "I mean it," I said. "Who are you?"

"I'm the girl who knelt in chocolate syrup and had to sneak out of the diner through the back way, that's who I am."

Personally, I thought ZiZi's long story was a lot more interesting than mine; it had much more drama and tension. For definite, it was funnier. ZiZi hiding under a table in a public eatery; ZiZi scaling a chain-link fence; ZiZi being outraged at the assumptions of men. Talk about tales of the unexpected. I really didn't know who she was any more.

"It is pretty ironic, Duane the Lame criticizing women drivers," I said when I'd stopped laughing. "Gender stereotypes aside, it's like a nuclear bomb calling a BB gun a dangerous weapon."

"Tell me about it," said ZiZi. "If I hadn't been terrified he'd see me I would have laughed out loud."

A new, unpleasant image came into my mind. "It could have been much worse, though."

"You mean if he had seen me?"

"I mean if they'd been talking about sex. It could have put you off it for life."

"If they were, I guess I would've had to kill him. Or at least push his face in his fries."

I have to admit to a certain amount of astonishment. Giselle Abruzzio isn't the first person you'd imagine sneaking out of her favourite diner. More astonishing was the fact that she was taking it all in her stride. As if it was a typical day in her life.

"Between Schonblatt haranguing me, spoiled brats trying to bite me and my brothers giving Neanderthals a bad name, it pretty much was a typical day in my life," said ZiZi. "And anyway, I'm pretty astonished, too. I can't believe you didn't tell me you have a crush on Gabe. I'm not saying I didn't suspect it. I saw the way you looked at him that time in town. But you never said a word. And I thought I'm your best friend. You're supposed to share stuff like that with me."

"You are my best friend. But I didn't want to jinx it." I let out a long, heartfelt sigh. I wasn't eighteen yet and I already seemed to be accumulating an impressive collection of regrets. "Only it looks like I jinxed it myself with Gabe. If you'd seen the way he backed out of the store…"

"Excuse me?" ZiZi eyed me as if I was a debatable shade of blue. "Backed out of what store? You mean there's something else you forgot to tell me? Maybe I should make a list of possible discussion topics to run through with you every day." She ticked them off on her fingers. "One: did they really find a baby bear on Mars? Two: what would Emma Goldman think about Internet porn? Three: do you have a major crush on Star Boy? Four: did you tell everybody except me that you're going out with Dillon Blackstock? And five—"

"Do you want to hear what happened or not?"

When I finished my tale of woe, ZiZi, whose knowledge of fashion is only matched by her experience with boys, said, "But that doesn't make sense." She frowned in thought. "I mean, if he came by Chelusky's, it was because he wanted to see you. Why would he run off? Maybe he just got a case of the shys."

Shy was good. I could live with shy. But he couldn't be that shy if he stopped by in the first place.

"Yes he can," said ZiZi. "He's not exactly a player, is he? He may be totally confident with meteors but I don't think he's the kind of boy who's that confident with girls."

"Maybe…" I replayed the doomed visit to the store in my mind. Gabriel. Me. Vinnie. "I don't know… I thought it was okay, but maybe it wasn't, after all."

"Thought what was okay?"

I explained about Vinnie coming in while Gabe and I were trying to think of something to say to each other. "Vinnie almost called him Dillon."

ZiZi groaned. "See, boys and girls? This is why your parents tell you never to lie." She eyed me sternly. "How close?"

"He got as far as 'Dillo', and then I shouted that this was Gabriel Schwartz. I thought I cut him off in time."

"Well, it doesn't sound like you did a very good job.

Not if Gabe bolted like that." She'd been lolling back against the pillows but now she sat up. "Here's the thing, Lo. Gabe must know Dillon, right? From school."

"Yeah, of course he does. Gabe even came to a special screening of Kubrick's *2001* at the Film Club, and Di—" And Dillon was there; the three of us sat together. "Oh God, do you think he thinks there's something going on with me and Dillon?"

"If he doesn't, that puts him in the vast minority," said ZiZi. "You have to do something, Loretta. Call him."

"I have called him."

"Well, call him again. Call him about the shooting stars or whatever."

"I did that." Two voicemails and three texts since his very brief visit to Chelusky's.

"And?"

"And I got one text back saying he's cancelling the Perseids watch due to lack of interest. Since then, there's been silence." So I knew where the lack of interest was coming from. And who it was directed at.

"Well, you can't leave it like that," said ZiZi.

"I can't?"

"No. Seriously, Lo. This is just a misunderstanding. I think he *likes you* likes you. I know he thinks really highly of you. Plus, he talks about you all the time."

"He does? All the time?"

"Don't get mega literal, Loretta. All the time when I see him. I mean, I don't see him every day or anything. And we don't always have a chance to speak. But when we do, your name always comes up."

"What does he say?"

"You know."

"Yes, of course I do. Because of my psychic powers. That's why I'm asking you what he says. To check I'm listening in on the right thoughts."

"He just asks about you. You know. 'How's Loretta?' That kind of thing."

Not exactly a declaration of undying love or a threat to spend the rest of his life floating through space like a chunk of debris if he has to live without me.

"I know what you should do," said ZiZi. "You're picking me up from work tomorrow, right?" The parent Abruzzios were still away; I was going to spend the night at ZiZi's so I could see Nightmare on Olsen Street for myself. My mother was letting me take her car. "Try to be a little early, so you're there at shift change. Park by the side entrance to the kitchen, not out front. You might run into him. Have a little conversation. Maybe it wasn't Vinnie. Maybe it was just the store scared him off. All those power tools and all that testosterone."

"Scientists use power tools, ZiZi. Besides which, I'm sure he has plenty of testosterone."

"You know what I mean. He's not exactly fullback of the year, is he?"

I mulled this over for a few seconds. Not the football part, the trying-to-run-into-Gabe part. Men often depict women as scheming and duplicitous, always trying to entrap them. Which, obviously, I disagree with, but it made me wary of acting in any way that might be seen as scheming or duplicitous. For definite that was a stereotype I didn't want to fall into. On the other hand, I couldn't see anything wrong with ZiZi's idea in principle. I was picking her up anyway. And Gabe is my friend. If I saw him it would be really odd if I didn't say hello. It would be rude; possibly hostile.

"Okay. I'll be there. I'm pretty sure Mr Chelusky will let me leave a few minutes early."

The next afternoon, I got to the Inn twenty minutes before shift change and parked by the far side entrance, STAFF ONLY. Some guys who were obviously kitchen staff showed up, but none of them was Gabe. Tired of standing, I sat down on the steps to wait. A waitress arrived and hurried inside. I was checking the time when a shadow fell over me. It could have been the shadow of a very large bird or a fairly small bear. I looked up. It was Mr

Schonblatt. I'd never actually seen him in the flesh before but ZiZi's pretty good at description and has an eye for detail. I would have recognized him even if I wasn't sitting on the steps of his Inn but had bumped into him in town. She got the fishing-line mouth and ball-bearing eyes perfectly. He didn't look happy to see me. I guessed I was probably breaking a couple of his rules.

"Can I help you, young lady?"

"You must be Mr Schonblatt." I got to my feet. "I'm Loretta Reynolds. I'm waiting for Giselle? Giselle Abruzzio?" Smiling as if I was selling something had become second nature. "She's told me so much about you."

It didn't seem to occur to him that everything she'd told me was bad.

"Has she?" He smiled back. "Loretta, is it?" He held out his hand. "Very nice to meet you."

That should have ended our conversation – it ended it for me – but Mr Schonblatt had other ideas. He started talking about the Inn and how busy it is in the summer and all the problems he was having with staff – because a great many people are useless and not accustomed to real work. Now that I was a professional listener, I nodded and murmured and acted a lot more interested than you expect a teenage girl on a Summer afternoon to act when the topic was less interesting than someone reading out batting averages for the last fifty years. I didn't so much as think of yawning. People walked past us, some going in and some coming out – and none of them Gabriel Schwartz – but Mr Schonblatt kept on talking. And then he said, "I suppose ZiZi's told you about the wedding reception we're having here soon."

Which would be the Bagley-Schreiber reception. Because it had amped up Mr Schonblatt's fascist tendencies to new levels, I'd heard more about it than anyone except the bridal couple actually needed to know. I said, "Yes. It sounds like it's really going to be something."

"It is, it is. It's a very big deal, let me tell you." He actually rubbed his hands together. "An event like this could really put the Inn on the map."

I was tempted to ask what map – the map of twelfth-century Asia? Of the Hapsburg Empire? Of southern Florida? – but I knew that ZiZi had enough troubles with Mr Schonblatt without adding a snarky friend to the list. I said, "Oh, really? That's great."

In case ZiZi had omitted sharing any detail of this affair with me, Mr Schonblatt filled me in. It was the wedding of the season – at least in Howards Walk. The bride's father was a mega-rich developer; from Mr Schonblatt's description, I guessed the bride's father was the kind of developer who bulldozes the Garden of Eden to build luxury apartments. The guest list included some very important people – very, very important. He told me what the menu was. He told me all about the flowers and how much they cost. He explained that the colours of the wedding party's dresses were being coordinated with the serviettes. A person can only retain so much trivial information and I was starting to lose the plot when he asked me if I'd ever done any waitressing.

"Excuse me?"

He needed extra staff for the wedding. People were letting him down – going away, not wanting to put in the extra hours. "You'd be amazed at how lazy some people can be," Mr Schonblatt confided. He could tell that a girl like me would be perfect for the occasion.

This time I was tempted to ask if, by "girl like me", he meant breathing. I didn't, though. I said, "No, I haven't really done any waitressing." Meaning none at all.

"Oh, you don't need a lot of experience." He dismissed my lack with a wave of his hand. "It's not like you'd have to take orders, you'd just have to serve," Mr Schonblatt explained. "This is a very sophisticated do, and, if you don't mind me being frank, you're exactly what we need."

Which meant he didn't ask me because I can breathe, he asked me because he thought I looked good.

I demurred. "Well…"

His smile made me wish he'd scowl. "What do you say? I'm paying time and a half."

This was another one of those moments when I was going to say no – when I should have said no – but right then Gabriel Schwartz strode past me without even looking my way. And, in that moment, it occurred to me that if he was working at the reception – which was likely; he was planning to get as many degrees as I was and would want the extra money – and I was working at it, too, I would have the opportunity I needed to confront him. You can't ignore someone who has you backed against a sink.

And that's why I said, "Yes."

Which, for me, was the biggest surprise of the last twenty-four hours; twenty-four hours that had for definite had their share of surprises.

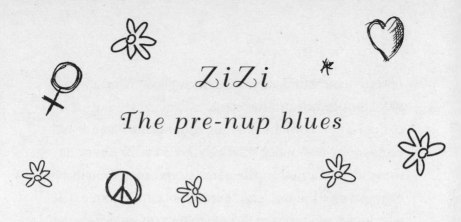

ZiZi

The pre-nup blues

Weddings are supposed to be happy, joyous occasions, but, as far as I could tell, the Bagley-Schreiber wedding (at least the reception part of it) wasn't bringing any joy or happiness yet.

Not to Mr Schonblatt, that's for sure. Where he was concerned, all it was doing was bringing out the worst in him, and, trust me, that's not a pretty sight. It was like all these evil demons had been hiding in a corner of the dungeon of his heart and just the words "sit-down dinner for two hundred and fifty" had called them to the surface, drooling and wailing and flexing their claws. God knows when he found the time, since he was always in such a state, but he came up with dozens of new rules to fit the occasion. How we should walk. How we should serve. What we should do when we weren't serving. What we should say. What we shouldn't say. Where to stand and how to do it. "Think of yourselves as ghosts," he repeated so often I heard it in my sleep. "Always there but never seen." He was constantly telling us how much stress and pressure he was under (like we couldn't tell!). Every day something changed in the plans (sometimes something changed on the hour), and Mr Schonblatt made sure "the wedding crew" (as he called us) shared his pain.

I could almost feel sorry for Mr Schonblatt when yet another thing was altered or when another waitress said she couldn't work the reception after all. But only almost. They were closing the restaurant for two days, one for the decorators to set it all up and one for the reception itself, and the hotel was booked solid for the guests. So even though he was having a hard time, he was making a fortune and couldn't really gripe. Plus, none of us was sorry to see him get some of the misery and blame he dished out back. (That's called "karma", aka "you get what you deserve"!)

But here's the thing. If the wedding was bringing any happiness and joy to the bride-to-be, she was making sure no one knew that but her. She was the one making all the decisions, but a day (if not less) after she made one, she didn't like it any more. *Change this. Change that. I hate this. I hate that. We can't possibly serve chicken…* (Or beef, or cheese, or potatoes, or lettuce. You can pretty much insert any food you can think of here.) *Why can't you people get anything right? What's so difficult about following my instructions?* She was on the phone at least twice a day (we always knew it was her, her voice really carried!) Sometimes she rang so often that Mr Schonblatt made one of us answer to tell her he wasn't there, and we actually did it. The days she didn't call up, she came in (stomped in, really, but very elegantly, and always in designer shoes), her mother in tow. (Two very sophisticated-looking and expensively dressed women who may not have been born with silver spoons in their mouths but absolutely ate with them.) *Isn't that true, Mother? Don't you think so, Mother? My mother agrees. My mother thinks so, too.* Mrs Bagley was the senseless victim here. She may have been wearing enough gold and diamonds to pay a ransom, but if you asked me she was a little downtrodden. All she ever did was smile and agree (kind of like the way a chameleon changes colour to protect itself from predators). All the bride-to-be ever did was shout or burst into tears. But I still had more sympathy for her than for Mr Schonblatt. I figured it was all the pressure and stress and pre-wedding nerves. Even if it was pretty exhausting for everybody else.

"I know Mr Schonblatt's going to wring every ounce of misery out of it that he can," I said to Loretta, "but

I'm really glad I'm working the reception." (I was really glad Loretta was working it, too, but that was because I wanted her to have the full Schonblatt experience. Then she'd really know what it's like to be me!)

Loretta had wads of cotton between her toes and was holding the polish in one hand and the brush in the other. She looked up. "Why's that?"

"Why's that? Seriously? Because I've only been to one wedding in my life and that was in a yurt. This is a real fairy-tale wedding. It's going to be awesome." The flowers alone cost thousands. I couldn't even imagine what everything else cost…

"A fairy-tale wedding?" Loretta put down the polish like she was stabbing something with a knife. "Is this the fairy-tale where the princess gets locked in the tower?"

"No, Loretta. It's the fairy tale where everybody lives happily ever after."

It was a full sixty seconds before she stopped laughing. (I know this because I was looking at her antique alarm clock so I didn't have to look at her while she was impersonating a gang of hyenas.)

"Oh, give me a break, Zi. You know that isn't true. Most marriages are just as likely to end in divorce as not."

"Everybody wants to get married, Loretta."

"No they don't. I don't."

She'd said this before (she's said everything before) but I thought she was just being Loretta (you know, difficult for the hell of it). This time, I believed her. She had that you'll-never-open-this-lock look on her face.

"How come? Because you figure no one will ever ask you?" Who would have the nerve?

She put the brush into the polish bottle and set her face for lecture. "Because historically, Giselle, marriage has been used to oppress and control women. To treat them like property. Like they're a bed or a horse. And that's all so the man has some guarantee that the children his wife has are actually his."

I said that was pretty cynical.

"I am or they are?" Loretta said that's why she believes in matriarchy. "You always know who your mother is. It makes so much more sense."

"Well, I think you're wrong. I don't think marriage is about oppression. I think it's about love. Love and commitment and making a life together."

"Love! You don't need to get married to love someone or to be committed and build a life together."

"Maybe not, but then you miss out on the wedding. Come on, even you have to admit there's nothing like a wedding. Queen for a day."

"Serf for a lifetime," said Loretta. "Besides which, it's

just a big party that costs a fortune and usually ends in somebody's tears."

"Then I don't know why you took the job if you think weddings are such a joke. Surely you're demolishing a couple of your precious principles here."

"Mostly, I took it for the money. The pay's good, and there's a solid chance we'll all get a nice tip if no one sets the bride on fire or knocks over the cake."

Quel negative attitude, or what?

"That and Gabriel Schwartz. If Gabe is there, I'll finally have a chance to talk to him."

"You see?" I said. "Deep down, you are a romantic."

"It's not romance," said Loretta. "It's biology."

Like I said, I was glad Loretta was working the Bagley-Schreiber reception with me, even though she was her usual major monsoon trying to wash out my parade about it. (I told her to remind me not to ask her to be my bridesmaid, and she said she would.) But I wasn't going to let her negativity throw even a tiny cloud over me. I was excited and I was staying excited. Plus, I guess I secretly hoped that once she saw what a real wedding's like (it's all civil ceremonies and a takeaway in her family), she'd change her mind about marriage being just another thing invented by some man to enslave women and ruin their lives (and about weddings being just a waste of a lot of money).

I was determined that the Bagley-Schreiber wedding was going to be the wedding you dream about from when you're little. Maybe the bride wasn't a princess and the groom wasn't a prince, but you can't have everything. And anyway, it was going to be almost as good as. The bride was going to be beautiful. The groom was going to be handsome. The guests were going to be glamorous. And my faith in romance and love would be restored. I was counting the days.

If I'd known what was going to happen, I might have stopped before I started.

Loretta

One girl's dream-cometrue is another's giant monster crushing everything in its path

By the time the Bagley-Schreiber wedding was looming over the horizon, shadowing everything around it like a berserk, giant monster set on destroying the world, I was already tired of it. And I didn't even work at the Inn, which meant I wasn't having it shoved in my face every day. I might have been tempted to back out at the last minute, but ZiZi found out for certain that Gabriel would be working in the kitchen; faint heart never won attractive astronomer.

Everything I heard about the wedding – which was a lot – I heard secondhand. Secondhand and through the deep pink, bubble-filled filter of ZiZi's enthusiasm. I said I hadn't realized she was such a fan of antiquated, oppressive institutions. She said what she is a fan of is romance and love; and that if she couldn't have romance and love for herself because Dillon Blackstock went to live in a tent, then she'd have it through the Bagley-Shreibers. "Just wait," said ZiZi. "You'll see. Even you're going to have to admit it's like a dream come true."

File under the heading: *Famous last words.*

It was an afternoon wedding, and the reception didn't start until five, but, of course, we had to report for duty hours earlier. Since it was the kind of wedding where nothing was left to chance – if they could have controlled the weather, they would have – professional wedding designers had done the decorations, but there were still tables to lay, two marquees as well as chairs and tables to set up in the garden and Mr Schonblatt's drill to go over and over again.

It was the hottest day of the Summer so far, thick and muggy; the sun so strong that the air was almost liquid, making everything appear slightly warped – as if you were looking through a bubble.

"What'd I tell you?" ZiZi was ecstatic. "Ohmygod, it's a totally perfect, gorgeous day!"

I ran a handkerchief over my forehead. "Except for the part where the air is wet."

The slightest exertion – for instance, breathing or moving one foot after the other – made you sweat and want to sit down.

"People in love don't care about humidity," said ZiZi.

I flung myself into the air-conditioned car as if it was a mountain pool. "But people hauling trays of food do."

The first thing I noticed when we got to the Inn was that if it had been a country it would have been on red alert with soldiers at every airport and train and bus station, and a police presence on every street. Everybody seemed to be running in circles, and Mr Schonblatt was dashing from one place to another, shouting and looking distraught.

Of course, that wasn't what ZiZi noticed.

"Ohmygod, will you look at it! It's totally awesome!"

It may have been Summer in the Sahara outside, but inside it was more like a snow palace – and not just because of the air conditioning, which felt as if it was cranked up as high as it would go. Everything was white and silver. Tiny white star and heart lights criss-crossed the ceiling and framed the windows; there were white and silver flowers at every table.

"But this isn't all," gushed ZiZi. "There's going to be this amazing ice sculpture in the shape of a swan in the centre of the room."

I said I could hardly wait.

Mr Schonblatt had a clipboard with all his notes on it, and he marched around the dining room and the terrace barking orders as if he was a general about to launch an invasion. We had to set the tables three times because there was always something not quite right. We had to hear again the sequence of events – drinks and photographs, dinner and speeches, dancing to live music more or less under the stars. He reminded us several times that we were to think of ourselves as ghosts, neither seen nor heard but always present.

At the point where there was so much tension in the restaurant that if we'd been a bottle of champagne we would have popped our cork, the wedding party and the guests finally began to arrive.

ZiZi and I stood side by side at a window, watching the cars pull into the parking area.

"Look at her," whispered ZiZi as the bride and groom got out of their limo. He climbing gracefully out of the car; she fighting her dress, which seemed to want to stay where it was. "Tell me she doesn't look like she stepped out of a fairy tale."

"She's lucky if she's able to step out of the car."

What the bride looked like mostly was a cream puff – one with mobility issues – and the groom looked like he was either a very upmarket mortician or in a clothing ad, but I had no chance to say anything because Mr Schonblatt clicked into gear right then and sent us all scattering like confetti being thrown at a bride and groom.

Two waitresses who the gods called lucky were sent to cover the garden – Claire and me. The garden was where the pre-dinner drinks and canapés were being served while the bridal party was having their photographs taken. Two marquees had been erected at the far end of the lawn – the larger one for the band and the dancing, the smaller one as an outdoor bar.

Mr Schonblatt might as well have sent us to hell, it was so hot outside. I looked back with longing at the Inn, which shimmered mirage-like under the broiling sun. Inside, it was cool and shady; inside, was the kitchen.

"Put a smile on your face and hope for the best," whispered Claire. "Here they come."

I turned. Surging towards us was a kaleidoscopic wave – a tsunami, really – of guests. There were so many, I couldn't believe they were all friends and family – some of them had to be strangers they'd picked up along the way or hired for the occasion. I put a smile on my face, and stepped forward bravely with my tray.

"Here they come" was the last thing Claire said to me for the next two hours – and more or less the last thing I heard besides the voices of the celebrants. After that, it was serve tray, load tray, smile, smile, smile. Besides serving and smiling, we were responsible for the general happiness and well-being of everyone in the garden. If a guest wanted ice, you had to get it. If you were offering a tray of caviar but a guest wanted "another of those cheese things", you had to scuttle off and get it. If someone wanted a coffee rather than a drink or needed tissues or had a bottle for baby that needed to be warmed, the smiling waitress was given the job. If they'd wanted a cup of water drawn from a distant mountain stream, that would have been our job, as well. We could have used Segways.

As involved as they were with themselves and the happy couple, the guests still found time to ask a lot of questions. *Is there anything that's gluten free? Do you know if this has nuts in it? Is this organic? I don't really eat dairy, does this contain butter or milk? What is this? What's in that? What happened to the shrimp? Aren't there any restrooms outside? Are you bringing some chairs down to the lawn?*

Within minutes, every nerve I have was tingling, but I was strong; determined. I channelled ZiZi. Her words ran through my head like a mantra: *You have to think of being a cute girl as your lever… You have to think of being a cute girl as your lever… You have to think of being a cute girl as your lever…* I was such a cute girl I could've moved a mountain. I smiled. I was helpful and eager to please. I was pleasantness with a tray of avocado and salmon on rye.

It wasn't just the men who thanked me and smiled back.

You didn't have to be listening to overhear conversations; and you didn't have to be paying close attention to figure out who was a guest of the bride and who a guest of the groom. The bride's guests were the ones who were better dressed and very obviously accustomed to parties where they were photographed talking to some movie star or politician. They were also used to bossing servants around. If you were looking for humility, you wouldn't be looking in that group. They didn't so much as glance at you as they reached for a canapé or set an empty glass on your tray. They gravitated to the limited shade like moss; they mingled only with themselves. The groom's guests were the ones standing in the sun looking as if they'd arrived at the wrong hotel – possibly in the wrong country. The groom's guests were the ones who said thank you and smiled.

Unfortunately, there was no leverage to use against the weather. Inside, there was air conditioning and, at least for the beginning of the reception, only a handful of guests and very little to do. Outside – unless you were in one of the marquees, where there were fans – the air was like a hot wet towel, and there were scores of party-goers schmoozing and eating and drinking and waiting – demanding – to be served. The guests, of course, weren't the only ones outside. There was the photographer as well, moving the bridal party around like traffic from one scenic location to another, always in search of the perfect shot. Besides the official photographer and the bridal party, there was some guy with a video camera filming the whole thing. He was everywhere and nowhere; there and not there at the same time – which means that he was either getting in people's way, or you thought he'd gone only to spot him lurking behind a bush like a spy. Not that I had time to pay attention to anything but the guests. Maybe it was the combination of the heat and the alcohol making everyone seem extremely intense, but working in the garden was to hectic what a supernova is to a sparkler. It didn't take more than ten minutes for me to realize that though some people might have a natural talent for waitressing I for definite wasn't one of them. Not only did you have to keep the trays coming, answer any questions, clean up any messes and make sure no one was left out or overlooked, you had to do it all with a pleasant attitude, smiling as if you enjoyed it.

It also didn't take long to dispel any idea I might have had way at the back of my mind that weddings bring out the best in people.

I was approaching the chattering throng with a loaded tray of canapes, trying not to think about how long this day was going to be, when suddenly the janitor, who was doing a last check on the marquees, bumped into me from behind. I pitched forward, struggling to keep my balance. I managed not to fall, but the canapes weren't so lucky. They flew into the air like miniature missiles decorated with parsley and olives. It's practically a natural law that if something like that's going to happen it's going to happen to the least equanimous person within a twenty-mile radius. Several rounds of toast, with lobster, pastry and possibly mayonnaise involved, hit their target – who, in this case, was the father of the bride. He let out a bellow of surprise, dropped the glass he was holding and stepped back into the woman behind him, who, of course, then spilled her drink. That a perfect chain reaction of people knocking into each other didn't result is only because Mr Bagley recovered from his surprise in half a nanosecond – and as soon as he did he started shouting. Which caught everyone's attention. Because he was a Master of the Universe type, Mr Bagley didn't shout the way a lesser mortal might have, but got this eerily calm but authoritarian tone in his voice – as if he was God telling Man what he was doing wrong and how much trouble he was in. "You!" he roared. Meaning, me. "Are you a totally incompetent idiot or have you been hitting the bar?" Behind him the video guy suddenly materialized. After I'd apologized I kept my gaze on the ground – I didn't want to meet those cold, dead eyes again – and concentrated on picking up as much as I could. While Mr Bagley rolled on. He not only questioned my sobriety and general ability to walk and breathe at the same time, but accused me of being a tray-wielding terrorist. All the while he was ranting, his wife, summoned by his booming voice, was dabbing at his jacket with a napkin and trying (unsuccessfully) to calm him down. When he finally ran out of insults, he marched off to the Inn, Mrs Bagley scurrying after him. Everyone around us went back to their interrupted conversations and I went for another tray.

The talk and laughter got louder. Smiling relentlessly, I filtered through the noisy throng, bearing platters of stuffed quails eggs and caviar on rounds of toast. I was so busy that I couldn't see the trees for the wood; all I saw was a blur of laughing, talking, chewing, sipping faces. I lost track of the bride and groom early on. I lost track of Claire, only occasionally catching a glimpse of her holding a tray and smiling like a corpse. Every now and then I'd catch a glimpse of Mr Schonblatt on the edge of the gathering, checking that the guests were having a good time and that Claire and I weren't. Besides getting an ache in my back and blisters on my feet because I'd been too cheap to buy a pair of pumps that fit and was wearing ZiZi's, I began to acquire a new respect for her. It was bad enough just serving, but at least I didn't have to take orders or explain the menu or do crisis control the way a real, everyday waitress does. The only person who spoke to me – except to ask for something – was the janitor. Who said, "I'm sorry, honey" when he nearly knocked me over.

Otherwise, I was the ghost of Mr Schonblatt's dreams; silent, invisible and excruciatingly busy. So busy that it wasn't until dinner was announced and people headed inside that I realized two things. The first was why the woman in the blue suit and hat that resembled a beached boat looked vaguely familiar. I'd seen her before, of course, but she'd always been wearing leggings and a tank top and carrying a purple mat under her arm. It was as I was passing behind her that I heard her say something about her yoga class. Yoga class? I stopped and took a good look. She was Magda Hornung, Dillon Blackstock's mother; which more or less guaranteed that the man beside her had to be Dillon's stepfather. He was wearing a carnation in the buttonhole of his jacket – as were the groom, the father-of-the-bride, and several young men I took to be the best man and the ushers – and Magda Hornung was wearing a corsage of tiny roses – as were the bridesmaids and the bride's mother. I was wondering if that meant that Magda and her husband were part of the wedding party when realization two hit me like a meteorite; who the guy with the video camera was. It was none other than Dillon Blackstock himself. Why hadn't I recognized him before? Because he was behind his camera? Because I was so busy? Or because I thought he was hundreds of miles away making a documentary about a man who was living without money, not in Howards Walk, filming the Bagley-Schreiber wedding – where money was being spent at the speed of light. Which meant that Dillon's brother's wedding was happening after all.

I watched Dillon stride towards the Inn, camera in hand, grinning as if he knew he was going to win a documentary award at the Sundance Film Festival.

There was no way I could warn ZiZi. Phones had been left in the staffroom, and even if I could escape the vigilant eye of Mr Schonblatt, I couldn't move fast enough in the shoes I was wearing to get inside before Dillon. My only hope was that she was in the mood for surprises.

ZiZi

Dadzilla and me

I woke up on the morning of the wedding to what was a totally perfect day for a celebration of love and romance, all sunshine and blue skies. Loretta (big surprise!) said it was too hot, too humid and was probably going to rain. I said it was probably going to rain somewhere, but not in Howards Walk. Not today. Look at that sun. Look at that sky. (If there'd been a couple of stick figures on the lawn, it could've been a picture by a little kid with only primary colours in her paint box.) Loretta (who'd rather wear a bikini than admit she might be wrong) said it was an afternoon wedding, so what did it matter what colour the sky was if it was going to be dark by the time the reception really got under way? See what I mean about negativity? Another patent pending.

The Inn may be just a really big old house, but the decorators had made the restaurant and the garden look magical. The dining rooms were all white and silver with lights and candles and flowers everywhere. In the garden there were two billowy white marquees (that looked like the tents of desert kings, not like the grubby old yurt my cousin was married in that looked like it'd been used to house goats) and metal arches covered with roses and tiny, heart-shaped lights. And, when the bridal party finally arrived, the bride looked like a princess (unless you were looking through the eyes of Loretta Reynolds, who thought she looked like food) and the groom like a prince (or an undertaker if you were the best friend standing beside me). If you ask me, all the shouting and crying had been worth it. This really was a dream wedding. A dream wedding planned by someone (the bride) who cares about appearances and knows the importance of getting every little detail right. (Over and over and over again, and no matter how long it took!) If Mr Schonblatt hadn't forbidden phones at the reception (staff phones, not guest phones!), I would've taken pictures so I could remember everything for when I get married myself.

Mr Schonblatt stationed Claire (who had a lot of experience) and Loretta (who had none) in the garden. But, because the regular staff had pretty much bailed on the reception for one reason or another (mainly being fed up with Mr Schonblatt!), I was the most experienced waitress left inside (and, because I'd been so determined not to let the back room beat me, also the most efficient), so the Schonblatt put me in charge of the dining rooms and of making sure everyone found their table and everything. (It'd been a long and ugly war, but if you asked me, I was winning!)

Almost everybody stayed down by the marquees or on the terrace, but some came inside (especially the older guests, because of the heat). I was kind of surprised that the parents of the bride were among the first to take shelter in the dining room. I knew who they were because I'd seen Mrs Bagley so many times before. Plus, as they swept through the French doors, he was saying to her, "We've had our pictures taken more times than necessary, and if anyone wants to talk to us, they can come in here. I'm not standing out there baking like a loaf of bread with that damn boy prowling around with his camera, getting in everybody's way, and clumsy waitresses bombing me with hors-d'œuvres, Adele. I want air conditioning, I want to sit down and I want a drink. Where's our table?"

By then, I was pretty used to men like Mr Bagley in his hand-stitched suit. Rich, successful and always expecting to get their own way (except that Mr Bagley acting like he owned the place made sense since he kind of did, at least for the weekend). I stepped forward, welcoming smile on face and clipboard in hand. "It's right over here, Mr Bagley." (They like it when you know who they are.)

Mr Bagley has the kind of vision that doesn't always see people he doesn't think are important, so he didn't seem to see me, but he saw his table okay. "I don't want to be near a window. I've had enough sun for one afternoon. You'll have to change us." (But he could talk to me even if he didn't see me.)

"I'm sorry but I'm afraid everything's set." I looked sorry. Sorry and sincere. I held out my clipboard as evidence. "See? It's all been agreed."

Mr Bagley is one of those people whose super power is to grow larger and more imposing the more displeased he is. And believe me, that did nothing to make him more charming or endearing. "Not by me it wasn't."

"Well, no, I know." I kept smiling but it was a sad, helpless smile. *If it was up to me, sir... But what can I, a mere waitress, do?* "The thing is..." I turned to Mrs Bagley, who knew all about the seating plan even if she hadn't made it herself. I was hoping she'd step in and explain. But Mrs Bagley wasn't going to rescue me. She was looking at the table, straightening a fork. I took a deep breath and tried again. "I really am so sorry, sir, but the place cards—"

"Move the place cards," said Mr Bagley. You couldn't call it a suggestion.

Loretta always asks herself, *What would Emma Goldman do? What would Gloria Steinem do?* I asked myself what Mr Schonblatt would do. Grovel. "Of course, Mr Bagley. Where would you like to sit?" I moved the place cards. So now he was in my section. It was then that I should've realized that my guardian angel had taken the day off.

Once he was seated out of the sun at the table of his choice, Mr Bagley wanted drinks. Wine was going to be served with the meal, but there was a bar at one end of the restaurant for anything else, and before the sit-down you were supposed to get your own.

The way Mr Bagley looked at me when I explained about the bar made me feel sorry for anybody who worked for him. "I'm the father of the bride, not the date of a distant cousin. I don't wait on tables. I get served."

I said, "Of course. I'm sorry. Just tell me what you want."

When I came back with the drinks, he wanted canapés. There weren't any canapés inside. Not in here. The canapés were all kept in a chill case in the smaller of the two marquees outside.

"Do I look blind to you?" asked Mr Bagley. He pointed

to the garden. "What's that on those trays out there? Rocks? I happen to know for a fact that there are canapés, because I've had quite a few of them thrown at me by your incompetent staff."

I stood up tall, looking competent. And oozed positivity the way a gateau will ooze icing if someone steps on it. "I think you're supposed to stay in the garden while the photographs are being taken and—"

"In case it escaped your attention, I am not 'staying in the garden'," Mr Bagley informed me. You know, in case I hadn't noticed that he was sitting there, getting bigger (and a lot less happy) by the second.

"I understand, sir, but—"

"You are aware that I am paying for this shindig, aren't you? I don't think it's too much to expect a cracker with some caviar smeared on it."

Okay, so maybe if it had been me in charge of the reception arrangements I would have had canapés in the dining room as well as in the garden, because people like Mr Bagley don't get where they are by being shy and retiring and making do and not getting what they want. But I hadn't been in charge. That was his daughter (who you'd think would've known better), with help from his wife (who should have known better, too). Sit-down dinner was indoors. Drinks and canapés were outdoors. That was what they'd ordered. I glanced around for a higher authority. The bride was standing under an arch of roses having her picture taken looking beautiful and happy (I'd never really seen her smile before). Mr Schonblatt was somewhere whipping his staff into shape. Mrs Bagley was staring at the ice in her drink as if it might speak.

I think I may have curtsied. "I'll be right back."

When I returned with a full tray, there'd been enough time for Mr Bagley to realize that there was something wrong with his drink. (Of course there was; how could there not be? The whole world obviously went out of its way to annoy him.)

He held up the glass. "This isn't what I asked for."

I wasn't the bartender. I'd only placed the order and carried it to the table. "It isn't? That's not scotch and water?" Even without actually sticking my nose in his glass I could smell the whisky.

"It is scotch and water, but it's not what I asked for."

I apologized. A lot. "I'm so sorry, Mr Bagley. I really thought you said scotch and water." I reached for his glass. "Just tell me again what you do want—"

"I want scotch and water."

Was there something wrong with my hearing? Or was there something wrong with the water? He wouldn't be the first man wearing a gold Rolex to send the water back. Not at the Old Clipper Inn.

"Excuse me? I'm sorry but—"

"Be a good girl and just get me my drink. I asked for a very specific scotch, and this is not it. I know you have it, because I ordered it in. I don't know what you told him, honey, but this is bottom shelf."

Loretta could tell you (and would) that I'm not the kind of person who objects to being called "good girl" or "honey". I'd always thought that, as words go, they were pretty sweet and affectionate. But they didn't sound sweet and affectionate coming from Mr Bagley's gleaming white and over-toothed mouth. They sounded patronizing and condescending. *Be a good girl? Honey?* If I'd been male he probably would've called me "boy".

My smile was intrepid. "I told him what you told me." I remembered because Mr Bagley had repeated it three times. "I'm really sorry. I don't know how this could have happened. I'll change it right away."

He spelled out the name of the whisky he wanted so I wouldn't get it wrong. "You got that?"

Loretta would have snapped at him "I can spell, you know", but all I said was, "Yes. I have it."

Mrs Bagley handed me her glass. "I'll have another of these."

I was starting to feel pretty sorry for her. Even though I'd only known Mr Bagley for ten minutes, I figured no one could blame her for drinking. She really was a senseless victim.

"And watch him pour it this time," said Mr Bagley.

The second time I went back to the bartender, he returned to the table with me and poured it in front of Mr Bagley.

More people started coming inside so I was kept pretty busy showing them to their tables and stuff like that, but no one kept me busier than Mr Bagley. He was like a one-man rush hour when orders get mixed up or forgotten and every word you hear is a complaint.

He sent back the cutlery. He sent back his water glass. He ordered a bottle of mineral water and sent that back. (There was no big mystery about which parent the bride took after. Chip off the old megalomaniac, or what?!) He couldn't make it to the bar to get himself a drink but he was able to get up and tour the dining room, talking to people he knew and noticing anything and everything that was wrong (eat your heart out, Otis Schonblatt!), and making sure I knew about it. He went on for at least ten minutes about the ice sculpture. It was a beautiful, intricately carved swan, the space between its wings filled with flowers. Everybody except Mr Bagley and one other person loved the ice sculpture (so, amazingly enough, he had something in common with Loretta Reynolds!). Mr Bagley doesn't like swans. Plus, he thought it looked cheap (it wasn't, Mr Schonblatt told us all exactly how much it cost). Mrs Bagley, who was on her third cocktail by then, murmured that Gloriana chose the sculpture. Mr Bagley made a sound like the bathtub backing up because it's clogged with hair. "Is that supposed to make me feel better, Adele? Gloriana has the taste of a salesgirl. Look at who she's married."

I was really looking forward to after the meal when everybody was free to wander around and go into the garden and dance and everything. When Mr Bagley wouldn't be constantly snapping his fingers at me. I thought things were bound to get better.

And then dinner was announced.

Loretta

Things are bad, then things get just that enormous amount worse

I was so relieved when the guests all went inside for dinner that I nearly wept. Which is probably the closest I'll ever come to crying at a wedding. All afternoon, while I'd been scurrying back and forth like an obedient servant, I'd had no time to think about Gabriel. I suppose, in a way, that was a good thing. One less agony in a day of torment. Then came the halcyon moment when I finally watched everyone stroll inside, and prepared to shrug off the yoke of servitude and fulfil my mission.

It was my and Claire's job to clean up outside and get things ready for the after-dinner party. We loaded the glasses on trays and put all the rubbish in bags. One of us had to stay in the garden because the band would soon be arriving and setting up in the large marquee; I volunteered to bring the rubbish to the bins outside the kitchen and the dirty glasses into the kitchen itself. We both had walked miles that afternoon – largely in circles, but the mere fact that a hamster doesn't get anywhere doesn't mean she doesn't cover a lot of ground – and Claire was happy enough to let me do the hiking up to the house and back. I took the bags first to get them out of the way. When I finished with them, I grabbed a tray and headed for the kitchen.

It had already been a very long day; exhausting and stressful. The main purpose of putting myself through it, was, of course, to speak to Gabriel. It was only as I trudged up the sloping lawn that I finally began to think about what I was doing. To question myself in a critical manner. I'm not what anyone would call bold or forward when it comes to boys, and yet here I was being forward and bold. Had I misplaced my mind, if not actually lost it? What did I think I was doing, barging into a busy kitchen where everyone was working flat out to confront a boy who'd given every indication that he wouldn't be disappointed if he never had to speak to me again? It wasn't even as if he was my boy – or ever had been. We'd never had a date. We'd never so much as joked about having a date. Now that I was about to stand, sweaty face to sweaty face with him, what exactly was it that I planned to say? I had no idea; I hadn't given it any thought. All I'd thought about was wanting to say it; wanting to look him in the eyes and say something. So much for all my lists and planning; so much for always being prepared. *You don't have to do this*, said a reasonable voice in my head. *All you have to do is leave the dirty glasses and go.* That was true, I thought. That was all I had to do.

I stepped up to the back door and went inside.

The kitchen staff weren't just working flat out, they were past frantic. Except for the absence of blood and crashing buildings, it was a scene from a disaster movie. Guys were running back and forth, shouting and cursing. Even the ones who were standing still were moving. Accompanying the urgent male voices was the clatter of pots, dishes and cutlery. Accompanying all of it was the heat; it was so intense that the sauna that was the garden was chilly in comparison. Even the pans hanging overhead seemed to be sweating. If I'd been a candle, I would have started to melt the instant I crossed the threshold; it was as if I'd walked in, not on the kitchen crew of the Old Clipper Inn, but on the crew that was stoking the fires of Hell. Or, in Gabe's case, washing Hell's dishes. Which is to say that I assumed he was washing dishes, but there were so many people and so much noise that I didn't see him at first. Wondering what I was going to do, I stood by the door for several seconds, holding out the tray of glasses smudged with lipstick and clouded by fingerprints like an offering. I finally spied him on the other side of the large but cramped room, bent over a sink with his back to me.

Everybody was so absorbed in their jobs that they hadn't noticed me come in – or, if they had, couldn't be bothered to care. I didn't think to myself, *Yes, I'm going to ignore the voice of reason and go over to him*; I simply went. I left the tray on the counter of dirty dishes and crossed to the sink where Gabe was working furiously.

I had to touch his arm before he realized there was anyone beside him. Gabe jumped, splashing us both with dirty water.

"Loretta?" His voice was pitched at a conspiratorial whisper. He glanced around. Nervously. I could almost hear him thinking, *How did you get in? Has anyone else seen you? How did you know where I was?* "Loretta, what are you doing here?"

"I'm conducting a survey on job satisfaction in local employment. How the kitchen staff would rate working at the Inn. From one to ten, with ten being the top score."

He blinked. "That's a joke, right?"

"Of course it's a joke." For God's sake, I was dressed as a waitress – one with the shadows of fish and wine on her shirt, and aching feet. "It's just that – it's…" He was staring at me, but not with the awe and affection I would have liked to have seen there. More as if I was an annoying fly and he was working out how to get rid of me.

I'd never realized before that you could be as rigid as a wall and still give the impression that you were stamping your feet. "What? It's what?"

When inspiration fails, the truth will have to do. "It's just that I need to talk to you."

"Now?" His face was shiny from the heat and the steam and sweat; he sounded fairly incredulous. "I can't talk to you now." He turned back to the sink. "I don't have time for this. We're in the middle of a reception here."

How had I not noticed that?

"I'm in the middle of a reception here, too," I told the side of his head. "But this is the only way I can get hold of you. Since you won't answer my texts or calls."

"I did answer you. I told you. Nobody got back to me about the Perseids, so I cancelled. That's all there is to it. There's nothing else to say."

"That's not true." A mist of hot, soapy spray fell over us as he scrubbed frantically. "What about me?"

"What about you?" He was looking at the brush in his hand. If there'd been a pattern on the dishes, he would have rubbed it off. "I didn't think you were interested any more."

"I don't know how you came to that conclusion. Because I don't remember being asked."

"I – you know. You seemed pretty busy." I wasn't sure if he was blushing – everyone in the kitchen was flushed – but for definite he was looking shifty. He started splashing water around even more, as if he was washing his way through the sink. "Loretta, would you please just go? Now."

The chef's attention had been focused on what he was doing at the stove, but some sixth, chef sense must have alerted him to the fact that something he wasn't going to like was happening in his kitchen. He was a large, stocky man who didn't give the impression that he was difficult to annoy, and now he was looking right at Gabe and me. "Oi!" he shouted. "Are you doing dishes, Schwartz, or exchanging phone numbers? Tell your friend to get out of my kitchen! This second!"

"Dishes!" yelled Gabriel, not looking at either of us. "Go, Loretta. Now."

"I don't understand what I did that you won't talk to me. Just tell me what I—"

"Hey, you! Girl who won't stop talking!" bellowed the chef. "Don't you have something better to do than disrupt my staff? Like a job?"

"Yes. You're right. I do. I'm going." I took a step

backwards, so he'd believe me. "I am sorry. Truly sorry. I know how busy you are, but this is very important." I was practically simpering. The cute-girl lever was working hard, while all my principles were dead and rolling in their graves. "I just need to talk to Gabriel for a minute more. Please. One minute. And then I'll go. I swear."

"Thirty seconds."

I leaned as close to Gabe as I could without being hit by his elbows. "Just say you'll talk to me." I wasn't sure that the kitchen guys couldn't stir, sauté and plate up and still eavesdrop, which made me whisper. "That's all I ask."

"Maybe later," muttered Gabriel. "Or tomorrow. Maybe tomorrow."

"You promise? Tomorrow?"

"That's your thirty seconds up," shouted the chef. "Now get the hell out of here before I throw you out myself!"

"Promise?"

"Yeah. Yeah. Now go."

I went quickly, thanking and apologizing as I hurried to the door. I was feeling optimistic. Not enormously optimistic, but solidly hopeful. ZiZi had to be right, it was a misunderstanding. This happened all the time in plays and novels. Look at Romeo and Juliet. On second thought, they were a bad example; their misunderstanding cost them their lives. My misunderstanding with Gabe had to be a lot less lethal than that. He'd thought I wasn't interested any more; he'd thought I was busy. We'd got our signals crossed, that was what had happened. All I had to do was uncross them; and then everything would be all right. I'd live through the ordeal of the reception. I'd straighten things out with Gabriel. I'd win the bet and go back to the way I'd been. Logic and order would be restored to my world once more.

This idyll of optimism lasted less than five minutes, because as I neared the large marquee, Mr Schonblatt burst out, Claire behind him. They were each carrying one of the fans that were intended to keep the dancers and the band from heatstroke. Mr Schonblatt looked the way a mouth ulcer feels; Claire looked like a hostage.

"You!" Mr Schonblatt roared. "Have you seen Abel? Where has he gone? Is he up at the Inn?"

"Abel?"

According to ZiZi, Mr Schonblatt's patience was a limited resource at the best of times – and even someone who didn't know him well could tell that this wasn't one of those.

"Abel! Abel! The janitor! He's supposed to be keeping an eye on things. But has he? No, he has not! The air conditioning's kaput. In the middle of dinner! In the middle of dinner this happens!" He waved his arms around, as if trying to attract the attention of the air-conditioning gods. "Could anything else go wrong? Could it?"

I took that as a rhetorical question. Which, considering what happened later, was just as well. "I was bringing things up to the kitchen," I said. "I didn't see him there."

"Well, find him," barked Mr Schonblatt. "Check the basement. I have to get back to the guests."

"But, Mr Schonblatt, I don't know how to get to the basement."

He looked as if I was purposely trying very hard to irritate him – and succeeding beyond my wildest dreams. "Through the kitchen. It's the door near the big fridge. Now get going."

"And when I find the janitor? Then what do I do?"

"Then you tell him to effing do something!"

ZiZi

And then the swan started to melt

You know those days when you feel pretty sure that nothing more can go wrong because it's all been downhill since the moment you woke up? And then it does. You're walking under a lamppost and a pigeon poops on your new blouse, and you're so surprised you drop your bag and it lands in the road and some bad driver (like Duane Tolvar) runs over it and mashes all your make-up into paste.

This day was something like that. It got off to a bad start the minute Mr Bagley rolled into the restaurant, snapping his fingers and being a general major pain in the butt. But, because Mr Bagley was really doing my head in, I figured things weren't going to get worse. I also figured that with my positive personality I could handle it – especially since the wedding had put me in such a good mood. (If you can't be in a good mood at a wedding, when can you?) Plus, even though there was a chance he'd find a lot wrong with his meal (meat overcooked, vegetables undercooked, lettuce too green), I was hoping that, once the dining room was full, Mr Bagley would see that he wasn't the only person who needed attention and chill. At least a little. And if he didn't chill, I'd be way too busy to jump every time he crooked his finger, so he'd just have to live with it.

I was coming out with a tray of starters, and thinking how I was really glad I wasn't working in the kitchen. I had noticed it was starting to feel a little warmer in the dining rooms than it should have (I figured it was me, because I'd been running around so much), but the kitchen was so hot it was amazing the plates weren't pools of glass. So anyway, I was coming out with the first course when who do I see but Dillon Blackstock. I stopped dead. I blinked. If I'd had a free hand, I would've pinched myself and rubbed my eyes. He had a good tan and his hair had grown, but it was Dillon (there couldn't be any doubt, he had his camera with him). The other waitresses glided by me with their trays, but I just stood there, wondering how this could be. What were he and his camera doing here? He was supposed to be in the Ozarks or wherever it was, living on berries and twig tea. What happened to his awesome social commentary? And then, because I guess I knew what the answers to my questions were, I looked over to the bridal table, where the groom was getting an earful from the bride. The family resemblance was unmistakable (same strong mouth and straight nose, same brooding eyes, same carnation buttonhole). So this must be his brother's wedding (the brother with a different last name). It had been called back on, after all. Only no one had bothered to tell me. I don't know how I managed to hold on to the tray, I was so surprised. Dillon was looking totally gorgeous in a very smart summer suit and a lemon-yellow shirt that really went with his colouring (I wasn't so surprised I didn't notice that!). You might expect me to go into shock-terror mode at the sight of Dillon where I wasn't really expecting him to be. Especially if you remember my reaction when I almost came face to face with Duane Tolvar. Red alert all the way! And a couple of months ago, or even a couple of weeks ago, I probably would've panicked. I would've turned around and gone back to the kitchen and not come out till everyone left and Mr Schonblatt dragged me out from under a counter. But here's the thing. Call it maturity or call it fatalism or call it being worn down to way past caring by Mr Bagley and all the other traumas of the Summer, but I didn't panic. Seriously? Next to Père Bagley, Dillon

Blackstock wasn't that big a deal. I could handle him being there. As long as I kept out of his way, everything would be okay. I watched to see where he was sitting. He headed away from my section and over to where the groom's family was hunkered down (as far away from the bride's as Gloriana could put them, by the looks of it).

I was standing there thinking, *Everything will be okay,* when I kind of blinked again and there was Mr Bagley right in front of me. Like an angry (and slightly perspiring) bull. If he got any bigger, he'd have to go outside. Behind him was the bride, crying. I'd seen her cry so many times before that I didn't think anything of it.

I smiled like I was glad to see them. I said they had to excuse me but I was just starting to serve.

Through her tears, the new Mrs Schreiber burbled, "Tell her, Daddy. Make her do something."

"You go sit down, sweetheart," Mr Bagley ordered. Gently. "Go back to your table. I'll take care of this." To me, he said, "Never mind serving. Get the manager. There's something wrong with the air conditioning." Sounding about as gentle as being hit by a sledgehammer feels.

"The air conditioning?"

"Yes, the air conditioning. Can't you feel how hot it's getting in here? If the a/c's blowing anything, it's blowing hot air."

It wasn't the only thing that was doing that. And anyway, it wasn't that hot. It wasn't cold like it had been, but it wasn't hot. If you were from India, you probably wouldn't even think it was very warm.

"I'm sorry, Mr Bagley, but there's really nothing I can do." I raised my tray a little to prove my point. "I have to—"

"The only thing you have to do is get the manager. Now."

What would Emma Goldman do? She'd probably wop him over the head with the tray. I said, "Consider me on my way."

If I'd served those starters any faster I'd've been clearing them away at the same time. I got one of the other waitresses to cover the rest of my section and (taking the long way around so Dillon Blackstock wouldn't see me) I went looking for Mr Schonblatt. He wasn't in the kitchen. He wasn't in the gardens. He wasn't in one of the marquees. He wasn't in the parking lot. He wasn't outside the kitchen, sneaking a cigarette. I finally found him taking an undeserved break with his wife in reception (where the air conditioning was working just dandy). Did he thank me for taking on the job of Mr Bagley's personal assistant? Did he thank me for looking all over for him (so that now I was so limp and soaked with sweat I looked like I'd been swimming)? Sure he did. And then he gave me a thousand-dollar bonus and the keys to his car.

"You go tell Mr Bagley everything's under control," Mr Schonblatt commanded. "I'll fetch Abel."

By the time I got back to the dining room, the swan was just starting to melt.

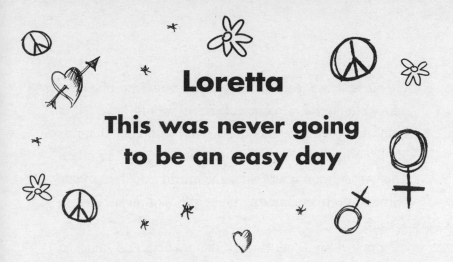

Loretta

This was never going to be an easy day

As I was a little unsure of my welcome – or sure that I wouldn't have one – I approached the kitchen cautiously. By now, it was so hot in there that they'd opened all the windows and doors, trying to get a breeze through. They were still working demonically, despite the temperature – as if by working fast they could finish their jobs before they collapsed with heatstroke. I hovered at the entrance while I looked for the door near the big fridge. The big fridge was a walk-in; the door closest to it was the only one that was painted blue. I took a deep breath, counted to three, walked straight to the blue door, pulled it open and went down the stairs. If anyone saw me, he kept it quiet.

Our basement at home is just a bare concrete space where the boiler, my workbench and a lot of cobwebs live. The basement of the Inn – which was enormous, of course – was partitioned off into a warren of rooms and sections that a colony of rabbits would have felt at home in. I tried several doors before I found one that was already slightly ajar, and behind it was the janitor's office. The janitor himself was sitting in an old armchair in one corner, asleep and snoring peacefully. I almost hated to disturb him.

I poked my head through the opening and knocked gently. I knocked not so gently the next time. "Abel?" He snuffled like my cat Gertie when she gets grass up her nose. "Hello? Abel?" With every word, I took a step inside and increased my volume. "Abel? I'm really sorry to bother you, but Mr Schonblatt's having a fit…." I went over and gave him a poke. "Abel?" I shook him. "Abel, you have to get up. Mr Schonblatt needs you." I shook him harder, despite the fact that by then I was close enough to him to know that he wasn't going to wake up any time soon; I could smell the whisky. Apparently, it had been a mistake to put him in charge of the marquees – especially the one with the bar. I tried a few more times to rouse him, and when that didn't work, I went to get Mr Schonblatt.

Just as in the kitchen, all the doors and windows had been opened in the dining room – which at least gave the illusion of making it cooler. A few people had taken their plates out to the patio, but most of them had stayed where they were. The bride and groom were still at their table in the corner between the two rooms, behind the dripping swan. The bride had turned her chair so she had her back to the groom and was fanning herself with a menu. The groom had taken off his jacket, rolled up his sleeves and loosened his tie, and was leaning over the bride's shoulder, trying to talk to her, but it was hard to tell if she was listening or not; there were tears in her eyes.

I guessed that the reason the guests hadn't abandoned the dining rooms was because of the drama unfolding centre stage. Mr Schonblatt was holding up his arms and trying to reassure everyone that things were under control. Mr Bagley stood near him – so angry he was red as a boiled lobster and the veins at his temples were throbbing – arguing, gesticulating and bellowing orders. ZiZi was between the two men – either trying to keep them apart or trying to calm them, it wasn't clear which.

ZiZi looked really glad to see me. "Loretta!"

Mr Schonblatt looked really glad to see me, too. In my experience, people in real life don't exclaim the way they do in old novels, they speak. But Mr Schonblatt for definite exclaimed when he saw me hurrying towards him. "Thank God! You found him? Is he on the job?"

Mr Bagley must have remembered who dumped

the canapés on him earlier because he didn't look glad to see me, but that didn't stop him from having something to say. "Is this the janitor we're talking about?" he demanded. "What's he doing about this infernal heat?"

I decided to lead with the good news and nodded. "I did find him. You were right, Mr Schonblatt, he was in the basement. In his office."

"And? What did he say? Did he look at the unit? Does he think he can fix it?"

I was trying to ignore Mr Bagley and only address Mr Schonblatt, but Mr Bagley is the sort of man who assumes that anyone talking must be talking to him. Before I could answer Mr Schonblatt, Mr Bagley took over.

"Presumably, he's already on the job," said Mr Bagley. "Did he give you any idea of how long it's going to take? Is he sure he can handle it?"

Both the men were glaring at me. That didn't make it any easier to say what I had to say. I turned to ZiZi. "I'm afraid the janitor's not going to be able to do anything about the air conditioning right now," I informed her. "There's a little problem."

ZiZi didn't say anything but her eyes got bigger and her mouth got smaller.

Mr Schonblatt said, "What are you talking about?

Mr Bagley said, "I should have known a place like

this wouldn't employ someone capable of dealing with emergencies."

I glanced at ZiZi again, for moral support, and then turned to Mr Schonblatt. "I did find him – but, as I said, I'm afraid there's a problem. It—"

"Of course there's a problem," Mr Bagley interrupted. "Problems are the only things you people get right. You should mention it in your advertising."

From the other end of a very long, dark tunnel, Mr Schonblatt said, "And what precisely is the problem?"

It's a strange aspect of human behaviour, but sometimes, people who go ballistic over little things – like a badly folded napkin or a misaligned fork – remain calm in the face of a real disaster. Mr Schonblatt took the news that Abel was passed out drunk with uncharacteristic equanimity.

He breathed very slowly and deeply. "All right," said Mr Schonblatt. "That's not an insurmountable problem. It can be solved. We'll just have to sober him up, won't we?"

"I'm going to sue," threatened Mr Bagley. "You mark my words. This is my daughter's wedding reception. I'm not going to let you get away with this fiasco."

Mr Schonblatt ignored him. "One of the other girls can hold the fort in here for the next five minutes. You two," he said to me and ZiZi, "come with me."

ZiZi and I followed him out of the restaurant. As the three of us marched through the kitchen, he shouted, "Somebody bring us a pot of very strong, hot coffee. Right away!"

Mr Schonblatt's estimate of returning to the dining rooms in five minutes was a little optimistic. He shouted at Abel, but Abel didn't stir. He shook Abel, but Abel kept on snoring. He pulled Abel to his feet, and Abel fell back in his chair. "God help us," muttered Mr Schonblatt. "He's one step away from a coma."

ZiZi tried the gentle, feminine approach. "Abel, do you know where you are?" she coaxed. "Do you know what day this is? Do you think you could take a look at the air conditioner?"

If Abel was one step away from a coma, it was a very small step.

Gabriel arrived with the coffee. He glanced nervously from me to ZiZi to Mr Schonblatt, but then he saw Abel. He gave a low whistle. "Oh, brother. This doesn't look good."

"Thank you for your professional opinion," snapped Mr Schonblatt. "Now put down that pot and help me get him to his feet. Let's see if we can walk him enough to get some coffee down him." He turned to ZiZi. "That'll be your job."

"But Mr Schonblatt," said ZiZi, "even if he wakes up, he's not really going to be in any shape to—"

"Don't argue with me. Just do as you're told."

"Right." ZiZi's mouth smiled. "I'll do as I'm told."

While Gabriel and Mr Schonblatt were trying to make Abel stand, ZiZi sidled over to me. "Do something," she whispered. "You can fix the air conditioner. Get us out of here."

"He's not going to like it if I interfere," I whispered back.

She gave me a withering look. "Like I care, right?"

I could see an orderly shelf of manuals on the workshop side of the office. There was bound to be one for the air conditioner, if I needed it; I had done this sort of thing before.

"You know, Mr Schonblatt," I said as, defeated, he and Gabe dropped Abel back in his chair. "It may not be anything major that's wrong. It's usually nothing more than that the filter needs cleaning."

Mr Schonblatt didn't bother to glance my way. "It doesn't matter what the problem is if we don't have anyone to fix it."

"I might be able to get it going." More able than Abel, that was for certain.

Mr Schonblatt turned so quickly he knocked into

ZiZi, standing at the ready with the pot in her hand. "You? We don't have enough problems right now?"

"I have cleaned filters before, Mr Schonblatt. Maybe not this exact model, but I've worked on commercial systems; I doubt that this is very different from them."

"Absolutely not. I can't have some girl monkeying around with the air conditioning."

ZiZi put the cup down with a bang. "She's not some girl, Mr Schonblatt," said ZiZi. "Loretta happens to be a terrific mechanic."

"It's true," chipped in Gabe. "She can repair just about anything. One time, my car wouldn't start and Loretta—"

"Is there something wrong with everyone's hearing?" shouted Mr Schonblatt. "I said no. It's out of the question."

I summoned every bit of cute-girl leverage I had. I said, "But Mr Schonblatt. What can it hurt if I try? If I just look at the filter? I swear, if it looks okay, I won't touch it." I implored him with my sweetest smile. "The swan is melting, Mr Schonblatt. Mr Bagley's melting, too." The mention of Mr Bagley made him wince; the way things were going, the only map the Old Clipper Inn was going to get on was one of places not to go. I pointed to the slumped body in the chair. "There's no way he's going to be fit to do anything until tomorrow, and you know it. Don't you think it's worth a try?"

"No," said Mr Schonblatt. "I do not think it's worth a try. You heard Mr Bagley. He wants to sue us! Mr Bagley's an important man. He has powerful friends. What do you think he'll do if you set his daughter's wedding on fire or blow us all up?"

"Are you saying you'd trust a drunken man to fix the air conditioning before you'd trust me? Because I'm a girl? You can't be serious."

He gestured to Gabriel. "I'd trust this boy with the earring sooner than you."

Gabe took a step backwards. "Not me. I'm useless at things like this."

I tried one more time. "Please, Mr Schonblatt, you must see how—"

"No! Don't touch a thing or it'll be your parents being sued. You stay here with him" – he nodded to Gabriel – "and try to bring Abel round. You," he said to ZiZi, "come back upstairs with me. You can do damage control." He turned back to me. "I just need to make an announcement, so don't get any ideas – I'm coming right back."

I could hardly wait.

ZiZi

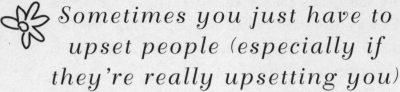

Sometimes you just have to upset people (especially if they're really upsetting you)

"You're making a big mistake," I said as I followed Mr Schonblatt up the stairs. "She can solve the problem in about five minutes and get Mr Bagley off your back."

"The only thing I want off my back right now is you," he snapped.

As we reached the top, one of the kitchen guys went by, carrying a box from the pantry. He'd left the pantry door open but I could see the key in the lock on the outside. I don't know what came over me. It really had been a long day, and this wasn't the fairy tale I thought it would be. And I guess the little bit of romance and love I'd been clinging to had started melting along with everything else. Plus, I was fed up. I'd been badgered and patronized and ignored all afternoon by one man or another and I was pretty tired of it by then. Anyway, I don't know why or where it came from, but I suddenly had this idea. I didn't think about it. I just did it. I stopped outside the pantry and said, "Wait! Mr Schonblatt! What's that?"

"For God's sake, now what?" But he stopped and looked over.

"In there!" I pointed. "There's something in the pantry."

A person not so fixed on controlling things probably would've ignored me and walked on. Mr Schonblatt had already passed me, but he came back. "Of course there's something in the pantry. It would be remarkable if there wasn't something in it." He stopped in the doorway and peered in. "What am I looking at?"

"There!" I pointed past him. "At the back. It could be a person. Is there someone asleep in there?" That was a stroke of genius; someone asleep in the pantry was the kind of thing that could make him forget Mr Bagley for at least a second.

He took a few steps in. "I don't see anyone. Where's the light?"

"It's over on the right." While he was looking for the light, I shut the door behind him and turned the key. He didn't start banging right away. He was probably too surprised. I looked around. Everybody was looking at me. "Just leave him there for ten minutes," I begged. "Just till the air conditioning's fixed."

I'd never seen the chef smile before. "Leave who where?"

I ran back to the cellar to tell Loretta what I'd done and then I went back to the restaurant. We were ready to serve the main course, but Mr Bagley had stopped that from happening. He was waiting for me. By then, he was about the size of King Kong.

"Where have you been?" he boomed. "Where's Schonblatt? What the hell is going on?"

"Everything's under control," I assured him. "Mr Schonblatt's seeing to the air conditioner. It'll be back on in just a few minutes."

He didn't believe me. "I've heard that before." He wanted everyone to go outside. "I haven't paid all this money to watch my guests keel over from heatstroke and dehydration," said Mr Bagley. He wanted more tables and chairs put on the patio and on the lawn. Like we just had to wave a finger and the furniture would all float outside without anything spilling or falling off.

Except for the guests who had already fled, everybody was standing around watching and listening to me and Mr Bagley. And even though I was trying really hard to keep my back to him, I knew Dillon Blackstock and his camera were recording the whole thing for the YouTube audience. You couldn't expect him to pass this up. It was social commentary gone straight into the stratosphere of awe! So because the eyes of the Old Clipper Inn (and possibly the rest of the world) were on me, I was trying to be as polite and reasonable as someone who had just shut her boss in the pantry could be expected to be. I said, "I know it's pretty hot in here, Mr Bagley." In case he thought that waitresses don't sweat. "But I don't really think we can just move everything into the garden. And there isn't any need. Mr Schonblatt said—"

He loomed over me like a tank over a toy car. "Mr Schonblatt isn't here. It doesn't matter what he said."

It mattered to me.

"He isn't here because he's getting the air conditioner fixed. So if you could just be patient for a little longer…" Like he even knew what patience is.

"I don't need the incompetence of the management made worse by the stupidity of the staff."

And I didn't need the nightmare that the dream wedding had turned into made worse by the arrogance of the bride's father.

"I'm just trying to be realistic, Mr Bagley. It seems to me that everything will be back to normal way before we get everything outside, and then we'll just have to bring it all back in."

His lips curled. "Oh, is that how it seems to *you*?"

"Yes. It is."

"Don't argue with me, honey," said Mr Bagley. "Put that little butt of yours in gear and start moving the tables."

Was it "honey"? Was it "little butt"? Was it just his negative attitude? Maybe it was just that tiny streams of sweat were running down his face, making him seem almost human and not a superior, if unpleasant, life form. Made him seem like a person. Like I'm a person. And the other sweating, exhausted waitresses were persons too.

"No." I stood up really straight. (If only I had on heels!) "It's not my fault or Mr Schonblatt's fault or anybody else's fault that the air conditioner's not working." I took a step forward. "So let me tell you what you can do, Mr Bagley." I took another step forward. "You can stop talking to me like that, that's what you can do. I am not your servant. And I am not a stupid girl. And I am totally not your honey." All the while I talked, I kept walking towards him. "So if you want the tables outside so badly, you can move them yourself."

And that's when Mr Bagley fell into what was left of the swan, bringing the whole table down.

Nothing happened for about half a second. It was like everything just stopped. Breathing. Hearts beating. Earth turning. Everything. Like the fairy tale this wedding was in was the one where the bad fairy casts a spell on everyone for not inviting her to the party. And then, just as I heard the air conditioner kick in, Mrs Bagley screamed, "Donald!" and the new Mrs Schreiber screamed, "Daddy!" I'm sure it wasn't everybody else, but a lot of people started to laugh.

I suppose I should've helped Mr Bagley out of the rubble, but I didn't even think of it. (Anyway, the groom jumped up and did that.) I was just kind of standing there. Stunned. I suppose I should've felt sorry for what happened, but I didn't. I was wondering how much trouble I was going to be in when Mr Schonblatt got out of the pantry and found out about it, because he was sure to blame me. On top of everything else (like locking him in the pantry). But weirdly, I didn't really care about that, either. And then I felt a hand on my shoulder. "Way to go, Giselle!" I turned to see Dillon grinning at me.

So at least two of us were happy.

Loretta

Things don't go back to the way they were

The Bagley-Schreiber reception turned out to be more of a fiasco than a fairy tale, but for definite nobody who was there was ever going to forget it. Except, maybe, Abel, since he slept through most of it. I wasn't going to forget it, either – despite the fact that I only ever saw the swan incident on Dillon's film.

After ZiZi gave us the all-clear, Gabriel and I left Abel sleeping and went into mission control where the restaurant's air-conditioning system was. United by disaster, we had our talk while I was making the repair. It may have been because it was the sort of day that invented stress, or it may have been because – according to Mr Schonblatt – I was about to blow up the Inn so, subconsciously, I knew I had nothing to lose, but I had no trouble saying what I wanted to say – and Gabe had no trouble listening.

I said, "Whenever I think one of us is going to ask the other one out, you run away."

Gabe said it wasn't like that, and, in any case, he didn't run; he simply walked very quickly. He said that the time he came to my house he was all set to ask me out but he hadn't expected ZiZi to be there and it completely threw him. In more ways than one. "I made such a complete fool of myself that all I wanted to do was leave," said Gabe. When he came to Chelusky's to see me, he was going to try again, but that time he hadn't expected to discover that I was dating Dillon Blackstock.

It was a little complicated explaining how I'd come to give the guys at work the impression that I had a boyfriend whose name was Dillon. "I know I should have said I'd made a bet with ZiZi, but it seemed easier to let them think I was dressing differently because of a boy."

Gabe said I was probably going to think he's a jerk, but that was what he thought, too. "When I saw you in town that time? You looked so – you know. I thought I'd waited too long to say something. And then in Chelusky's... Then I knew for sure I'd missed the shuttle."

I said, "I don't think you're a jerk."

The day after the wedding-reception-no-one-will-ever-forget, ZiZi and I called the bet a draw. Each of us figured she was right. Which probably we are – more or less. We both always said a woman is judged on how she looks; but we didn't deal with that fact in the same way. It was as if we were standing on opposite sides of the same mountain, trying to work out how to get across it. The bet had made each of us see things from a new perspective. ZiZi said there was no way she'd give up her dresses, her make-up and her curls, but that she knows that none of those things define her as a person; she can use them rather than be used by them. "Plus," said ZiZi, "I figure you have an advantage if you look all girly but have a kick-ass attitude because they're not expecting it."

I'd learned a couple of lessons, too.

I wasn't going to stick with the pink and the hour-long beauty regime, but I was letting my hair get a little longer and putting on a little make-up and wearing a dress every now and then. It doesn't mean I abandoned all my principles; it just means that I also have longer hair, make-up and a couple of dresses, and if anybody thinks that implies that I'm naturally better at cooking than theoretical physics they're in for a major surprise. There's more than one way to solve most problems; there's more than one way to be a girl.

On the night of the Howards Walk High School's Astronomy Club outing to view the Perseids, Gabe picked me up after supper and we drove out to a bluff overlooking the beach. We spread the blanket on the ground. We lay on our backs, staring up at the busy sky, feeling as if we were swimming through the stars.

"This is fantastic." Gabe reached for my hand. "You want to know the truth, I'm glad no one else wanted to come. It's better with just the two of us."

I wasn't going to argue with that.

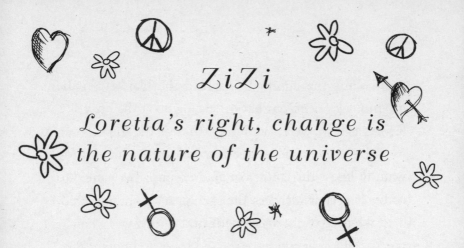

ZiZi

Loretta's right, change is the nature of the universe

After Mr Schonblatt got out of the pantry and Mr Bagley went to his room and changed his clothes, things pretty much went back to normal (in a weird kind of way!). The kitchen staff swore up and down that they didn't know how he got locked in the pantry. They figured someone shut and locked it without thinking in all the chaos and rushing around, and then no one could find the key for a while. I doubt that Mr Schonblatt believed them, but he went along with it. At least the air conditioning was back on, and anyway, he had Mr Bagley to worry about. (Mr Bagley is a man to make a few minutes in a pantry seem like a vacation in Hawaii.) We finished serving dinner and they had the toasts and the speeches and then almost everybody went outside to dance the night away. Everybody agreed that Mr Bagley had been pretty psycho, plus he'd been drinking, and that bringing down the swan was just an unfortunate accident. So I didn't get into trouble for that, either.

And Dillon was totally thrilled with the footage he got. He said it just showed how things had a way of working out, didn't it? If Tobias's cousin hadn't given up his year in the wilderness after a month (too hungry, too dirty, too tired of chopping wood and getting wet when it rained), Dillon would have missed the wedding and my Emma Goldman moment (I couldn't believe it, he knows who she is!).

But here's the thing. When Dillon and I looked at what he'd shot, it was pretty obvious that I'd backed Mr Bagley into the swan. Maybe not consciously, but pretty deliberately. Dillon said he didn't think I had it in me. (Who did?!) "I always thought you were one of those girls who depends on guys to take care of them." Mainly that was his opinion because he was always seeing me when there was some guy doing something for me. And because I was so girly. (Girly and helpless isn't his type. His first girlfriend wants to be a fighter pilot!) "I thought you were a princess like my sister-in-law. I never thought you'd stand up for yourself like that." *Quel ironic*, or what? "I guess I should've known if you were friends with Loretta, you must have more going on, but I always saw you hanging with some jock."

I said I hoped he wasn't going to have a problem now that Loretta and I had settled the bet and I was going to go back to looking like a girl again.

He said, "No. No problem. You're still you."